Best Seller

MARTHA REYNOLDS

DEDICATION

for Jim

CONTENTS

ACKNOWLEDGMENTS

Writing is a solitary venture, but I couldn't complete this book without help.

Thank you to my friend Donna Annicelli, who grew up in the small New England town that was the inspiration for this novel. Over coffee on Main Street, we chatted about days gone by and growing up in the seventies.

To Diane Hogan, who helped me find back issues of periodicals and newspapers from the Bicentennial era. The fashion! The music! You're a treasure to the library. Thank you.

To Darcie Czajkowski and Carolyn Aspenson – thank you for taking the time from your own writing schedules to provide honest feedback. Your comments helped me to craft a better, tighter story.

Francine LaSala, author, editor, and friend - once again you demonstrated your brilliance to me.

Heather McCoubrey and Carol Wise of WiseElement for the beautiful cover of this book. Thank you for your kindness and patience in helping me find just the right design!

To my Review Crew and my loyal readers! I'm nothing without you. I wish I could write faster sometimes (ha!). Your support and encouragement over the past three years has kept me going, and will keep me writing until I can't do it anymore.

1

My father stopped speaking to me the day I was
expelled from college, and a few weeks before he paid
my fine to the court. That was a month ago. One day
after my appearance in front of the judge, I moved
into my apartment, in a house he owns. I pay rent to
the property management company he also owns. So
I'm not really independent. Not yet, anyway.

I flip my calendar to July before June even ends. I
can't wait to circle three dates with my red magic
marker. On the Fourth of July there'll be a giant
bicentennial parade in town and fireworks over the
harbor. Plus, I don't have to work. One red circle.
Three days later, my twentieth birthday. Probably no
family celebration this year, though. Another red
circle. Used to be, you couldn't drink until you turned
twenty-one, but they changed that law when I was
seventeen. The year before that, they changed the law

so I could vote when I turned eighteen. Turning twenty? No big deal.

I draw two red circles around Friday the twenty-third, because that's the day Maryana Capture will make an appearance at the Thousand Words bookstore. She's my absolute favorite author of all time. I've read all of her books and can't believe she's going to make a stop here. Well, one town over. Her newest book came out a couple of years ago, and I read it right away. I guess she's been traveling all around the country and will finally end up here.

Today's my day off, so I take the bus to Westham and walk to the bookstore. It's across the street from the new mall, in a low brick building that used to be a dance studio. Since I come here almost every Tuesday, I know Dorothy, who owns the store.

"I can't wait to see Maryana Capture," I say. Dorothy's eyes light up like fireworks at the mention of her name. Obviously, it's a big deal getting a famous author to appear at her little bookstore.

"Oh, so are we! Isn't it exciting!" Dorothy is exactly the kind of woman you'd imagine running an eclectic bookstore like the Thousand Words. She wears her long gray hair in a single braid down her back, and sports a necklace made of feathers and beads. When she steps out from behind the counter, I notice an ankle adornment, some kind of bracelet, made of copper wires and more beads. Her skirt is long and wrinkled, but I don't think she cares. She shows me where the event will take place, in a cleared area off to the side. "This is where we have our book club meetings on Wednesday nights, Robin, if you're interested in joining us."

"I wish I could, but it's too late for me. I start work at six o'clock in the morning."

"Oh! That *is* early." She smiles sympathetically, as if I think waking up at five o'clock is horrible. I don't mind.

"Dorothy, it says on the poster that attendance is limited to fifty fans? Please tell me you don't have fifty people signed up yet. Please." I lean forward on the counter, my legs suddenly unsteady.

She chortles, and a drop of spit shines in the corner of her mouth. The skin on her neck is wrinkled and wobbles like that thing on a turkey. I wonder how old she is.

"Oh, don't worry about that." Her voice drops to a whisper. "They say that to make you think you'd better sign up quick. See? It worked." She grins. "If more than fifty people show up, they'll be thrilled." She reaches under the counter and pulls out a red vinyl binder. There's an index card taped to the front, and the word "CAPTURE" written in black magic marker. "Here, I'm making a list. Her publicist suggested it." She rolls her eyes behind round wire-rimmed eyeglasses. "Let me see, Robin. Look, you'll be number two." She laughs as she writes my name in perfect script. Then she swivels the binder around so I can see. Yes, there's my name on line number two. Only one name is above mine: Carole Keller. I know Mrs. Keller. Her daughter Miranda was a year behind me in high school.

"So there are only two of us signed up for the event?" I'm surprised. After all, it's Maryana Capture, best-selling author. We don't get many famous people around here.

Dorothy shrugs. "There'll be plenty more. No one thinks they have to sign up to attend a book signing. You're one of the few who read that line on the poster, dear."

"Okay, well, I'm glad I'm signed up. See you later, Dorothy." I turn to the door and head outside. The humidity is worse now, and the air is so thick it's like walking through steam. I just want to go back to my apartment and lay in front of my fan.

The Fourth of July is less than a week away. Every shop on Main Street is decorated. There's a red, white, and blue stripe painted down the middle of the street, from the First National grocery store to the post office. I've been working at the Liberty Diner, every day except Tuesday, since a week after I was kicked out of college. George was the fourth shop owner I approached for a job, and he hired me. He yells a lot, sometimes to tell me to hurry up, sometimes when there's an order ready, sometimes for no reason at all. But you'll never meet anyone more patriotic than George. He told me he arrived in America at age twenty-two, and started working in his uncle's restaurant in New York City. By the time he turned thirty, he had saved enough money to open this diner, and he called it the Liberty Diner after the Statue of Liberty. George loves America so much he closes the diner on the Fourth of July, even though this year the holiday falls on a Sunday and Sunday is his busiest day. People like to eat pancakes after church, but George says the holiday is important. I think maybe he just doesn't want to pay us extra.

Anyway, the Fourth should be fun this year, even if my father's mad at me. I'm meeting up with Speedy Mello, or Frank as he now wants to be called. We've been pals since elementary school, and now that I'm back in town doing my penance, we've caught up. Frank was the fastest runner in high school, breaking all kinds of long-held records, and everybody called him Speedy since he was twelve. On graduation night, the car he was driving was hit by a truck at the intersection of McCormick Street and Soldiers' Highway, where there should have been a traffic light (there is now). His girlfriend was killed and Speedy broke both of his legs. He lost out on a full scholarship to Penn State and people started calling him Frank after that. The accident wasn't his fault, but judging from the way folks in town have treated him, you'd think he set out that night to kill his own girlfriend. The cops tested him for alcohol, and he had a little in his system, but hey, who didn't on graduation night? It wasn't enough to rule him legally drunk or anything. And now he lives with those horrible memories and a slight limp. The parents of the girl who died moved away to Florida, and who can blame them. I'd move to Florida if I could.

He and I were always just friends growing up, but we're looking at each other differently now. Hanging around together and being older makes that happen. So Frank and I plan to watch the parade together. My parents have a huge cookout every year, right after the parade. This year I'll pass. Hey, I'm probably not invited, anyway. Everyone else in town will show up, because half the people in town suck up to my father, and the rest of them want a chance to see inside the house. Surprise for them, he rents those portable toilets and places them back along the woods line, so no one except family goes inside. They may not be allowed in the house, but they can drink his beer and eat his hamburgers and hot dogs. I'll head to the beach and maybe I'll have the whole place to myself, unless Frank comes with me.

I first smoked pot when I was seventeen. Everybody was doing it, and most of my friends had started earlier. My friend Deb's older brother had gone off to Vietnam the year before and she tried it at his going-away party, the one his buddies threw for him out in the fields of McCarron's Farm. By the time I said yes to a joint, I was pretty much the only one left who hadn't at least tried it. I didn't really like pot, though, so I never developed a habit that would cost me my baby-sitting money. Instead, I started selling it.

At first I just sold to a few friends the summer after high school. A dime bag here and there. But soon after I arrived in Boston for college, word spread and I, or my product, was in demand. I got my supply from a guy in Amherst, and once I'd saved up some money, I bought a kilo from him for about three hundred bucks. Since a kilo's a little over two pounds, I had about thirty-five ounces. I could get fifty bucks for an ounce, because the stuff was really good, so I'd net close to fifteen hundred bucks. Then I'd buy another kilo and do the same thing. By the time I got caught I'd banked a few thousand bucks.

So, I was kicked out of school and my parents drove up to get me. It was late March, and we only had another six weeks left in the semester. I don't think I've ever seen my father so mad. I mean, this was his alma mater and all. My mother had to drive home, he was so angry. At one point, he turned around in the front seat to glare at me, and he said, "Do you have any idea how much I've sacrificed for you? Do you?" His neck and face were very red. I wouldn't look in his eyes. "Was it about the money? For Chrissakes, Robin, we've given you everything!"

"Hap, calm down, dear, you're going to give yourself a heart attack," my mother said, as she pointed the car toward the highway.

I didn't say anything.

"You treat us like shit!" he yelled before turning back around in his seat. That was basically it; he had nothing more to say to me after that. All communication from then on went through my mother. If I had anything to say, I'd say it to her. A couple of weeks later, the three of us drove back up to court, where I was sentenced to probation. I avoided jail time, the judge said, because my parents were here with me. But I'm pretty sure my dad wrote a check to someone to get me that probation. In his world, everything can be fixed or bettered by writing a check.

We drove back home, to the big house my father built before I was born. The house with a wing on either side, for us, he'd said once. Skip and Kay live in one of the wings now, just like they were supposed to do. The other wing is empty, and I figure it'll stay empty, unless my dad decides to rent it out to someone more deserving of that residence than I would ever be.

Once we got back to the house, my father disappeared, and my mom sat me down to tell me that I'd be moving the next day. Moving out of the house I'd always lived in, out of my lavender bedroom with the white canopy bed, and into a tiny apartment on the ground floor of a house down the hill from Main Street.

This apartment I live in, it's really small, but still bigger than the dorm room I had at college, and I don't have to share it with anyone. My father owns the house, which is comically ironic, I suppose. Or ironically comical. I pay the rent with a check (fifty dollars a month, so I figure it's just symbolic for him to charge me), and I always make sure I mail the check the day before the first of the month, so he can never accuse me of being late with the rent. My mom slips me money every week, thank goodness, because what I make at the diner might cover rent and food, but there would never be anything left over. Frank said my dad is being stupid, that he should just make me pay rent for the wing, but I know my father. He's thick-headed that way. It's all about principle with him, and all about payback in this instance. Like the wing is a prize that I don't get now.

Is it the life I thought I'd have? No, of course not. When I started college, I dreamed about being a writer. I did well in my courses, and I loved the novels I was assigned to read. I learned to write better. I went on a few dates, nothing memorable. Some of the girls I met freshman year were stuck on finding a husband at college. My freshman year roommate, Belinda, wanted nothing more out of college than an engagement ring.

"But what about a career?" I remember asking. "It's 1975, you can do anything!"

She laughed and curled a strand of golden hair around her index finger. "I don't want to work," she said. "I want to be a mommy! Three times!"

Belinda went as far as to say that, if the opportunity arose before she'd finished four years of college, she'd drop out. I couldn't believe what I was hearing. Of course, Belinda was still in school, looking for Mr. Right, and here I was, kicked out before I'd finished my sophomore year.

Anyway, I'm glad to have the Fourth of July off from work, and I'll enjoy the big parade on Main Street. I don't even really care about my birthday anymore.

But when Maryana Capture comes to town, well, that's exciting.

She's my absolute favorite author, and she's written five books, all best sellers. I devour them like chocolate, until I'm near the end, then I slow way down, because I hate for the story to end. I've read and re-read her books, and can't wait until she releases another one. Dorothy in the Thousand Words bookstore said she'd be there to sign her books, but she doesn't have a new one out yet. That's a disappointment, but I'm looking forward to seeing her anyway.

2

June's been a hot month, and the air inside this apartment is stifling. The less time I spend inside, the better. I finish work at two o'clock, and run home to change into shorts and a tee shirt, then walk down to the harbor, hoping for a breeze. The outside deck of Flynn's is packed with people. They look to be in their twenties, but I don't recognize any of the faces. Out-of-towners, all of them. They're laughing and drinking. Men hold bottles of beer like torches. One woman pulls her hair into a ponytail and tosses her head. I turn and walk in the other direction.

This is a parochial, foggy town, built upward from the wharves over the past three hundred years. Generations of unfortunate men have plied the bay waters for clams, quahogs, littlenecks, cherrystones, returning to the docks at the end of the day and spending a good portion of their pay at the local watering hole. Then they stagger home to their dreary hovels, snarl at their wives and maybe even their kids, eat some slop, fall onto a thin, lumpy mattress, and rise at four to start all over again. No wonder they die young.

Over the years, the town built upon itself. The "low end" is exactly that. The old stately houses that perch on the hill above Main Street belonged to sea captains and mill owners. Usually three stories high, some with a widow's walk, they're painted blindingly white or soft kitten gray, with black shutters and shiny brass fixtures and the occasional red door. Some of the houses have plaques nailed next to the door, stating the original owner and the year the house was built. Ezekiel Cooper, 1743. John Weston Booth, 1699. Roger Knight, 1750. Some of the houses have remained with the original family members. Those people make sure you know that they've been residents of the town since its inception. Really, who cares if this is your great-great-great-grandfather's house? He's dead, move on.

The waterfront is fine as long as it's daytime, but once it gets dark, I don't like to be out here alone, even though I thought I knew this town like I know my own skin. It's changed in the past few years. My father would say it's all because of the drugs. Well, of course he would say that. There's only Flynn's and a couple of biker bars, and they all get pretty rowdy late at night in the summer. I can hear the noise from my bedroom window, even with the fan running at full blast. Revving motorcycles and breaking glass.

I check my pocket for money and pull out four one-dollar bills. There's a little clam shack at the far end of the marina. A small basket of fried clam strips and fries is $2.95, and I decide I'll have that for supper. At least I can eat at the picnic table next to the take-out window.

I stay there until almost seven, then hike back up the hill to my apartment. If I wanted to, I could sit outside on the little wooden porch, but the mosquitoes are out in force this evening and I'd rather not get bitten. I head in, close up the windows in the kitchen and lock them. I turn on the fan in my bedroom and feel hot air blow over my sweaty skin. I hop in the shower for a quick, cool wash-off before I lay on my bed in just a clean, dry tee shirt. I turn off all the lights because I live at street level and there are some weirdos who walk around this part of town.

Frank had to do some family thing today, but he said he'd call when he got home. At this point, I'd rather he didn't call, because I need to sleep, but we've gotten into the habit of talking to each other late at night, even if just for a few minutes. I think it helps us both to sleep. And I did tell him to call me. I don't want to call his house, where he lives with his parents and his two sisters. His sisters are okay, and his dad is nice to me when I see him, but his mom is kind of standoffish. I guess because of what happened to me up at school. Now she thinks I'm a bad influence on her son. Ha.

I'm just about to drift into a state of semi-consciousness when the phone next to my bed rings. I pick it up on the second ring and murmur, "Hey."

"Hey. You were asleep."

"Almost. It's okay. Did you have a good day?" I roll over onto my back and play with the telephone cord.

"It was boring. We had a birthday party for my uncle tonight. My aunt Rose asked me about my future plans and when I told her I was working for my dad, she made a face. Then my dad got mad at that and accused her of being a snob. Then my uncle got into it and said I should have an education. It was like I wasn't even there. I went outside and threw a ball to my little cousin, who can't catch to save his life. Then we came back inside for cake. Then my aunt made up some excuse about having to get back home early."

"Oh, sorry. Well, I'm gonna try to get to sleep now. Early day for me tomorrow."

"Yeah. G'night, Robin."

"G'night. Talk to you tomorrow."

My brother Skip is eight years older than I am, so we didn't hang out much as I was growing up. When I was six, he was fourteen. When I was twelve, he was away at college. He joined our father's construction business right after graduation and now, almost thirty, he's very successful. And very wealthy. They have two kids, a boy who's almost five and a girl who's three. Perfect family. I don't say this with bitterness, they just are. Perfect. Skip and Kay are both really nice to me. They even have a nanny, so Kay can do her charity work during the day. The first nanny they had was from Norway, or Sweden, and she was blonde and round, unlike Kay, who is brunette and so thin you could fold her up like one of those origami birds. Anyway, the first nanny left after a few weeks, or maybe Kay got rid of her, who knows. But now they have Nancy, who's old and wears thick glasses.

Kay's real name is Katherine. But it didn't surprise me when I met her and she said everyone called her Kay. It's as though Kathy is too common a nickname for someone like Kay. My mother told me she comes from "old money," which I didn't understand when I first heard the term at age thirteen, but I understand now. Kay can trace her ancestors all the way back to the Mayflower, for crying out loud. As if that should matter. But it does, especially around here. Family lineage and all that. She's from Newport originally,

and met Skip at college in New York. I remember
Skip was really nervous the first time he brought her
home to meet us, and he and Mom had a long
conversation about what she was planning to serve
for dinner. Mom was nervous then, too, all worried
about the roast beef and the cheesecake she made for
dessert. No vegetables out of the can that day, I can
tell you that. No, it was springtime, and everything
had to be fresh. I remember we drove to the city to
buy everything from Shiravo's Fresh Fruits and
Vegetables. Flowers for the table. The good
tablecloth and Gram's china from the cabinet. Even
the good silverware, which I had to polish with a
paste and a soft cloth until my fingers were as gray as
nickels. All for Katherine Winslow Britteridge.

Skip and Kay married the following June, just before I
turned fifteen, and I got to be a bridesmaid, the
youngest one of the eight bridesmaids. We all wore
mint-green long dresses with matching floppy hats
and had bouquets of carnations tinted mint green. My
parents paid for my dress, and the shoes I had to have
dyed to match, and the hat, and even a thin gold
bracelet I gave to Kay for her wedding ensemble. I
tried champagne that day, but didn't like it, and I
danced with my dad and with Skip. And I made out
with a seventeen-year-old boy named Lionel, Kay's
cousin who came down with his family from Old
Orchard Beach in Maine. We ended up on the floor

of a gazebo on the grounds of the mansion in Newport where they had the wedding.

I never saw Lionel again. But I got better at kissing, that's for sure. And other things.

Kay's always been pretty cool, for old money, and I think of her as a sister. I get along better with her than I do with Skip. Of course, Skip takes my father's side in everything, and especially in this latest thing.

"God, Robin, you can be such an idiot for a smart girl," he said. I was at their house for dinner. My parents were right next door in the main house, but they weren't invited over. Well, maybe they were, and maybe my father refused, knowing I'd be there. It was a few days after the court date and I think Kay felt bad for me. She made ziti casserole with little meatballs and plenty of cheese and even offered me a glass of red wine.

"I'm not sure that's a good idea, Robin," Skip had said, reaching for my glass.

"Geez, Skip, you think I've never had wine before?" I rolled my eyes in Kay's direction. My sister, my pal. She poked her fork into her ziti and said nothing. I was hoping she'd stick up for me.

"We're not going to enable you, Robin. You've brought a lot of embarrassment to this family. Do you know how much Dad gives to BU every year?"

"Apparently not enough to keep them from kicking me out," I said. "Come on, Skip, everybody there smokes pot. It's no big deal."

He held his fork in mid-air. A thread of melted cheese connected his fork to his plate, and I watched it, mesmerized, until he must have remembered and lifted his fork to his mouth. Snap! The thread broke.

"Don't be a wise-ass," he said. "You need to think about your life. What are you going to do now?"

I shoveled food into my mouth and moved my jaw around to break it up. I didn't really have to chew it. But I made him wait, raising my index finger as a sign that I wouldn't want to speak with my mouth full. After I swallowed, I said, "Skip, I'm working. Six days a week."

"At the diner," he said. I took a long drink of water.

He leaned forward. "Robin, you're waitressing in a diner, for God's sake. You're better than that and you know it."

I sat back, glanced at Kay, whose eyes ping-ponged back and forth from Skip to me, and said, "I'm happy about it, for your information. I may do this for the rest of my life." Even I knew how lame that was. Of course I wouldn't be a waitress for the rest of my life. I mean, look at Jenny, who trained me for the morning and noontime shifts. She was in her forties and looked about seventy. I was only going to do this to prove to my father that I could work. By September I'd be back at college.

Skip shook his head with disdain. "Fine, Robin. Your choice."

"And you'll love me either way, right?" I gave him the same goofy grin I'd given him when I was eight and he was sixteen.

"Yeah, you nut, I'll love you either way. But you're almost twenty years old. Time to grow up."

3

Every morning at the Liberty Diner (except for Tuesday, my day off), I arrive at 5:45 sharp. It's only a five-minute walk up the hill from my apartment to Main Street. George is always there ahead of me, preparing for the breakfast crowd. I slip into a bright blue smock that covers my tee shirt and fasten the snaps that parade down the front. I take a knife, fork, and spoon and roll them inside a paper napkin, tucking the edge just under to fasten it. The roll goes to the left of where the plate will be. I make sure the salt, pepper, and sugar containers are full, then check ketchup and syrup. I start the coffee, two pots of regular, one pot of decaf, and fill the little silver pitchers with half-and-half from the big refrigerator. George is usually singing in the kitchen, some old Greek song, but it won't be long before he starts yelling. That's just George. He yells a lot, but the customers are used to it, and so am I. He's just very devoted to his diner. This morning he's in a good mood because it's almost the Fourth. The parade will go right past the restaurant, which will be closed to honor America's birthday. I think of that when he starts yelling.

Lately, the yelling's been directed at Jenny. Thank God. What I mean is, she's been messing up a lot, and I hope he doesn't fire her, but I'm glad he's not yelling at me. I like working with Jenny, and even though she's a lot older than I am, we get along great. I can talk to her about anything. We help each other out when it gets crazy with customers. But she told me her husband's sick – something, I can't remember, but he was in the hospital, so she's probably worried about him and her mind isn't on the job. I try to cover for her where I can, so George doesn't see, but he's got those beady little eagle eyes and misses nothing.

My mom called last night and asked me if I wanted anything special for my birthday. It's not like I could say, 'how about if Dad started talking to me again?' It's ridiculous, really. I know I embarrassed him by messing up at school, although I do think he and the college overreacted. Come on, if the college only knew how much drug-taking and drug-selling was going on. I just happened to be the one who got caught.

So anyway, I told my mom that I could use some new sneakers, and maybe we could go shopping for them together. I know what I'm getting from Skip and Kay, because Nancy the nanny let it slip last week when I saw her on Main Street after my shift. They bought me an electric typewriter! I hope it's that Olivetti I saw in the window of Helger's Office Supplies. It has a key that you hit and it automatically corrects a mistake. I could use that.

Having a new typewriter means I can type up my novel, the one I've been writing in spiral-bound notebooks for the past year. I wouldn't say it's autobiographical, not really, but some of it is based on my life. Like the part where my Uncle Lester accidentally on purpose saw me naked and didn't leave the room *immediately*. I put that in the book, only I renamed the guy Mr. Crane. Anyway, I still have to write the ending. Maybe a happy ending. That's what readers like.

I told George I'd stay after work today to help decorate the place. There's nothing else to do, and at least it's not the apartment.

I pull my shirt away from my chest, knowing it's soaked through in the back, and twist my hair into a knot on top of my head. Even with the air conditioning unit at the front of the diner, above the door, the heat from the kitchen renders it impotent. George brought red, white and blue bunting from his house and together we drape it around the inside windows. He has me climb a ladder to hang red, white and blue paper lanterns, and garlands of pinwheels with the American flag on them. All made in Japan. I know because I looked, and it's stamped on everything. "Made in Japan." I wonder what the old guys who come into the restaurant, wearing their "WWII Veteran" ball caps, would think about that.

"Here, Robin, climb down now," he says. "Let's have a look together."

I step down carefully, looking over my left shoulder as I descend. George and I stand side by side, hands on our hips, and survey the room. I think it's overdone, but I'm not about to say that. In George's mind, there can never be too many American flag decorations.

"Looks good," I say, nodding. "Very patriotic."

He crosses his arms over his barrel chest and when he raises his arms, I catch a whiff of his sweat. It's manly and tinged with what I think is Old Spice deodorant. I have to say, George has been very sweaty at times, but he's never been stinky. I don't think I could work for him if he was smelly. He's very hairy, but clean.

And as far as I know, no one has ever found a black hair in their eggs.

"Hmm," he buzzes, his thick black eyebrows drawn together as he no doubt ponders whether he could stick more junk around the diner. "Okay, okay. For now, we done inside. Come, Robin, we drape the bunting outside now."

He gathers up the polyester fabric in his big arms and heads to the door. I follow, carrying a hammer and a pack of small nails. The window boxes are at street level, so we don't need the ladder. George drapes the bunting in no time, making grand sweeps of the fabric from one corner of the window box to the other, then repeats it at the other window box. His wife has planted bright red geraniums and it really does look good. I'm proud to work here. I turn and smile at my boss.

"You're more American than a lot of people I know, George." He narrows his eyes at me and I'm sure I said the wrong thing.

"That's too bad then." He lays his right hand over his heart and I think he's about to pledge his allegiance to Old Glory stuck in a flag holder to the right of the diner's door. "I love this country. I am proud to be citizen. Is very important."

I nod and wonder if I would feel the same way if I went to Greece and wanted to be a Greek citizen. But then, I can't imagine that.

"Is it okay if I go now?" I glance at my watch. I've already been here an extra hour, and he's not paying me for this.

George's mind is somewhere else, I can tell. Maybe back in Athens, at the Acropolis or something. He snaps out of it, looks at me, and says with a wave of his hand, "Go, go."

I leave before he changes his mind.

There's a guy who comes into the diner. Andrew. He stops in on Wednesday and Friday mornings, always around six-thirty. Coffee and a grilled blueberry muffin with butter. Wednesdays and Fridays. Like clockwork.

When I first started working at the diner, Jenny was Andrew's waitress, but Jenny has Wednesdays off now, and that's how I first met him. Now, even on Fridays, he makes sure to sit at one of my tables. He comes in by himself, so really he should sit at the counter, but there are enough empty tables that early in the day. Usually it's just the truckers, the big beefy guys who work construction or haul freight, or Mick who works down at the docks with the fishermen. They all take stools at the counter. Andrew wears a suit, and he always looks nice. He's a lawyer, he said, in the city. Moved here from South Carolina and he's still getting used to the area, but he likes the ocean. He's very cute, and he wears a shiny gold band on his left ring finger. He's never mentioned a wife, or whether he has any kids, and I don't ask. All I know is that I look forward to Wednesdays and Fridays more than the other days of the week.

4

Today is Monday, and I'm sweating here in my bed. I have a fan in the window, something the landlord (my father) actually provided. It fits snugly in the window, but when I leave the apartment, I take it out and pull the window down to lock it. Living at street level has its worries, too, and this part of town, "below Main," as the locals refer to it, is rougher than the hill where I grew up. Someone could get inside this apartment so easily. Not that I have anything worth taking, and I'm not afraid. The most valuable thing in this place is my pile of notebooks that contain my novel. I should get them copied at the shop up the hill. Another item on my long list of things to accomplish.

I switch off the fan and listen to the sounds of the early morning – birds chirping their greetings and in the distance, the noise of men on fishing boats heading out to work. I might as well get up and shower. Standing under cool water, not even wanting to turn the knob toward 'H,' I stick my head under the spray before I realize I can't bear to use a hair dryer today. Oh well. I'll pull it back and hope George doesn't yell at me for having damp hair. I usually tie it back in a tight braid anyway when I'm working.

The air is steamy and clings to my skin with tenacity. Even the fresh towel is damp. After turning the fan back on, I dress quickly, in tee shirt and white slacks, and pull white cotton socks over my feet before slipping them into the sneakers I keep for work.

The guy who lives upstairs from me is clomping around and I'm glad I wake up so early. I'm usually gone before he leaves for work, so we hardly ever see each other. Just as well. I did run into him once, on my day off. I happened to be up early, because it's hard to change your schedule when you're used to getting out of bed before dawn. I don't even know his name, but he's a really big guy, just as I suspected from the heavy footsteps. He wore khaki pants and a shirt with a patch on it, like maybe he's an electrician or a plumber or something. I don't know, and I don't really care. He lifted his hand to wave at me and I nodded back, then turned away.

If I get to work early enough, and complete all my chores before we open, George will cook me a breakfast, usually a fried egg sandwich. But I don't want him to think I expect it. I mean, I do have some pride. So I wolf down a bowl of corn flakes before I head out the door. George also lets me take food home, as long as it's something he can't serve the next day. He always says he can't use it, like I'm doing him a favor by taking it, but I know better. "You too skinny," he says, giving me the once-over and shaking his head. George doesn't leer, he's not like that, but he's always telling me women should have some meat on them. "Men like a girl who's not so bony," he says, making me blush, because my old boyfriend Corey used to say the same thing when we were together. He used to say there wasn't enough for him to hold on to. We had some good times together, and then he met someone else, a blonde girl who had something for him to hold on to.

I walk up the hill to Main Street. At the top of the hill, I stop and stare. There's yellow paint all over the bunting George and I put out yesterday afternoon, like someone took a can of paint and just threw it at the fabric. Someone must have done it last night. The street's still quiet at this early hour. Where's George, I wonder. Maybe I should take the bunting down. I approach the diner and pull open the door. The little bell tinkles, signaling my arrival. I see George's dark head in the kitchen.

"Morning, George," I call, so as not to startle him. He raises his left hand in greeting but doesn't turn around. Surely he must have seen it, I think, unless he used the back door. Maybe he used the back door. Then I should tell him about this.

"George?" I step toward him and he turns his head just a little to the right, so I can see his profile. Still he doesn't say anything. "Um, did you see the bunting outside?"

He turns back to chopping ham into tiny pieces. He'll use this ham for omelets and again at lunchtime for ham salad sandwiches. "Yes, Robin, of course I saw it." His voice is soft, so soft it doesn't even sound like George. He keeps chopping. I watch the knife twinkle under the fluorescent light. He's deft with that knife.

"Do you want me to take it down? I have time before we open." Not much time, I think, so let me get to it.

Now he sets down his knife and turns his whole body to me. His face looks as if something was pulling the skin down, like there are weights in his neck making his face longer. "Robin, I want the peoples to see it. To see what someone did to a symbol of freedom." He turns back to the ham.

Well, I don't agree with that, but he's the boss, so I head out into the dining room to prepare for the day. I know that when customers come in, they're all going to say something about the yellow paint, and what am I supposed to do then? George will be in the kitchen, so he's not about to tell them what he just told me. Maybe I can sneak out and take the bunting down.

"Hey!" Jenny announces her arrival. "What the hell happened out front? Did you see that? George!" She yells into the kitchen. "Someone defaced your bunting! Want me to take it down before everyone sees it?"

I shake my head and hold an index finger to my lips. Then I wait for the explosion. But none comes. George's face appears at the little pass-through where he usually puts the plates of food. He stares at Jenny for a few seconds, until she shifts her weight from one foot to the other.

"Go take it down," he says, again in that strange new George voice. I look at Jenny, who turns on her heel and marches out the front door. Within a minute, she's back, with the yellow-spattered bunting wrapped in her arms like a pile of dirty laundry. She glances at me before hurrying into the back storage area. Well, at least we have our flag. Maybe George's wife can wash the yellow paint out of the bunting. There's still time before the Fourth.

An hour later, George is back to his usual self, yelling at us to pick up our orders. Jenny's handling the counter, because she's better with the guys. She tells me they're harmless, and I'm sure they are, but they always say things that make me blush, and I wish I had a smart remark for them. Jenny says it comes with practice.

I have two tables of customers, but they're nice people. Andrew won't be in until Wednesday, and tomorrow's my day off, so I can make it through whatever today has in store for me, I'm sure. I clean the table after two old ladies leave. They come in once a week and order the same thing. Coffee, small prune juice, and Raisin Bran with skim milk, times two. They stay forever, and leave two quarters on the table as my tip. On a total bill of $3.50. If I could flirt with the guys who sit at the counter, I bet I could make more money. I'll have to ask Jenny to let me take the counter once in a while, so I can have it on her day off.

"You got big plans for the Fourth, Robin?" Jenny asks during a lull, around mid-morning. I've been on my feet since before five, and would love to just sit for ten minutes, but we never have a chance. I know Jenny wants a cigarette. Sometimes I spot her a quick smoke in the back when she thinks George won't notice. She could probably smoke right at the counter. Her cigarette would be lost among all the other ones going. By ten, the gray-blue haze in the diner is noticeable. I switch on the ceiling fans to move the air around. George runs the air conditioning on low, and as much as I want to turn it higher, he'll know, and I don't want him yelling at me in front of everyone.

"I'm gonna watch the parade with Frank, then maybe we'll just spend the day at the beach." Frank and I haven't talked about the Fourth yet, but that's what I'd like to do, and Frank'll probably go along. He and his family are always invited to my parents' house for the Fourth, like everyone else in town. My father acts like the friggin' mayor, for crying out loud. Well, this year I won't be there, that's for sure.

"You're always welcome at my house, you know that," she says.

I know she means it. I'm always welcome at her house. I'm not welcome at my father's, though. Funny.

By the time I get back home, the clouds are dark and heavy and I smell rain in the air. Maybe even a thunderstorm, with all this humidity. Fine with me, I think. I open the door to stifling air and unlock the bedroom window, then hoist the fan into it and turn it on high. Come on, rain, I implore silently. Wash away this heavy, choking air and cool things down.

I'm starving, and George didn't offer anything today. I open a can of deviled ham and make a sandwich. My cupboard is almost as bare as old Mother Hubbard's, so I make a mental note to do the grocery shopping tomorrow. I wish I had some potato chips to go with the sandwich. Or an icy-cold beer. We have a First National supermarket at the end of Main Street, and hopefully it won't be raining tomorrow. Big plans for a day off, I know. But if that's all I plan, then maybe I can get the rest of this writing done. I'll dedicate myself to working on the ending. If it's all written by my birthday (when I'm getting a typewriter!!), then I'll be in good shape. I've read and re-read these pages so many times, I think I could recite the entire book from memory. And now I know how I want it to end.

After I gobble down my sandwich, I lean out the front door to pick up the mail from the box that hangs on a shingle next to my front door. There's an electric bill and flyer from the market featuring this week's sale items.

"Howdy."

I look up and into the pink face of my upstairs neighbor. He opens the mailbox next to mine and pulls out a few pieces of mail.

"Hey," I say and edge back inside. Guess we'd have to meet officially at some point.

He sticks out a meaty paw. "We haven't met, but I'm on top of you. David," he adds.

He's *on top of me*? Oh, I don't think so. I grip his hand and give it one shake. "Robin," I say.

"Nice to meetcha, Robin. You been living here long?"

Ha. He's clueless, and possibly the only resident in this town who doesn't know the story of Robin Fortune's fall from grace. I shake my head. "Couple of months." Please let this end our conversation.

"Me, too. Nice enough place. You work?" He leans against my doorframe and sticks his hands in the pockets of his Dickies pants. He's in my way.

"At the Liberty Diner, on Main Street."

"Oh, no kidding? I've been meaning to stop in there. Well, now I will." He nods to himself, like he just came up with a brilliant decision.

"Great. Okay, well, have a good night." I stand in front of him, waiting for him to move so I can get in my own apartment.

"Sure. Okay, Robin. I'll see you." He turns away and goes around the side of the house, where the door that leads upstairs to his apartment is. And within a minute, I hear his leaden footsteps above me.

5

It's the Fourth of July and everyone in America seems to be celebrating. I didn't get any sleep last night because it was so noisy down by the harbor. Even with the fan going full-blast, the fireworks pounded in my head, and then the sirens went all night. I probably fell asleep around five, just as the morning light filtered in through the gauzy curtain at the window. The parade doesn't start until ten, so I turn away from the window, hoping for another hour or two of dozing. But then I start thinking about everything. My writing. My parents and the barbecue. Frank. He told me last night he wanted to go to the beach with me. I have this feeling that something's going to happen between us tonight. I mean, I'm willing if he is. We've been friends forever, but I'd like to see how it would be if we were physically closer.

Frank said he'd bring a bag of food to my place, because I didn't have time (or money, or inclination) last night to pick anything up. I have a couple of cans of beer in the fridge, but he doesn't drink anymore. Not since the accident. He'll smoke pot, though, if he has any. Might make it easier for us to move to this new level of intimacy.

He comes by at nine and we have an iced coffee in the apartment before walking up the hill. It's early enough that we're able to find a good spot to watch the parade. Main Street is filling up, but we have beach chairs and my little cooler, with one can of Tab and one Coke, and a bag of pretzels in case we get hungry. He points to a place that has shade, and we set up there, right at the curb so no one can sit in front of us. We each have a little American flag to wave, thanks to George. I see people who look familiar to me, mostly friends of my parents.

"Robin? Is that you?" I twist around to look over my shoulder and see bare legs that go on forever. It's Melissa Bornberg. We went all through school together, but I wouldn't say she's a friend. She went away to Ohio for college and I haven't seen her since we graduated from high school. I scramble to my feet, using Frank's shoulder for leverage. He stays seated and ignores her. Melissa is golden and blonde and has an arm draped around the waist of a guy I don't recognize.

"Hey, Missy," I say, forcing a smile. "How's it going? You home for the summer?"

She licks her lips before smiling wide, showing off a mouthful of straight, white teeth. Missy wore braces until just before we graduated, and I can see it paid off. "Yeah, home for a couple of weeks before we go to Colorado." She seems to remember the guy next to her. "This is Mark." I see her pull him a little closer. "Mark, this is Robin Fortune. We grew up together."

I notice she doesn't say we're friends, and have to give her credit for her honesty. We're not, and never have been. "Hi," I say, and extend my hand. He stares at it before taking it and squeezing.

They all come back home for the summer, the kids I knew from high school who all went out of state for college. Missy goes to Bowdoin in Maine. Jayne's up in Minnesota, and probably staying there this summer. Laura's family moved to Georgia a couple of years ago. All of us scattered after high school, landing at good colleges, mostly chosen by our parents. They paid the tuition, they made the decision.

Melissa's eyes travel down to Frank, sitting low to the sidewalk in my beach chair. She peeks around to catch his eye and I see her expression change as she recognizes him. "Speedy Mello," she says dully. Looking back at me, she gives me a look, her lower lip dangling as if to say, 'Are you crazy?'

Frank stares straight ahead. Melissa was Janine's best friend, and she still blames Frank for what happened.

I feel my muscles tense before I speak. "Nice of you to stop by, Missy. Have a good day." I want her gone. Her and her Ken-doll boyfriend.

"Yeah. We will." Her pale eyes, now hard as glass, hold mine, but she looks away first. Bitch. She takes Mark's hand and they head off in the other direction. I drop into my chair next to Frank.

"That was pleasant," he says quietly. "Never gets old."

"Hey." I reach for his hand. "She's a bitch, always has been. Some people never change."

He turns his face to mine. "I wish to hell we could move away from this place."

"Me, too. Wanna skip the parade?" I'm thinking we both have so much pent-up frustration, there might be just one way to get rid of it. I lean in close. "Come back to my place."

"You sure?" He pulls back. "You're too good a friend, Robin, and I don't want anything to mess it up."

"It won't," I assure him, all the time trying to assure myself. Frank and I need each other right now. I know we're both screwed up, but we're old enough and we know each other so well. Maybe we could help each other mend. Maybe not, but we could have fun trying. I stand up first.

A stranger sees us folding up our chairs. "You guys leaving? The parade ain't even started yet."

"She doesn't feel good," Frank says quickly. "We'll be back. But go ahead, you can have these spots."

"Hey, thanks!" He steps forward, signaling his wife and kids to follow. "I hope you feel better," he says to me.

"I will."

Frank and I make the short walk downhill to my apartment. Just as we step on the wide, planked porch and lean the chairs against the wall, my upstairs neighbor comes around the corner, carrying a case of beer in his meaty arms. We make eye contact and I fumble for my key. What was his name again?

He looks at Frank and lifts his chin. "How ya doin'? I'm David. Sorry, can't shake."

Oh right, David.

"Hey. I'm Frank," says Frank, tapping his chest. He eyes the case of beer. "You need a hand?"

"Nah, I'm fine," David says, shuffling to the pickup truck parked in one of the paved spaces reserved for tenants. The tailgate is down, and he slides the case into the bed, then lifts the tailgate and slams it shut. He ambles back to us. "I'm headed up the hill to a house party. Seaview Avenue, the big yellow house. You're welcome to stop by. If you want." He looks at me the whole time, ignoring Frank.

I stare back at him, and wrap my arm around Frank's waist as I let my eyes linger on David's protruding belly. When I lift my eyes to his, he glances away. "We have plans. Thanks anyway," I say coldly. I turn back to the front door, taking Frank's hand and leading him inside even as I know David stands there, staring.

We have a little beach in town. It's actually called Little Beach, and it's a tiny strip of sand where the bay juts inward like a stuck-out tongue. It's good for people like me who don't have a car to get to the ocean, which is an hour's drive south. Families like it for their kids because it's calm, no surf. In the summertime, there are ice cream and hot dog carts parked under the pines at the edge of the beach. The only way to get to Little Beach is past my parents' house. House? I should say compound. My father bought twenty acres of land back when he and my mom were first married, when he was starting out in the house-building business. Their spread is on one of the many hills in town, but the land sweeps down to Main Street, so anyone who walks by can't help but stop and stare at the estate set way back from the road, with the long expanse of manicured green grass leading up to a two-story faux Victorian house with a wraparound porch. After Skip was born, my father built the additions. Yes, even as we were just children, he'd already planned our future residences. We would live there, too, with our respective spouses, Skip on one side, me on the other. He built wings, only one story high, but perfectly symmetrical. There's a covered walkway that connects the wings to the main house. When we were kids, my grandparents lived in one of the wings, but they ate dinner with us every night. Then they died, and for a while, one of Dad's employees lived on the other side, the side where Skip and Kay live now. But then there was a big fight and the man left in the middle of the night. That's what Skip told me. I was only six at the time.

So Skip and Kay live in the wing on the right side, with their children, Harold Fortune III, who everyone calls Happy now (but come on, how long will that last?), and Samantha, who everyone calls Sammy. There's a separate driveway to their house, off Juniper Street, thank God, because I do visit them from time to time. Once in a while I see my father by the pool in the back, when he's not working, but if he notices me (his own daughter), he never lets on.

The parade has ended and some of the town workers pick up litter from the street. I spot a couple of cardboard containers, a blown-out balloon tied to a stick, and even a small American flag. I pick up the flag, habit from my days as a Girl Scout. Flags aren't supposed to be on the ground.

Frank holds my hand, and even though I'm not quite comfortable with it, I let him. I guess we're a couple now. It's fine, I suppose. Now that we've had sex, it's not like either of us would just turn away. We've known each other so long. I just hope I don't screw it up. Already it feels weird, different, being with him, like he's a thick blanket on a hot summer day.

All the people who lined the street this morning have meandered off to their cook-outs and pool parties. It should be peaceful now in the afternoon for a few hours, until the parties start up again tonight. We head toward the beach for some sun.

"So, you're quiet," Frank says, slowing his staggered stride.

"Shocking, huh?"

"Sort of, yeah." He stops, and because he's still got my hand, I stop. There's a bench on the sidewalk. We're almost to my parents' house. He motions for me to sit, so I do. I put the cooler between us, but he picks it up and moves it to his side so his thigh is up against mine.

"Please tell me things aren't going to be weird between us now," he says. He pushes his hair away from his face and his forehead glistens in the sun. Frank has dark good looks. A thin nose, large eyes that look black most of the time, a good jawline. Plenty of thick black hair that falls over his eyes a lot.

"Well, it's different. It's going to take some getting used to." I know I was a willing participant, even an initiator, but we can't deny it. Things *are* different now.

"Are you sorry we did it?"

Am I? No. Definitely no.

"No," I say, and I mean it. "It was really good, Frank. I don't want things to get weird, either. Jeez, you're my only friend around here. I couldn't stand it if we messed that up."

As if he could read my thoughts, he said, "I won't smother you, Robin. I know you like your independence." He squints at the storefront across the street. There's a sale on patio furniture. "As long as we're honest with each other and say what we mean." He lifts a shoulder in a half-shrug. "I had a great time today, you know."

I let my hand rest on his thigh, just where his shorts end. My finger plays on his skin. "I had a great time, too." I did.

"But you're still edgy," he counters. He won't let it go.

"We're near my parents' house, that's why," I say in the most honest voice I can manage, because I don't know why else I'd be this way.

The Little Beach isn't crowded, and we stay until well after six. I fall asleep on the sand, and even the scratchy old blanket and the high-pitched voices of children playing at the water's edge don't bother me. When I wake, I feel Frank's hip against mine, warm and solid, and I don't move. He sits with his elbows on his knees, watching small boats out on the bay. I fold myself up to sit next to him.

"You hungry?" he asks. "I ate all the saltines, sorry."

"It's okay, they were for you, anyway. Is there anything to drink?"

He pulls a can of Tab from the cooler, dripping. I pop the top and hand the pull tab to him.

"I stepped on one of these once. Can you just put it in the cooler?"

We pass the can back and forth until it's empty. Frank tosses it in the cooler.

"You didn't say if you were hungry."

"I am," I say. "But I hate to leave here."

"We could crash your folks' barbecue," he says, nudging my shoulder.

I imagine the spread they must have, so much food you wouldn't know what to do with it. My mother was always worried about running out of food, and then we'd have leftovers for days after the Fourth. Hamburgers, hot dogs, chicken. I want that food. But damn if I'll walk up there.

"Not in a million years," I say.

"Robin, you have every right to be there. My parents are there now, I guarantee it. We could hang with them."

I turn to face him square on. "It's not happening. My father hasn't spoken two words to me since I came back home. He doesn't want me there. You wanna go? Go." Case closed. I stand up and pull on my shorts.

"You mad at me now?" He's still sitting and looks up at me with a hand flattened over his eyes, like a bad salute. The sun's not behind me, I don't know why he thinks he has to shade his eyes.

"Look, go. I'm sure my parents would love to see you. Make an appearance, have a burger. I'm going home to shower." I didn't need a shower; I'd taken one after we'd had sex earlier in the day. And he knew that.

He wraps his hands around my ankles, holding me in place. "I could go and grab some food and bring it by," he says. "Chicken? Potato salad?"

"No, but thanks. I'll find something to eat at home. I'm actually beat, didn't sleep much last night. Think I'll call it an early night."

Now he stands. Facing me, he puts his hands on my shoulders, like a father would do to a daughter.

"Robin, we're okay, right?" I nod my reply. He leans in and kisses me, tenderly, right there on the beach where everyone can see. Won't that get back up the hill in a hurry, I think.

I lay my hand against his cheek. It's stubbly. "Call me before you go to sleep," I say.

"Like I'd forget," he says, with a quick kiss on my lips. He heads off and I wait a few minutes before I gather up my stuff and walk home.

6

The day that I got caught selling pot at college, and
the next day when my parents found out about it, was
one of those late days in March that still feels like
winter, even though the calendar said spring was a
week old. The wind was cold and brisk, and there had
been drizzle that felt like tiny shards of ice falling
from the sky. Spring break had just ended, and I was
back on campus. My business was thriving; I'd
banked well over two thousand bucks since
September. And then it ended with a knock on my
dorm room door at six in the morning. The following
day, my parents drove up to the campus and, after a
meeting with the dean and bursar, we packed my stuff
into the station wagon. Back then, I figured I'd be
suspended, maybe miss the rest of the spring semester
and have to make up my classes to stay on track for
graduation. I didn't think they'd kick me out. I bet my

dad didn't think so, either.

Maybe I don't need a college degree. Maybe if this book is any good, if Maryana Capture can help me to get it to a publisher, maybe I'll prove them all wrong. But first, I have to celebrate my birthday with my mother.

My mom calls early to say she's taking me out today, a "birthday luncheon," she calls it. It's lunch, but she insists on saying "luncheon," like it's more important or something. We're probably going to the steak house at the mall. She'll want me to dress up like a debutante, in case we happen to see any of her friends. She'll pretend that I'm still in college and courted by all the "right" young men, as if it's 1954, for God's sake. But I let her have her little fantasies, because if I call her out, if I refuse to go along with her delusions, I wouldn't have a relationship with *either* of my parents.

So I'll wear a skirt and a blouse and my dressier sandals. I told her that Speedy Mello had invited me out for pizza on Wednesday, my actual birthday, so she wouldn't think I was going to spend the evening alone. She still refers to Frank as Speedy, as if the accident never happened. If I said "Frank and I are going out for pizza," she'd say, "Who's this Frank fellow?" That's my mom.

Besides, I have to work tomorrow. George isn't one of those bosses who says, "Oh, it's your birthday, Robin, you take the day off." Besides, I had Sunday off with the holiday. I'll see Andrew tomorrow. Jenny mentioned something about my birthday last Friday when he was there, and I know he heard, because he said, "So, someone's got a birthday next week!" And I said yes, my twentieth birthday is on Wednesday, and yes, I have to work. He smiled and said he remembered turning twenty. I just shrugged and said, no big deal, I have to work, and went to another table. It's not like he's going to buy me a birthday present or anything. Maybe he'll throw a couple of extra dollars on his bill.

So here I am, awake at four-thirty on my day off. I roll over and try to fall back asleep, but twenty minutes later, my upstairs neighbor David starts clomping around. Then I hear the water whooshing through the pipes and I know he must be in the shower. I picture him naked in the shower, then squeeze my eyes shut, trying to obliterate the image. Frank is skinny, but he has muscles. I don't have any complaints about Frank's body.

David takes a long shower, and when I finally hear the water stop, I figure I should wait a half hour at least or there won't be any warm water for me. And there's no going back to sleep. Six days a week I wake up before five, so it's not like my body knows it's Tuesday and should just shut down. I lay on my bed and the breeze from the fan is cool, probably as cool as it's going to be all day. The guy on the radio said we're in the middle of a heat wave. Yeah, tell me something I don't know.

Clomp, clomp, clomp. He is so annoying. I turn up the radio and sing along with Carole King.

My mother picks me up at eleven, which is early for lunch. She must have something planned. I was right, we're going to Gracie's Steak-out in the mall. It's her favorite place. I'd rather she just take me grocery shopping, but I can't say that. Maybe I'll order something big and just eat half of it, then I'll have food for supper.

When my mom knocks on my front door, I'm still getting dressed.

"It's open," I yell and she walks in.

"You should keep your door locked, dear, even during the day," she says as a way of greeting. I walk out of the bedroom, buttoning my blouse. In a polyester pantsuit from Country Casuals, my mom looks like every other middle-aged well-off woman in town. Lime-green double-knit slacks, a white knit shell and navy short-sleeved cardigan, also polyester.

My mom loves double-knit. "Drip dry," she calls it. Her shoes are white platform sandals. She wears white shoes during the months of June, July, and August, but once we hit Labor Day, those shoes are packed away until the following Memorial Day.

"Hi Mom," I say, accepting an air kiss. "You look nice."

She strikes a pose, as if there's a photographer hiding behind the stove. "You like it? I love this color combination," she says. She turns her eyes to appraise my outfit – a white Levis skirt and a pink blouse she'd given to me last year on my birthday. The only sandals I own are the Doctor Scholls, but they're white, so I figure she'll be okay with that. Her gaze lingers on my feet.

"Well, I think we'll begin our day with a pedicure for the birthday girl!" Her voice is bright, but it sounds fake to me. I look down at my feet. They're clean, but apparently in my mother's eyes, they're not complete without toenail polish. "We have time for that before lunch, and we can shop this afternoon. Come, Robin, let's go." She has her hand on the doorknob. Her fingernails are shiny red. I won't allow that color on my toes.

After my pedicure (the palest of pink), we walk through the mall to the restaurant, situated at the far end. This is the kind of place I'd never go to on my own, or even with Frank. It's filled with women just like my mom - women whose husbands make plenty of money, whose primary focus seems to be fashion and hair. We're led to a table along the wall and my mother greets at least four other women on the way. She doesn't introduce me, though, and none of the women seems to know I'm Ruth Fortune's only daughter. Or maybe they do know, and they know I was tossed out of college, so that's why they ignore me.

A tall young man in a light gray suit holds my mother's chair for her while she sits down, then pushes it in slightly. I seat myself, not wanting anyone to hold my chair. I mean, it's 1976, not 1956, right?

"Well, Robin, it's your last day as a teenager. How does that feel?" My mother clasps her hands on the table.

I shrug. "Pretty much the same, Mom. It doesn't really feel any different."

She frowns for a second, then probably realizes it'll cause wrinkles and she relaxes her face. "Let's have a celebration drink."

I glance at my wristwatch. It's ten minutes after twelve. Other than a beer now and then, I don't drink much, and really have no interest in sharing a cocktail with my mother in this restaurant, but I had promised myself I'd be a good sport today. "Sure, Mom. Whatever you think. I don't know cocktails very well."

"Well, I do, dear. I'll order for both of us." She raises her right hand just a bit, and a waiter appears almost instantly. She turns her face up to him and smiles sweetly. "Two Manhattans, please, and we'll both be having the chef salad."

I slump in my chair. Really? I didn't care that she ordered a drink for me, but my lunch, too? I would have asked for one of those roast beef sandwiches that comes with a cup of broth for dipping. But I guess not. Happy birthday to me.

Our drinks arrive, and my mother raises her glass. "Happy birthday, sweetheart. I hope the year ahead brings you everything you wish for." She touches her glass to mine before taking a long swallow. When she sets her glass down, I see half her drink is gone.

"Thanks, Mom," I say. I take a sip and feel the alcohol burn down my throat, but try to be adult about the experience and not grimace. "My favorite author is coming to the Thousand Words bookstore at the end of the month, you know. Maryana Capture."

My mom was looking around the restaurant, and I knew she probably hadn't heard what I'd said. When she realizes I've stopped talking, she turns back to me with a pasted smile on her face. "That's nice, dear."

"Would you like to go with me?" I smile back at her. Now she'll either have to admit she wasn't listening to me, or continue to fake her way through it.

Her glass is empty and our salads haven't arrived yet. She signals the waiter for another, then turns to me. "I'm sorry, dear, what were you saying?"

Oh, screw it. It isn't worth an argument today. "Maryana Capture is coming to the Thousand Words at the end of the month. Want to go with me?"

"Oh, I don't think so, honey." The waiter places another Manhattan in front of her and picks up her empty glass. "I'm not much of a reader anymore. Maybe your friend from the diner would like to go!"

"Jenny? Probably not." I let the subject drop.

Here come our salads. Before the waiter hurries away, I ask for some bread.

"That's just for you, Robin. I'm trying to stay away from bread these days. Just adds the pounds." She shivers with drama and spears some lettuce on her fork.

"Mom, you've never had a weight problem." For that matter, neither have I. I eat what I want.

"I just want to stay slim," she murmurs, raising her glass to her lips. I watch her eyes roam around the room.

"You *are* slim. And attractive, Mom. You're the most beautiful woman in town," I add. Her cheeks grow pink and she sets down her glass, which is nearly empty again.

"Are you excited to get your new sneakers, dear? Are you sure you wouldn't like to have a new skirt? Or a cardigan?"

"No, I really need new sneakers." She could just give me the cash, for that matter. But I think she's trying to make up for this thing with my dad by spending money on me. "This lunch is really great," I say. A bag of groceries would have been a great gift, too.

We finish our salads and my mom raises her hand again to signal our waiter, but instead of coming to the table, he disappears into the kitchen. In a minute, I understand why. He approaches our table carrying a slice of cake on a plate. There's a little twisty candle stuck in the cake, and he places the plate in front of me, then lights the candle with a cigarette lighter. In a low voice, he says, "Miss, we do not sing 'Happy Birthday' here, but I wish you all the best today."

I don't tell him my birthday is actually tomorrow. I just sit up a little straighter and murmur my thanks. I close my eyes for a second and say a silent prayer that Maryana Capture will want to read my manuscript. Then I open my eyes and blow out the little candle with a puff of air. While I was busy with my wish-making and candle-blowing, the waiter brought my mom another Manhattan. Was that three or four, I wonder. And all she ate was some salad.

"Mom, please help me eat this cake," I say, and she waves her hand in my general direction.

"My little girl, all grown up," she says, but it comes out sounding like, "Mylillgull, allgrump." I'm glad the shoe store is right here in the mall. She can't drive like this. She stares down into her glass and speaks to it. "But no husband. No one to sleep with."

I stare at her. She's drunk. My mother never talks like that. She lifts her head slowly, as if it weighs a thousand pounds. Her eyes are watery. "Don't you want to have sex?" she asks. "Don't you want a hard body in bed with you?"

"Mom!" I hiss. "I can't believe you!" I mean, the topic didn't offend me as much as it shocks me to hear those words come out of my mother's mouth.

She laughs, too loudly, and leans forward. "You're a prude, Robin. Don't let life pass you by. Go have some fun."

I press my hand onto hers, using my thumb to give it extra pressure. She stares at me. "I have plenty of fun, Mom. And whatever I do in my bedroom is my business. I don't ask about you and Dad, do I?" I say it pleasantly; after all, this is my birthday lunch and it's supposed to be fun. I release the pressure on her hand and shift in my chair. "Are you ready to get me some new sneakers? The shoe store is at the other end of the mall." I eat the rest of the cake, all of it. There's no food to wrap up and bring home. Even the bread basket is empty.

"Oh, we're going to Silverman's," she says, referring to the small shoe store on Main Street.

"Mom, you can't drive," I say, eyeballing her glass. Admittedly, she hadn't had more than a tiny bit of this one. I reach for it. "Let me have a sip." I drink most of it down, leaving just a small amount for her.

"Finish it," she says. "I'm done." She turns in her chair and the waiter scurries to our table. "Just the bill," she says, her voice clearer than before. I watch her carefully, and she actually looks like she's sobered up. But she's still not driving.

I notice that the restaurant is mostly empty. My watch reads almost two. We've been here a lot longer than I thought. I need my sneakers, and I need to drive to Silverman's.

"Can I have the car keys, Mom?" I ask as we walk out of the restaurant and through the mall. I take her elbow, hoping she'll see it more as an expression of daughterly love than the fact I think she's unsteady in her white sandals.

She digs her keys from her purse and hands them to me. "Be careful, you're not used to driving, Robin. And your father will kill me if you get us in an accident."

I unlock her door and help her slide into the seat. My mother's car is a blue Buick convertible. It's pristine, because she never drives more than five miles a day. I haven't driven for over a year, and it takes me a few minutes to reacquaint myself with the car. My mother flips down the mirror and fusses with her hair, then pulls out a lipstick and applies a fresh coat of Really Really Red. She pulls a tissue from a small package in the glove compartment and blots.

"How do I look?" she asks as I back the boat from its parking space. I glance at her and say, "You look wonderful, Mom." It's just the shoe store. Jeez.

Ten minutes later I park the car in the big lot at Silverman's, and we get out. My mom fidgets with her hair again, and brushes her shoulders for possible dandruff. She pulls her shoulders back, lifting her chest, and marches to the entrance. I can only follow in her path.

Inside, Silverman's is nearly empty. Since the mall opened, a lot of the business has left Main Street. Everyone loves the mall, but I still like it here, among the small, eclectic mix of shops. A man rushes over to us. Oh, it's Mr. Newman. He looks different, though.

"Ruth!" He takes her hands in his. She holds them for a few seconds before pulling them back. I see his face redden all the way up to his hairline, and then I realize: he has more hair than I remember. How did that happen?

"Robin, say hello to Mr. Newman. He'll measure your foot." She spins around to inspect a row of beach sandals.

Mr. Newman recovers and smiles at me. "Come with me, please, Robin." He's all business. I glance over my shoulder at my mother, who trails behind us, patting her hair. Mr. Newman has measured my feet since I was six years old and got my first school shoes, a pair of dark red leather lace-ups that my mother may still have in the back of her closet.

I step out of my Dr. Scholls. Don't my feet look pretty, I think, grateful now for the pedicure.

"Do you have a pair of socks with you, Robin?" He
sits on a low stool and has to turn his face up to mine.
I shake my head. I wasn't thinking about socks today.

He reaches behind him and grabs an old shoebox
that's marked "nylon feet." It holds a bunch of
stockings that were cut off at the ankle. There must
be hundreds of them in the box and he hands me
two. I pull them over my feet. They just barely cover
my heels. My mom sits in an upholstered chair next to
me and crosses her feet at the ankles. I see Mr.
Newman glance at her feet and smile. He must like
those red toenails. Well, he's a shoe salesman, he must
like feet. He lifts my right foot and places it on a
metal device meant to measure the size of my foot. I
peer at the top of his head and wonder if he's had a
hair transplant.

"Seven and a half, medium width," he says with a
glance at my mother, then does the same with my left
foot. He inadvertently tickles my foot and I try not to
flinch. Once I'm measured, he sits back on his stool
and I get a good look at his face. He's handsome, in
an older man kind of way. His hair is still thin on top,
even if he did have that transplant, because I can see
his scalp through his hair. It's shiny and pink. He has
a long, thin nose and a full lower lip, almost like a
woman's. He's lean, like a runner, and very unlike my
father, who is barrel-chested, with legs like the trunks
of the old oaks in our backyard. Thick, sturdy,

unbendable, that's my dad. Mr. Newman has a fluidity about him as he glides to the back storeroom for sneakers in my size.

My mother uncrosses her ankles and stands. "I'd like to find a pair of dressy shoes," she says. "Maybe in silver."

"That would be pretty. For something special or just to have?" I know my mom and her penchant for shoes. Her closet floor is covered with pumps and platforms and ballet flats, and there are shoeboxes on the upper shelves with what she calls her "seasonal" shoe collection.

She doesn't answer me, but wanders off toward the display of fancy shoes. Mr. Newman returns with four boxes stacked in his arms. He lowers them to the floor at my feet and takes the tops off each of the boxes.

"Those," I say, pointing to a box with the word "Adidas" on the side and he pulls out a white sneaker with two blue stripes and one red stripe.

He holds it in the palm of his hand and lifts it to within inches of my face. "Pretty neat, huh? You'll look like an Olympian." He looks down at my feet and adds, "Robin, you should have athletic socks on for the fitting. I'll get a pair for you." He hurries away to get the socks and I see him talking to my mother.

She inclines her head to him and he leans in close to her ear. She laughs and pushes him away. I look down at my feet as he approaches.

"Here we are, Robin. Go ahead, put them on." I pull off the nylons and roll the thick white socks over my bare feet. I wonder what he said to my mother to make her laugh and touch his arm.

He puts the sneakers on my feet, laces them up, and tells me to walk over to the other end of the store and back. I'm kind of happy to walk away from him then, and the sneakers are really great. My feet almost bounce along the carpeted floor and I wish I could take off down Main Street, running like an Olympian, never looking back.

As I return to my chair, I see Mr. Newman helping my mother try on a pair of silver high-heeled shoes with a thin ankle strap. He holds her foot in his hand as if it's made out of porcelain, and when I look at my mom, her eyes are closed, but I don't think she's asleep. I walk backwards away from them, and hide behind a tall rack of Florsheim shoes for men, where I can spy on them. I see his hand move up the back of her leg and her chest swells, like she's taking the deepest breath she can manage. My mom opens her eyes and shakes her head, and before she can see me spying on her, I bounce back to my chair.

"These are great," I say to my mother, ignoring Mr. Newman, whose hands are no longer touching my mother's leg or foot. "Thanks, Mom."

She stands and touches her fingertips to her throat as Mr. Newman fumbles about with the boxes.

"Will you have the shoes, Ruth?" he asks softly. She nods and walks to the counter in the middle of the store, where a young girl stands behind a cash register. I follow behind her, leaving Mr. Newman to clean up. When the young girl tries to put both of the shoeboxes into one large shopping bag, my mother's voice is sharp.

"Two bags, for heaven's sake! Sneakers for my daughter, shoes for me." She lets out an exasperated sigh, and I think she's overreacting. Typical, Mom.

Just as we're walking out the door, there he is again. Mr. Newman opens the door for us.

"I'm glad you're happy with your new sneakers, Robin. Ruth, it was good to see you again." His voice is totally different when he says those two sentences. I walk out first without saying goodbye. I'm enveloped in the thick moist air and unlock the car doors. We slide in and I lower my window. My mom raises her index finger and says, "Oh, I forgot something in the store. I'll be right back, dear."

I sit in the car, clutching the shoebox, and wonder what in the world my mother could have forgotten.

7

It's my birthday. Happy birthday to me. Frank and I had a long phone conversation last night. I told him all about the day with my mother, from the pedicure to the Manhattans at lunch to Mr. Newman. I wanted to get his take on the whole thing with Mr. Newman. He said maybe it was just my mom having a couple of drinks and being flirtatious. But I was there. I know what I saw.

"How old is your mom now?" he asked as I lay in bed, with the fan on. The phone was pressed against my ear, making it sweat.

"She turned fifty last December, why?" We had a small celebration Thanksgiving weekend, when I was home from college. I remember, because she didn't want any fuss about it, and she was adamant.

"So she's fifty, she's probably feeling old, and maybe this guy Newman paid attention to her, you know, made her feel pretty. Maybe your dad doesn't do that much anymore."

"How did you get to be such an expert on relationships?" I smile at the ceiling.

"My parents went through it. I remember my mom crying about turning fifty, and my dad brought her flowers, then he took her on a trip to Bermuda. When she came back, things were a lot better. That was a couple of years ago."

"Well, I don't see my dad taking her on a vacation, or bringing her flowers," I mutter. But Frank has a point, I guess. My dad never has been the kind of guy who shows affection. I think I saw him kiss her once, I mean, a kiss other than a peck on the cheek. So if Mr. Newman plays with her foot, maybe it's all harmless fun. "So maybe it's nothing," I say. "But she should be careful. This town has ears and eyes everywhere. People gossip."

"Next time you talk with her, bring it up," Frank suggests. "Just carefully. You don't want her to think you suspect anything. 'Cause you don't, right?"

"Right. Okay, good night, Francisco."

He laughed. "Good night, Robina."

As much as I don't want to go to work today, I get up, remembering that it's Wednesday. Andrew will be in the diner this morning. And that's enough reason to get out of bed.

I open my eyes and throw off the cotton sheet that covered me during the night. I didn't hear David clomping around upstairs this morning, so either he's still sleeping or he already left. I run the shower, figuring I'll get the hot water first.

I straighten up the apartment, eat a banana, and put on a clean shirt and slacks. I haven't broken in my new sneakers, but I'm going to wear them anyway. I love them. Between the Fourth of July and the upcoming Olympics, I'm feeling very patriotic.

Frank offered to take me out for dinner tonight, but I said pizza would be fine. He suggested going to Flynn's, because he knows I like fried scallops, but I said no. I do like fried scallops, and Flynn's is supposed to have good ones, but some of the guys who hang around Flynn's can be a mean bunch, and Frank, well, Frank isn't a fighter. Even before he broke his legs, he wasn't like that. He's more likely to walk away from a confrontation. I think he'd fight if he had to, though. He's not a wimp or anything. So we can order a pizza tonight, and I'll have birthday sex, too.

Anyway, I don't have time to think about it. I head up the hill in my new sneakers with the red and blue stripes. George grunts at me when I enter the restaurant. Hey, I'm not late. Jenny's not even here yet.

"Morning to you, George!" I sing to the kitchen. I do all my preparations. It's Wednesday, and I'll see Andrew, so I'm thinking about that. I'm thinking about that more than I think about Frank, which is weird.

A lot of people are on vacation this week and the diner is nearly full, even at six-thirty. Folks on their way to somewhere, stopping in for a quick breakfast. I'm covering up to six tables at once, but as long as everyone has a full cup of coffee, they seem to be happy. One of the guys at the counter starts it up with Jenny, and she banters back and forth with him for a bit, until he takes it too far. When she rebuffs him, he gets nasty, and George tosses him from the restaurant. It's about as much excitement as everyone can handle.

The sight of Andrew walking into the diner is as good as a jolt of caffeine this morning. He grins at me and takes his usual seat at a table for two along the wall by the window. He's lucky that a couple just left.

"Hang on, let me wipe this," I say, grabbing a damp rag and swiping it over the table. Toast crumbs fall to the floor. I pick up the dollar bill left under the salt shaker and stuff it in my pocket.

"Good morning, Robin," he says. "And happy birthday." He winks.

"You remembered!" I'm surprised. Andrew remembered.

"I'm sorry you have to work on your birthday," he says, but he doesn't look sorry.

"No big deal," I say. "I spent yesterday with my mom." I want to show him my sneakers, but he'll probably think it's silly. So I don't. As I pour coffee into his cup, I say, "My brother is giving me an electric typewriter, so I can finally type up my pages." My mom confirmed it yesterday, but she did feel bad about blabbing and made me promise to act surprised when Skip and Kay brought over the typewriter. Andrew knows I've been writing a book. We talk about it sometimes, and he's been very encouraging. The first time we really talked, after he'd been coming here for a while, he asked me about my dreams. No one had ever asked me that before and it caught me off guard.

"My dreams?" I'd asked.

"Not what you dream of at night," he said quickly, a bit of red creeping up his neck. "What you want to do with your life, what you dream of doing."

I had told him I wanted to be a writer, and he hadn't laughed.

"A typewriter is a perfect gift for you," he says. I blink away the memory of our early conversations and focus.

"So, blueberry muffin?" I know that's what he wants, but a good waitress will always ask.

"Not today," he says, smirking. "This morning I'd like eggs over easy, a slice of grilled ham, toasted English muffin. Small tomato juice." He waits while I jot it down. "Are you ready to start typing?"

"I think so," I say, ripping the paper from my pad and slipping the pad back in the pocket of my smock. "Let me get this order in. So many people, it might take a little longer." I hurry to the back and set the paper on the counter for George. On my way back to Andrew's table, I stop and ask my customers if they need anything. Other than extra napkins for table five, everyone seems happy. Pancakes can do that. I walk back to Andrew's table, all the time keeping an eye on the kitchen pass-through. If George sees me idling at a customer's table, he'll yell at me in front of everyone.

"Robin, listen. I'm sure you know all about spelling and punctuation, but my wife is a librarian, and I'm sure she wouldn't mind proofreading it for you when you're done. It's always good to have another pair of eyes look it over. If you wanted."

His wife. He's never mentioned his wife before. And she's a librarian. I picture her, hair done up in a tight bun, thick black eyeglasses. Maybe she's unattractive and fat. But Andrew is so handsome, I imagine he has an equally beautiful wife. Good-looking men always have pretty wives.

"Okay. If you think I should."

"I do think you should, and Barbara wouldn't mind. Did I tell you? She's expecting!"

I swallow. "Oh! Congratulations!" No, he didn't tell me. And thanks. Now I have an image of the two of you doing it. Thanks a lot. "Let me check on your order." I hurry away from him to the stainless steel counter along the back wall.

"Robin!" George bellows from the kitchen. "How many times do I tell you, clip the order here?" He snatches up the paper and attaches it to a string of clips hanging above the counter. "Otherwise, if it flies away, you lose the order." He glares at me, his thick black eyebrows like angry caterpillars over flinty black eyes.

"Sorry, I thought I did," I say. I stand and wait, as I can see George is plating up Andrew's breakfast. There are blueberry pancakes and an omelet for table nine as well, so I pick up their food and deliver it to the customers, a couple unfamiliar to me. The woman gets the pancakes and frowns at them as I place the omelet, home fries, and toast in front of the man.

"Is everything okay?" I ask her.

"I didn't want butter on them," she says, and I know she didn't say that when she ordered.

"Oh, I'm so sorry," I say. "Let me tell the cook and he'll take it off." I pick up her plate. George will scrape it off, reheat the pancakes on the griddle and I'll bring it back to her.

"I'll need a whole new plate of food," she says, as her companion begins eating, ignoring her. Every once in a while I get a customer like this, someone who thinks they're in a five-star restaurant. It's a diner, for crying out loud. Blueberry pancakes. Two seventy-five.

"Let me take this back," I say. Meanwhile, I know Andrew is waiting for his breakfast. I bring the plate into the kitchen and tell George. "She's mad because there's butter on them, but she never said 'no butter,' George, I would have remembered that."

He starts to utter words in Greek, and that's how I know he's really mad. He doesn't want anyone else to understand what he's saying. He takes the pancakes, hands me the dirty plate, which I lay in the big plastic bucket under the counter, and he lays them carefully on the griddle. He's careful not to overcook them, and I hand him a clean plate.

He lifts a tin shaker that's filled with confectioner's sugar? "What about this?" He holds the shaker, waiting. Oh God, what if she didn't want the powdered sugar either?

I take the shaker from him. "Let's not risk it," I say, taking the plate and bringing it, and the shaker, to the table, where she sits glumly, watching her companion tackle his omelet.

I place the pancakes in front of her and say, "Would you like me to sprinkle some powdered sugar on top?" She eyes the shaker and tosses her head. I don't know if that means yes or no.

"Yes to the sugar, ma'am?" Poor Andrew, waiting for his breakfast.

"No, thank you," she says, lifting one pancake with her fork and looking underneath it. "These are fresh?"

"Yes, ma'am, the cook made new pancakes for you. Very sorry about the butter." She nods and I see her pick up the maple syrup dispenser before I walk away.

I hurry to Andrew's table, only to find him already eating.

"You got your food? I'm so sorry," I say, with a tilt of my head in the direction of table nine.

"Jenny brought it to me. She knew you were tied up. No worries, Robin! It's your birthday!" He spreads butter on his English muffin, and suddenly I'm jealous of that piece of bread. "Do you have plans for later?" He takes a bite and chews.

"Um, I'm having dinner with a friend later," I say uncertainly. Plus sex. I'll be having sex with Frank, maybe even before the pizza. Or after. Or both. But I don't think Andrew needs to know that. I feel the heat on my face. Fortunately, he's busy eating and doesn't seem to notice.

I turn to leave, to attend to the other tables I have, when he speaks.

"When do you think you'll have your manuscript typed up?" He picks up the pepper and shakes it over his eggs.

"Maybe in a couple of weeks?" I say. "I only have Tuesdays off and I don't type very fast."

Andrew pours sugar into his coffee and stirs it with his spoon. He sticks his tongue in his cheek, making a bump on the clean-shaven skin that I want to touch.

"I have an idea." He looks around the restaurant. "But I don't want to keep you from doing your work."

I'm still holding the coffeepot. "You're right. Okay, give me a second and I'll be back." I cast a glance into the kitchen, where George's back is to me. My customers all have their food, and no one has walked in. I rush to the other tables, check to see that they all have everything they need, refill a couple of cups, make sure the woman at table nine is happy with her blueberry pancakes, and return to Andrew's table.

"Well, I thought maybe Barbara could type your manuscript for you. She's very good. Then she could proof it at the same time." He lifts his eyes to mine. "I know she'd be glad to help."

How does he know that? And what would it be like to be married to someone who knows you so well that he can speak on your behalf without even checking with you first? I can't even imagine.

"Your wife would type up my manuscript for me?"

He nods. "Sure she would. She's a fast typist, too. She went to secretarial school before she became a librarian. I'll mention it to her tonight, you think about it, and when I come in on Friday, let me know." He grins, seemingly satisfied that he figured it all out.

I don't know what to say. "Wow, that's really generous. Thank you." I feel like I shouldn't give him a bill for his breakfast. I should pay for it out of my tips. But I don't.

"Happy to help," he says, wiping his mouth. "Well, I should get going." He pulls his wallet from his back pocket as he stands. He takes out a ten-dollar bill and hands it to me.

"I'll be right back," I say and turn to walk to the cash register, but he lays a hand on my bare arm. It sizzles in the cool, air-conditioned diner, like he's branded me or something.

"It's all set, Robin," he says in a soft voice, and I feel his thumb press ever so slightly into my skin. I look up at him, unsure if there's a hidden meaning in his gesture.

"Thanks," I say, because what else can I say? He just gave me a six-dollar tip. "I'll see you Friday."

"Bring your notebooks with you," he says, then his face splits into a wide grin before he turns to leave.

I watch him go out the door, until George yells at me to pick up an order.

8

I get home from work and run into David. No, really, I run right into him as I round the corner.

"Whoa! You're in quite a hurry, Robin." He's on my porch. Well, it's not really my porch, but it's where my apartment is. All three mailboxes are lined up outside my door, black metal rectangles with lids. The box on the left has a number one on it, the middle box (David's) has a two, and there's a three on the box at the end, but no one is living on the third floor right now.

He has a few pieces of mail in his left hand and one envelope in his right hand. It's a yellow envelope and he hands it to me.

"This was in my mailbox by mistake," he says. He looks at the envelope again as I take it from him. It has 'Happy Birthday!' written on it in pink Flair and I know it's from my cousin Denise. "Is today your birthday?"

Good work, Sherlock. "It is," I say. I want to go inside so I can change out of these clothes and shower. And open my birthday card in peace.

"I would guess twenty-three," he says, fondling his bushy mustache. I know he's trying to be a pleasant neighbor, but it's all so tiring. I don't want to be his friend, and I certainly don't want to be his girlfriend. But I smile anyway, because I don't want to be in a bad mood on my birthday.

"You'd be wrong," I say lightly, then add, "I'm twenty today." I reach in the pocket of my khakis and pull out my key, hoping he'll simply wish me a happy birthday and go wherever he was headed.

"Wow, only twenty years old. Barely legal," he says, and his fat pig eyes drift down from my face.

"My boyfriend's on his way over," I say, hoping he'll get the hint. "I need to go inside."

"Well, I hope you get everything you want, Robin," David says in a voice that turns my skin to gooseflesh. "Don't make too much noise." He laughs and turns to go. I rack my brains for something really witty and nasty to say, but I've got nothing. What a fat prick is what I'd like to say. I go inside and slam the door. I stomp into the bedroom to change my clothes, then stop, return to the kitchen and turn the deadbolt on the door. Fat loser.

Frank isn't coming over until five, after he finishes work. And I have a feeling Skip and Kay might swing by with my typewriter, so I pick up the place a little. I have a couple of cans of Coke and Tab in the fridge and an unopened bag of Fritos in the cupboard, in case they want a snack. It's nice to be able to offer something when guests pop over. I made oatmeal cookies last night, but those are for Frank and me later. Besides, Kay won't let Skip eat cookies before dinner. Even when I'm married, no one's going to tell me when I can have a cookie.

They show up just after four, and I'm guessing Skip took off early from work. I imagine him saying to our father, "Hey Dad, I'm going to leave a little early, swing by Robin's for her birthday." And I picture my dad, grunting in reply, or turning his back and walking away.

"Happy birthday!" they say in unison. Skip has a big box in his arms, wrapped in shiny paper with purple and red balloons on it. Paper for a kid's birthday present, but it's probably all Kay has in the house. Sure looks like the right size for a typewriter.

"Where are the kids?" I ask, looking behind them.

"Come on, isn't it a gift not to have to deal with them?" Kay laughs, her eyes twinkling. She can be that way because Nancy the nanny watches those kids so much. If Kay had to be home with them all the time, I don't think she'd look so pretty and relaxed.

Skip lays the box on my kitchen table and Kay hands me a card. She sees the yellow envelope on the table and points. "That's cute."

I hadn't even opened the card. The yellow envelope reminds me of fat David. "That's from Denise. I know her handwriting," I say, pulling the card from the envelope and propping it up on the table. I toss the envelope in the trash. Kay pulls a card from her bag and hands it to me. It's a white envelope that has my name printed on it. Black pen.

"You can open this later," she says quietly, turning her face away from Skip.

"So, happy birthday, Robin. Open it," Skip says, gesturing to the box. Am I supposed to act surprised?

"Well, what could this be," I muse. "Should I shake it?" I smirk at my older brother.

"Fine. You know what it is already. Come on, you've done nothing but talk about it ever since it went into Helger's window." He sighs dramatically but I see the corners of his mouth turn up.

I tear off the wrapping paper, dropping it on the floor. It is a beauty, this Olivetti.

"See, it has an auto-correct. It uses an extra ribbon. Now you can write that novel," he says.

I haven't told anyone that I've already written it. No one, not even Frank, knows about the spiral notebooks under my bed. Only Andrew knows, and probably by now, his wife knows, too. Pregnant Barbara.

"Thanks," I say, looking at them both. "This really is the best present I've ever received."

"Even better than sneakers from Mom?" Skip says with a chuckle. He pulls out a chair and sits at the table. Kay and I do the same.

"You want anything?" I ask, but they shake their heads. They know I have a nearly empty refrigerator.

"Nah, we can only stay for a few minutes. Mom's watching the kids," Kay says.

I turn to Skip. "Listen, this is probably nothing, but yesterday at the shoe store, Mom was acting kind of goofy with Mr. Newman."

"The shoe salesman?" Kay raises her eyebrows.

"Yeah, she was practically flirting with him. I mean, she had a few cocktails at lunch," I add. Skip gives Kay a dark look. "What? What's going on?"

He waves his hands dismissively. "Ah, nothing. She and Dad had a big fight the night of the Fourth. She accused him of flirting with Sandra Fox." He rolls his eyes. "They act like teenagers sometimes."

"Sandra Fox was flirting with Hap," Kay says, defending my dad. "I was right there. She couldn't have been more obvious."

I want to hear more, but Skip pushes away from the table. "Listen, we should go. Speedy taking you out tonight?"

Skip still calls Frank Speedy, just like my mom does. I tend to want to call him Speedy, too, but mostly I stop myself. "He's coming by, but maybe we'll just order pizza."

Skip points an index finger at me. "Keep it clean, Robin." Then he grabs me in a big hug. "Love ya, little sister." Kay gives me a kiss on the cheek when he releases me.

"Thanks, you guys. Really, I love my typewriter." I open the door to let them out.

So my parents are fighting. Again. They're so petty about things. My father has always been a flirt, it's part of who he is. And even if Mrs. Fox, who's divorced, was parading around in front of him in her bikini, I'm sure my dad was flirting right back. As far as I know, he's never cheated on my mother, even with plenty of opportunity. Lots of women have thrown themselves at him over the years. I can remember parties at the house in the summertime, my mother in a long white caftan moving among the guests, offering drinks and food. Mrs. Wagner spilling out of the top of her pink swimsuit. Miss Randall, in a red skirted suit, her hand resting on my dad's bicep. These images stay with me. Mom being stoic through it all. But I don't think any of that flirting meant anything to my father, even if he thrived on it. I think I would have known if he'd had an affair. Although I've been living away from home for the past two years, so who knows.

Frank and I spend the evening in my apartment, eating pizza and oatmeal cookies and drinking soda. He brings me a small flat box wrapped in pink paper and tied with a white ribbon. The box is from Marchand's, so I know it's jewelry. Jewelry is definitely a boyfriend kind of gift, and Frank and I have moved from initial awkwardness of two friends starting a relationship to a more comfortable place as boyfriend and girlfriend.

I lift the lid and find a silver bangle bracelet inside. It's pretty. I like silver, and Frank remembered that. Not that he could have bought me a gold bracelet. Not that I would have wanted him to. The bracelet has a hinge to get it on and off, and I like the way it looks on my wrist.

"Thanks," I whisper. "Perfect gift."

He seizes on the opportunity to collect his reward, and I'm feeling generous, so we stay in bed for over an hour. He leaves at almost eleven-thirty, which means it's going to be a very early morning for both of us.

"You could stay," I say, my words muffled against his neck. "There's room." He's never slept over, and I know he won't stay tonight.

"I should get home," he replies, without saying that his parents will wait up for him. Frank's from a very traditional Portuguese family, and he's expected to live at home until he gets married. And no staying over a girl's apartment is included in the rules. But I don't really mind. I need to sleep, and I imagine neither of us would sleep much if he stayed over.

"Okay," I say sleepily, hoping he'll just get dressed, kiss me goodbye, and let himself out. Then I have an image of fat David in my head and know I should lock the door. So I get up, pull a long tee shirt over my head and walk him out. He kisses me again at the door, lingering. "Go," I say with a laugh, opening the door and giving him a light push.

"You want me to call you when I get home?"

"I'll be asleep," I say, closing the door and turning the deadbolt.

9

I finished the ending for my novel last night. Now, I gather up my notebooks and put them in order. The ending is the way I want it to be. I know my work needs editing, and proofreading, but I'm so excited that Andrew's wife is going to type it up that I'm moving at lightning speed this morning. There are five notebooks in all, and I set them inside the bottom of a box I found at work yesterday. If I can get to the diner early enough, I'll stow the box in my locker and slip it to Andrew when he comes in, without Jenny or George finding out. I just don't want to hear it from either of them. 'Oh, you wrote a book, Robin? What's it about?' 'Can I read it?' 'Is it spicy?' (That would be Jenny). George would be more concerned that I wouldn't be working as hard. That's always been George's concern.

We're so busy today that I barely have a moment's rest. Everybody wants breakfast, it seems. Jenny and I are whizzing around, pouring coffee, setting down plates, picking up plates, wiping down tables, and I don't even see Andrew walk in. Well, that's because he doesn't walk in alone, like he usually does. I stop just short of his usual table when I see a woman sitting with him.

"Hi, Robin!" he chirps. I take a step around the table to look at the woman with him. She doesn't look like a librarian, that's for sure. "This is my wife, Barbara. Barb, this is Robin, the girl I was telling you about." Doesn't he look all proud of himself, sitting there in a yellow knit polo shirt. Where's his suit?

Barbara extends her hand to me, and I take it. Her skin is soft and I know my hands must feel like sandpaper to her. "Hi, Robin. Andrew wanted us to meet." She gives me a warm smile. She might be the prettiest woman I've ever seen. Shiny hair the color of coffee, pulled back from her face with a thin red headband. Giant blue eyes with dark lashes, and I don't think she even has makeup on. I mean, I think Andrew's cute, but he really hit the jackpot with her. They look like movie stars.

I snap out of it. "Would you like coffee?"

"Tea, please," Barbara says, with a look at her husband that is so intimate, I have to avert my eyes.

"I'll be right back," I say, and practically run to the alcove to get the coffeepot and the hot water. Jenny meets me.

"Tell me that's not his wife," she says, with a backward glance to the couple.

I nod glumly. "Barbara," I mutter. "Aren't they perfect?"

"Come on, you always knew he was married," she says.

"I just didn't expect him to bring her in, that's all."

She gives my shoulder a gentle push. "Ha, Robin. You want Andrew all to yourself in here, don'tcha?"

"Shut up," I say, but smile at her as I bring coffee and tea to the happy couple.

After they've eaten (scrambled eggs and dry toast for her, the usual grilled blueberry muffin for him), I bring the bill and lay it face-down on the table in front of Andrew.

"Did you bring it, Robin?" he whispers. I almost laugh out loud, remembering my pot-selling days at college when I'd hear the same question from my classmates. I swallow down the laughter and nod.

"Let me get it," I say. I pick up their plates and bring them to the kitchen before walking to the back room. I pull the box from my locker. There's no way to hide it, so if Jenny or George see it, there's nothing I can do. But George is still cooking, his back to me, and Jenny's having a go with one of the guys sitting at the counter, so she doesn't notice. I lay the box on the table next to Barbara, the only place there's room.

"Um, nobody in here knows about this, only you guys. I don't want to have to tell them right now. You know, in case the whole thing is crap."

Barbara lays her hand on the box. I see the diamond ring on her finger. It's small, tiny, actually. I thought she'd have a big diamond. Maybe that's all Andrew could afford when they got married. "I'll take good care of your book, Robin. How many notebooks are in here?"

"Five," I say. "I numbered them, and they're in order, so you should be able to follow it."

"Do you have a telephone number? In case I have any questions as I go along?"

I didn't anticipate talking with Andrew's wife on the phone. And I really hope she doesn't have to call me. She could just tell Andrew what she needs and he could ask me. I think all of this, but I don't say any of it. She's doing me a huge favor and I should be grateful. I *am* grateful. So I write down my phone number on the back of their bill. She pulls out a little pad from her purse and copies it down.

"I'll work on it a little every day," she says.

"I know you must be busy," I say. "Don't worry about how long it takes. My handwriting's pretty good, so you should be able to read what I wrote. And thanks," I add.

"It's summer. School's out, so I have time," she says, with another secret smile to her husband. "I don't know if Andrew mentioned it, but I'm expecting a baby. Not until January, though."

He did mention it, and I don't know what that has to do with our conversation about my book. But now I have to say something about it.

"He did, and congratulations. I hope you feel okay," I say. She sure put away that breakfast, I noticed.

"I feel great," she says, as Andrew pulls money from his wallet. He picks up the bill and hands me more than enough money, saying, "That's all set, Robin. Have a good weekend."

I fold the bill over the money, not even looking at it, and stick everything in the front pocket of my smock.

"You guys have a good weekend, too." As they turn, Barbara catches my eye.

"I'm really looking forward to reading this, Robin," she says, picking up the box and clutching it to her chest. Andrew puts his hand on her back and they walk out of the diner together. I forget where I am for a moment and just stand there like an idiot.

"Robin, pick up!" George yells, bringing me back to my wretched reality.

10

My mother usually comes into the restaurant on Sundays, after church. She comes alone. My father doesn't go to church anyway. If he did, he doesn't ever hear the priest talk about forgiveness, that's for sure. My mom asked me once if I had to work every Sunday, and with an exasperated and exaggerated sigh, I answered, "Yes, Mom, Sunday is our busiest day."

"Well, you could always attend the Saturday afternoon Mass."

"It's not important to me like it is to you," was my response to that.

Sometimes when she shows up at the diner, there aren't any tables available. And she refuses to sit at the counter. I can't let her sit alone at a table for four, so she has to wait for one of the two-seaters to open up. I try to ignore her as I fly around the restaurant, doing what George pays me to do. She sits on a straight chair near the entrance and folds her hands in her lap. She's wearing her church clothes, a dark pink skirt and pastel blouse with short sleeves that look as if they might fly away on their own. White pumps and sheer stockings.

I wonder if she's still fighting with Dad. If I ask her, she'll dismiss the question as inconsequential. Even when I was a kid, they fought. But Skip and I were supposed to be oblivious to it. They never acknowledged it in front of us, even though we could hear them yelling late at night. One time someone threw a lamp (probably my mom), and when it crashed against the living room wall, both Skip and I ran out of our bedrooms. I was about nine, which would have made Skip seventeen. My father made us go back to bed immediately, which I did, but I know Skip stayed up, because I could hear my dad talking to him in the hall. Their voices were muffled and I couldn't hear what they were saying. The next morning, it was as if nothing had happened. There was no trace of the broken lamp, and there was even another lamp on the table where the old one had been. So no one said anything about it.

"Mom, you can sit at the table by the window," I say to her. She glances at her wristwatch.

"Thank you, honey. May I have some coffee, please?"

"Uh, yeah." Gee, Mom, it's a diner, so yes, I think you could have some coffee. I smile to myself and grab the pot, making the rounds after I fill her cup.

When I return to her table, she orders the diet special, fruit cup and cottage cheese. And she adds one hard-boiled egg.

"Toast, Mom? English muffin?" I jot on the pad.

"No bread, dear." She pats her stomach. "No bread." She looks around the diner, and I'm thinking she's wondering if there's anyone here she knows. She motions with her index finger that I should draw my head closer. "Is that Rhonda Ewing over there? I can't tell."

I turn to look at the far wall, at a strawberry blonde with her back to us. "I don't know, Mom. I haven't seen Mrs. Ewing in a long time. But I'll sneak over and find out for you." She grips my forearm.

"Don't be obvious, dear. I was just wondering."

Mrs. Ewing owns the picture frame shop on Main Street. She's separated from her husband, I hear, and has a son who was a couple of years behind me in grade school. Derek. I think he's still in high school. I saw him down at the beach last week, smoking a cigarette.

I bring food to my mother and leave her to eat. I'm too busy to stand and talk with her, anyway. But I glance over every now and then and it's weird, but I actually feel sorry for her. She sits alone in the diner, overdressed, picking at her fruit and cottage cheese. She must still be fighting with my dad. He would never come in here, not while I'm working. God forbid he might have to speak to me if I took their order, right? But it's Sunday morning and they should be eating breakfast together. At least she shouldn't have to eat alone.

Frank calls me at nine on Sunday night. I'm already in bed, with my fan on, reading *Looking for Mr. Goodbar*. I picked it up at the library last week and probably shouldn't be reading it just before I go to sleep, but it's riveting. I tell Frank about the book.

"It's about this woman who lives in New York and goes to bars by herself."

"She's looking for guys?"

"Yeah, but she picks up the wrong guys. Guys who aren't as smart as she is. Guys who come from a different place."

"Why?"

"For sex. She gets beaten up a lot. I guess she needed that rush."

"Jesus, Robin."

"I know. It's disturbing. I'm not getting off on this, you know. But the story is fascinating. I like to read exciting books."

"Okay. Well, I don't want you to have nightmares from this. Why don't you read something else? Like Michener or even Harold Robbins?"

"Yeah, I just want to finish this."

"Well, don't expect a happy ending."

"I never do," I say, laughing.

"Robina," Frank says quietly. He's the only person who calls me that. Skip called me Robbie when I was little, because that's how I pronounced my name. He doesn't do it anymore, though.

"I love you."

Wow. That's the first time he's ever said he loves me. And on the phone. Maybe he was afraid to say it to my face the first time, scared of what my reaction would be. And I can't bring myself to say it back.

"Francisco," I whisper. I squeeze my eyes shut. "Good night."

There's maybe two seconds extra before he speaks. "Good night," he says before hanging up.

I mark my place in the book and turn out the light.

When Andrew shows up on Wednesday, he's back to being dressed for the office, this morning in his lightweight summer suit. And he's in a rush.

"Coffee and grilled blue, Robin, please," he says before he's even pulled out his chair.

"Sure thing," I say, scribbling on my pad, ripping off the sheet, and clipping it up for George to see. I pour coffee for him as he pulls a manila folder from his briefcase.

"Did you have a good weekend?" I ask.

He doesn't look up, just mumbles, "Very nice." I get it, no time to talk. No time to tell me how the typing is going. As I walk away to wait on another table, a feeling of utter dread washes over me. Barbara hates my story! And he doesn't want to tell me. That's it. I'm sure of it. Oh God.

I take orders and clean tables and do everything I can to avoid him until George calls me to pick up. I grab another plate and set that down at table two first, then bring Andrew his muffin. I stand there for a moment while he continues to pore over documents pulled from his folder. Finally, he glances up at me. Well, at least he doesn't look mad.

"Robin?" His face, so adorable, looks tired.

"Does she hate it? Is that it?" My skin feels itchy, like I want to tear it to shreds with my fingernails. It's hard to stand still.

"Hate it?" He gets horizontal lines across his forehead before slapping his hand on the table. "The story? Oh, Robin, no! No! She's working on it. I'm just tied up with a difficult case here." He gestures to the papers. "I've been working long hours and..." He glances at his watch. "I've gotta go." He gathers the papers, shoves them back in his briefcase, pulls a five-dollar bill from his wallet and hands it to me.

"Andrew, you always give me too much money," I say, digging in my front pocket for some change.

"It's fine, Robin. See you on Friday." He rushes out into the sunshine.

11

I can't believe it's already Sunday again. But if I ever forget, the rush of weekend customers reminds me.

My mother comes in toward the end of my shift. She finds a table in Jenny's section and sits there, even though I have empty tables. Jenny brings her a glass of water and I trail behind, stopping just next to her. Three tables just cleared out all at once, so I can breathe for a minute.

"Mrs. Fortune? Would you like coffee? I have a fresh pot. Or I could make an iced coffee for you." Jenny must have noticed the perspiration, too. There's a sheen all over my mother's made-up face.

My mom raises the glass of water to her lips. I see her inspect the glass first, and she drinks half the water down before setting the glass back on the table. "Iced coffee would be very nice, dear, thank you." Jenny walks away. I look around one more time before pulling out the other chair at the table and sitting. I lean forward and say, "Mom, are you okay? You look, um, sweaty."

"It's very warm outside, dear, and I had to park almost a block away." She retrieves a cotton handkerchief from her purse and blots her face delicately. She looks down, then to her side, before leaning toward me. "I should let you know before you hear it from someone else. Your father and I…well, your father is staying at a hotel in the city."

I sit back. That's big news. Not that they had a fight, I already knew that. Well, maybe that it's still going on. Usually my parents make up within a couple of days, a week at the most.

"What was the fight about, Mom?" More customers have left, and Jenny is cleaning up the tables, giving me a chance to talk with my mother.

She shakes her head and runs a fingertip around the rim of the glass. "It's silly. It always is. But it was a big fight nonetheless." She peeks up at me. "We just need some time away from each other. It happens even in the best of marriages, dear."

But theirs isn't one of the best. I know that much.

"When did he leave?" I check my watch. We could still get customers, but Jenny will cover for me. I catch George watching me from the counter, but I know he likes my mother, so he doesn't say anything, just gives me a pointed look.

"Yesterday."

An image of Mr. Newman from the shoe store pops into my head. Skip said Mom was jealous about some woman flirting with Dad at the Fourth of July party, and then a couple of days after that, I witness her girlish behavior with Mr. Newman.

"Mom." I lay my hand over hers and feel her flinch, but she doesn't pull it away. I admit, we don't do things like that. We were never very touchy as a family. I squeeze her hand before asking, "Did it have anything to do with Mr. Newman?"

Now she yanks her hand away. It disappears under the table, where I imagine she grips the other hand, maybe twists the wedding band on her finger.

Her shoulders sag and she exhales. "Was it that obvious, Robin? I'm afraid I've become a smitten schoolgirl around Russell."

"That isn't enough to make Dad leave." I take a sip of water from her glass.

"It's more complicated than that," she says.

"Well, Mom, I'm twenty years old. I can hear it."

She pats her hair. "I'm really not hungry, Robin. I just came in to see you."

I stand and catch Jenny's eye. "Okay if I leave now?"

Jenny approaches our table. "Sure," she says. "Go on, George is cleaning in back, I'll cover for you."

"My goodness, you have to ask permission to leave a few minutes early?" my mother asks.

She just doesn't get it. "It's my *job*, Mom. These are my hours." And in a lower voice, I add, "It's just common courtesy to ask your co-worker. Jenny and I take care of each other, but George may not like it." I'm quiet as we walk out. George isn't in the kitchen, anyway. It's weird that the restaurant emptied out so early today. I mean, we're busy for breakfast, but the fact that George closes at one on Sunday means folks don't normally come in after eleven. They want a place to linger on a Sunday morning, and by noon, George is usually making noises in the kitchen, and growling about closing in an hour. I understand he wants some time off, I mean the guy works every day, only closing on Thanksgiving, Christmas, and the Fourth of July. But maybe it would be smarter to close one day a week, like a Monday. Lots of restaurants are closed on Monday. And extend the hours. Weekdays he stays open until two. I tried to broach the subject with him once, even though it probably would have meant longer days for me, but he didn't want to hear it. He yelled about getting up every morning at four, something like that, so I just let it go. After all, it's his diner.

My mom and I walk up Main Street together. We're an odd couple, I have to admit. She looks like a watercolor and I have a ketchup stain on my tee shirt. She stops to look in the shop windows, but I'd rather just move along.

"Why don't you stay with me tonight?" I stop walking and stare at her until she turns back to face me. She pushes her big white-rimmed sunglasses up and squints at me. "What's wrong?"

"You want me to stay in the house? Mom. I have an apartment. All my stuff is there. And what if Dad decides to come back?"

She pulls her white purse closer to her body, like a shield. As if a mugger might decide to sprint down Main Street and snatch it from her. "Your father isn't coming back tonight, Robin. And I just thought it would be nice for us. Foolish thought, never mind about it." But she doesn't resume walking. She just stands there, in front of the Bud Gallup Pianos and Organs storefront window, like she's never been on Main Street before and isn't sure which way to go next.

"I get up so early, Mom," I say carefully. "I wouldn't be any fun."

I link my arm through hers and gently pull her along. We're on the opposite side of the street from the shoe store, and I try to keep her engaged as we walk by. They're not open today, anyway. We arrive at the supermarket, almost at the end of the street and close to her house. It's a glorious afternoon, with a cloudless sky, and the humidity finally has broken, even if the heat remains. I concentrate on that and push away any thought of whether my mother is having an affair with Russell Newman, shoe salesman.

"I need bread and cheese," I tell her as we enter the cool air-conditioned comfort of the grocery store. The First National is open on Sundays in the summertime. I release her arm.

We're in the dairy aisle and I drop a package of extra sharp cheddar in my basket. She slips a hand into her flat white purse and extends her fist to me. "Take this." I hold out my hand and we make the exchange, there in front of the milk, but it feels like I'm a junkie and she's my pusher. I look down and see two fifty-dollar bills.

"Mom, this is a lot." It is a lot, even for her. She's very generous with me, always has been. She usually hands me a twenty once or twice a week, and my rent is low, presumably discounted by my phantom father, who at least has the decency to not let his daughter be homeless. But a hundred bucks. That's pissed-at-my-dad kind of money. Still, I curl my fingers inward and drop my fist into the front pocket of my slacks, feeling not one but two fifties lining that pocket.

"Think of it as an extended birthday gift. Spend at least one of those on yourself, Robin." She smiles, but there's so much sadness in that smile it makes me want to cry. I hold back the emotion, though, because that's what we do in our family. No tears.

We move to the far end of the store and I pick up a loaf of rye bread. I'll put it in the freezer so it keeps longer. On impulse, I buy a box of Entenmann's donuts, the kind with the cinnamon sugar on the outside.

"I'm all set. Mom, do you need anything?"

She's somewhere else, I can tell. I touch her shoulder, feeling the slippery silk of her blouse. I repeat the question. "Do you need any food, Mom?"

She shakes her head and smiles. "I'm fine, honey."

We walk up to the cashier's line and I lay my purchases on the conveyor belt. The girl at the register has pimples all over her face, and I feel sorry for her. Even when the acne clears up, she'll have pockmarks. She picks up each item, squints at the price tag, and punches the numbers in on the register, then hits total.

"Two-twenty," she says, slipping my items into a brown paper bag. I pull two ones and a quarter out of my other pocket and hold out my hand for the nickel. I lift the bag and hold it against my chest as my mom and I walk out of the store.

I touch my cheek to my mom's. "Thanks. I'll talk to you tomorrow, okay?"

"Okay, dear," she says, giving me a brave, fake smile before turning and walking up the street to her big, empty house. I want to run along the sidewalk until I'm safely back inside my crappy little apartment.

The real reason I bought the donuts is because they're Frank's favorite. He said he'd bring Chinese food from the place up the hill. I asked for sweet and sour pork and fried rice.

And when my mother asked me to stay overnight in the house? Yeah, I didn't tell her the real reason. Of course, it's true that I didn't want my father coming home to find me there. Oh God, I can't even imagine what that would have been like. But she seemed pretty sure he wouldn't be home. I need to talk with

Skip and find out what's going on. And one day I guess I should tell her that Frank and I are together, before she finds out from someone other than me. Maybe Frank's dad has mentioned it to my dad. Not that I'd know, unless Frank says something. And I'm hoping I can convince Frank to stay over. Time to cut those apron strings, right?

I take a quick shower and change into shorts and a halter top. In the kitchen, I open the cupboard and stare at the measly contents. Two cans of Campbell's soup - one tomato, one chicken with stars. Two cans of Bumble Bee tuna. Two boxes of Kraft macaroni and cheese. I buy two of everything, it seems. Cans of green beans and carrots and corn. And now, rye bread and cheddar cheese and donuts.

Fat loser David is stomping around upstairs. Just park your lard butt and stop walking, I think. And the stomping stops. I smile at my powers.

Andrew said his wife was typing, but he didn't say whether she liked the story. Maybe she's just typing and not reading. But it would make more sense for her to read it first, and make corrections, before she starts typing. She'd only want to type it once. I tried to correct the spelling and grammar, but I know a real editor would make more changes. Still, I'm proud of my story. It's called *The Way to Remember*. A novel by Robin Fortune. I close my eyes and see the book cover in my mind, and I know exactly how I want it to look. My fantasy continues, as I am seated behind a table right in front of the big window of the Thousand Words Bookstore, smiling and signing copies for the hundreds of people lined up to see the small-town girl who is now a best-selling author. The girl who brought shame to her family while in college, now redeemed with a magnificent book detailing lives fraught with sadness and pain, but where hope lives on, like the bulbs that lay dormant in the ground under a thick blanket of snow, only to sprout up through the dirt when the ground is warm and the sun is stronger, blossoming into crocus and tulip and daffodil. I am one of those bulbs.

I open my eyes and realize I don't care about fame. Of course more money would be nice, but I want redemption. I want my father to welcome me back. I want him to be proud of me. Proud of me again.

I won't have to do dishes tonight, because Frank and I ate right out of the cartons, each taking turns with fried rice, sweet and sour pork, and spicy shrimp. I tried to use the chopsticks that came with our food, but I can't get my fingers to work. Frank tries to teach me, but I just can't get it right.

"A fork is more practical," I say, plunging my stainless-steel utensil into the shrimp carton.

He laughs and deftly uses the sticks to lift a sticky chunk of fried rice to his mouth.

"I want you to come over for dinner on Saturday. With the family."

"As your girlfriend?" I've known Frank's parents forever, and I like them. His little sisters are fine, too. But this would be different. Very different.

"Uh, yeah," he says, watching me. "Because you are. Let's do this, Robin. Let's let people know."

We've been sneaky up to now. Robin and Speedy, friends since grade school, hanging around together, best buddies, almost like brother and sister. Except for the sleeping together part, of course, which they don't know about. How will his parents react to this? They're pretty conservative, and of course they know about me, about my fall from grace. Everyone knows in this town. I'm just afraid they won't think I'm good enough for their darling Francisco.

I haven't said anything, and he continues to watch me.

"What is it?" he asks softly.

I lift a shoulder. "I hate small town life," I say. "Everybody gets involved in your business."

"Yeah. But we're here. We live in this small town. So who cares?"

He has a point. I shouldn't care. I'm certainly not ashamed of being with Frank. That's not it.

I squirm in my chair. I bounce my left leg. *Say it.* "Your parents aren't going to like me."

He laughs, almost spitting soda from his nose. "Get out! They've known you forever."

"They've known me as Robin, childhood pal of their son. Not his *girlfriend.* And now they think of me as the girl who was kicked out of college for selling pot. They're not going to approve of this." I shake my head back and forth for emphasis.

He pulls my hand away from the food and clasps his fingers through mine. "Stop," he says gently. "Don't do this to yourself. You're a good person. I wouldn't waste my time with someone who wasn't." He squeezes my hand and I look up at him. Those brown eyes bore into me and it makes me uneasy, but I don't look away. "Leave the food and come with me, *girlfriend,*" he says, pulling me to my feet and leading me away from the kitchen.

12

When Andrew walks in, it's like he's giving the sun a piggyback ride into the restaurant. No, I don't mean that to sound cheesy. He's wearing a light jacket the color of French vanilla ice cream, and navy blue slacks, and a white shirt with a tie that has yellow and blue in it. He just looks like summer at the beach. And then he grins at me and it's like I'm looking at Robert Redford. He makes it hard not to stare.

"Morning, Robin!" He pulls out a chair at his table, and lowers himself into it. "And happy Friday."

Friday for him is the end of the week. Friday for me is, I don't know, Wednesday. But I'm happy to see him. I always am.

"Good morning," I say, trying to sound detached – courteous, polite, warm. I pour coffee for him. "The usual for you today?" I will not ask him about Barbara's progress, as much as the question tears at me from the inside, trying to claw its way out.

His eyes scan the restaurant. I look around, too, and see three tables occupied. When he turns his gaze back to me, he states, "Today I would like two pancakes, some crisp bacon, and a glass of tomato juice."

"Wow, you're really turning things inside out, aren't you? Okay, let me put that in for you." I will not ask, I will not ask. I jot down "SS Bac," for short stack, bacon, and clip the paper at the counter for George.

I keep busy with my other customers, who begin filing in like robots. Ernie and Fred to the counter, Ernie joking with Jenny before they've even seated themselves. Mr. and Mrs. Budlong at table nine, picking at their food in silence. A guy I know only as Earl, on his third refill of coffee at table one.

I pour tomato juice into a standard glass and leave it on the counter while I wait for Andrew's order to be cooked. George's wife is in the kitchen with him today. She's making meatloaf and preparing fish for fish and chips. It is Friday, after all. And George hums when his wife is there with him.

"Your tomato juice," I say, setting it in front of Andrew. He's only ordered tomato juice once before, the time he came in with his wife. And I don't think he's ever asked for pancakes and bacon. A new Andrew, maybe. "I'll be right back with your breakfast." He doesn't reply, and is focused on a pad of yellow paper in front of him. I want to ask him about his work, because I imagine he must have some interesting cases, but it wouldn't be appropriate. And besides, all I really want to know is how far along Barbara is with the typing and what she thinks of the story.

I stand at the counter and wait while George plates Andrew's pancakes and bacon. He turns and scowls at me. I disarm him with a grin.

"How's it going, George? This morning's really flying by," I chirp. "Hi, Mrs. L." She raises her hand from the sink where she's washing dishes.

He glowers at me behind his thick black glasses. "Short stack bacon," he mutters, handing me the warm plate. I inspect the bacon to make sure it's crisp (it is), then I twirl and hold the plate high, knowing it bugs him. George needs to relax. After all, he's working alongside his wife.

"Short stack bacon," I repeat as I place the plate in front of Andrew. He pushes the yellow pad aside and picks up the bottle of syrup. "How's your wife?" I add just at the last minute.

Andrew pauses, holding the syrup bottle in his hand, tilting it toward the pancakes. He looks up. "She's just fine, Robin, thanks for asking." With a small smile, he resumes the ritual that every pancake-eater engages in. I skulk away, too embarrassed to ask any other questions. Like, 'Has she started?' Or, 'What does she think so far?' I'm afraid to hear the answer.

"Robin!" George bellows from the pass-through.

I scurry over to him. He has a dark look on his face. "Pick up your orders on time, Robin. Enough chatting and more serving." At least he didn't scream it for everyone in the diner to hear. "We're busy, and you don't have time to waste with your boyfriend." He turns back to the grill.

"He's not my boyfriend," I mutter, picking up three plates of food to bring to table seven.

I manage to see Andrew briefly before he leaves. He pays his bill, again leaving a generous tip, and says, "Don't expect anything for at least a couple of weeks, okay?"

"Of course. Please thank Barbara again for me." I say her name, and any fantasy I had about him dissipates like the blue cigarette smoke around the counter.

"Have a good weekend and I'll see you next week, Robin." He touches my arm on his way out and I tingle at his touch.

Frank has a thing tonight, so he's not coming over. I agreed to go to his house tomorrow night for dinner, but I told him I couldn't stay long, since I get up so early on Sunday. He said his mother understood, and we'd eat at six. I'm still nervous about it, but he's persuaded me that it'll be fine. Besides, his mom is making a pork roast, so how can I say no?

I head home after work, glad for some alone time, but my good mood is ruined when I see David hanging around his truck. He's fiddling with something in the pickup bed, but it looks empty to me. I ignore him, stepping onto my porch. Not my porch. The house's porch.

"Hi there, Robin," he calls from twenty feet away. He's parked under the big oak tree, in the shade.

I raise my hand. "Hey." I lift the lid on my mailbox, but it's empty, and for a split second I wonder if he stole my mail.

"Done with work?"

I'm just about to put my key in the lock. I turn halfway toward him and call back, "All done. Well, have a good weekend." Hoping he'll get the message, but no, of course he doesn't. I open my front door.

"Robin?"

I stop in the doorway and turn all the way around. He's walking toward me, big heavy steps that make no noise on the ground. I wait.

"Uh, I just wanted to ask you. I'm going out on a date tomorrow night, and you know this town better than I do. Can you recommend a restaurant that would be good for a first date?" He pushes his hand through his mass of hair, but it only makes it messier.

I lean against the doorway. He seems sincere, at least, although for the life of me I can't imagine David out on a date. Must be a blind date.

"Flynn's down at the harbor has good seafood. It gets kind of rowdy at night, but sometimes they have a band. There's an Italian place up the road." I point north. "It's in the next town, but right on the road, just a couple of miles. Giuseppe's. I've never been, but my parents used to go there a lot. It's expensive, though." That should be enough advice, I think. "Well, good luck," I say.

"So which one would you choose? You know, which of those two would you want to be taken to?" He's still standing there. I notice sweat stains under his arms.

"The Italian place. See ya later, David." I smile and close the door behind me, turning the lock. I watch through the sheer curtain as he turns back to his truck, gets in, and drives away.

He doesn't return until well after midnight. I know this because he makes a lot of noise and wakes me up. At first I don't know what the sound is. I mean, I was fast asleep. It sounds like he's doing jumping jacks upstairs, for crying out loud. Then I hear the water running through the pipes we obviously share. I'm going to have to buy earplugs.

Frank picks me up on Saturday. He comes by at five-thirty, and I'm not ready.

"Why are you here so early?" I snap.

"Nice to see you, too," he says, leaning in to kiss me. I let him, but squirm away from his embrace. He wins. He holds me in the kitchen and eventually I let the stiffness in my limbs give way.

"I've known your parents forever, Frank. Why is this dinner making me such a nervous wreck?"

He eases away from me, but rests his warm hands on my shoulders. "I don't want you to be nervous," he croons. "They love you."

"They used to," I counter. "Before I got busted and shamed my family."

As if on cue, he drops his hands to my backside. Pulling my hips closer, he's nose to nose with me. "They still love you. So do I. In different ways, of course."

We kiss and I wish he'd shown up earlier. Or that dinner was later. "Come on, help me decide what to wear."

Fifteen minutes later, we're on our way out. Frank opens the passenger-side door for me and I slide in. Just as he's backing out of the driveway, David comes into view. He's wearing dress slacks and loafers, a polo shirt and a jacket. He's combed his hair and he looks nice. Well, for David.

He waves and motions for me to roll down the window.

"Don't you look spiffy," I say. "Frank, you remember my upstairs neighbor, David?"

"Hey," Frank says.

"Your girlfriend gave me a good tip for a restaurant," David says. "I'm on my way to pick up my date."

I wonder what his date looks like, where she lives, where she works. It shouldn't matter, and it doesn't, but I wonder what kind of girl would find David attractive.

"Enjoy," I say, rolling up the window.

"Friendly guy," says Frank as we head toward his house.

"Yeah," I murmur, hoping David doesn't bring his date back to his apartment tonight.

13

If I were to describe dinner with Mr. and Mrs. Mello in three words, I would choose difficult, strained, and awkward. Strange, too, given our long history, but I entered their house not as Speedy's little pal Robin but as Frank's girlfriend Robin. It changed his parents, and not in a good way.

"Robin, so good to see you," Mrs. Mello said. She was overdressed for Saturday supper, and I was glad I wore a skirt. I was hoping Mr. Mello didn't show up in a jacket and tie. I handed her a bunch of flowers I picked up that afternoon. They were a little wilted from the heat in my apartment, but she didn't seem to notice.

"How thoughtful! Thank you, dear," she murmured, taking the flowers into the kitchen.

Frank took my hand. It was sweaty, but so was mine.

His dad was friendly, overly-friendly in that fake-friendly way. He talked a lot about my father's Mercedes and how fine a car it is. Like I cared. He talked all through dinner, which consisted of a really tasty pork roast and sliced potatoes. That kitchen must have been as hot as hell, but I just wiped my mouth with a heavy linen napkin and said, "What a delicious meal, Mrs. Mello." I was really trying to be on my best behavior.

"And how is work, Robin?" she asked.

"It's fine, you know," I said. "I meet a lot of interesting people." I thought about Andrew when I said it, and for some reason I felt my cheeks burning hot. I drank water and hoped Frank didn't notice. "I'm always busy. Early mornings." I smiled as she stared at me.

"You going back to school, Robin?" Mr. Mello scraped the last bit of food from his plate.

Ugh, the dreaded question. Everyone stopped eating to wait for my reply. Even Frank's two younger sisters watched me in silence.

"I sure hope so, sir. That'll have to be worked out." I wanted desperately to change the subject. I'd already complimented Mrs. Mello on the food. I had nothing to say to Frank's sisters. I mean, they're ten and twelve.

"Good," he said, pushing back from the table. "College is important, unless you learn a trade, like my Frank here." Mr. Mello pulled a fat cigar from his shirt pocket and snapped his fingers at his daughter to bring him his lighter. She jumped up from the table and scrambled to retrieve it from a drawer that was more within his reach than hers. And he couldn't get up and find it himself??

The girls cleared the dishes. Apparently, this is girls' work, because Frank just sat there. Or maybe it was because I was the guest. His girlfriend. There was no mention of our relationship, not one word.

We ate rice pudding quietly. I waited for Frank to say something, but he was practically silent through the entire meal. He never had a problem with conversation when we were together, but it was as if he'd been instructed to be a quiet little boy.

After the girls cleared the dessert bowls and coffee cups away, we all stood and Mrs. Mello directed us (yep, she directed us) to the living room. She picked up a fancy glass plate full of chocolates and held it out to me.

"Oh, no, thank you, Mrs. Mello, I'm full. That was a wonderful dinner. Thank you so much." Even I was being formal. I was sitting next to Frank, and I picked up his hand to hold. I saw Mrs. Mello eye us. Her lips pressed together and she set down the plate. She didn't even offer any of the chocolates to Frank.

I squeezed his hand and looked at him. Screw it, I remember thinking, if he won't do this, I will. I turned slightly to look at both his parents as I spoke.

"Frank and I have known each other for such a long time, since second grade. Now we're adults, and we're finding that we have so much in common." I squeezed again and turned to him. "He makes me very happy. And I think I make him happy, too." I didn't need to explain some of the more intimate ways we make each other happy.

I waited for him to say something, to extol my charms. He crossed his left leg over his right and stared into his lap.

Mr. Mello cleared his throat. "Yes, well, you know we like you a lot, Robin. And we know what good friends you two have been through the years. You stuck by our boy when he had all that trouble at graduation." *Trouble?* That's what you call it?

"A summer romance is an inevitable thing. But we assume you'll be heading back to college in the fall, and who knows what lies ahead, right?" He laid his big palms on his knees. The backs of his hands were very hairy.

"Well, we're not looking to get married!" I said with a laugh. Frank laughed, too, and started to cough. "Right, honey?"

"No! Of course not!" he said. "We're just really good friends," he added, finally looking at his parents, but not at me.

Really. Good friends. Yeah, that's what he said. And it wasn't like me to just sit there on their nice clean sofa, with my knees together, in my skirt, holding my boyfriend's hand as he conveyed to his parents that we were *not* together as a couple. So I spoke up again.

"Well, I'd say more than really good friends, Frank, wouldn't you?" I leaned against him. "Frank and I are a couple, Mr. and Mrs. Mello. He makes me happy."

His mother looked as if she might faint. I released Frank's hand and stood up, smoothing my skirt like a proper lady, which I'm not.

"Dinner was lovely, thank you again. Frank, honey, would you drive me home?"

I crossed to shake Mr. Mello's hand. He stood up and I wrapped my arms around him, knowing it would make him uncomfortable. Mrs. Mello was probably afraid I'd do the same, which is exactly why I didn't.

In his car, Frank came to life.

"Glad that's over with, right?"

"What the hell was that? You hardly said two words all night. And 'really good friends'? That's what we are? Because I had a completely different idea. I don't go to bed with my really good friends." I leaned against the car door, as far away from him as possible.

"Come on, Robin, it was my parents. I didn't want to freak them out. They'd have us married next week."

"That's not my problem, Frank, it's yours. Move out of your parents' house. Grow a pair, for God's sake."

"Are we fighting?"

I uncrossed my arms and turned in the seat as he shifted the car into park in front of my house.

"You better believe it," I said, getting out of the car and slamming the door hard. He didn't follow me, but he waited until I was inside before he drove away. Idiot.

Now that I'm alone, I throw off my clothes and get into bed. My boyfriend needs to grow up.

An hour later, I'm just about to fall asleep when I hear them. David and his date. Upstairs, and making a lot of noise. Great. I get to listen to this.

And it goes on for a long time. Every time I think they've stopped, they start up again.

14

I call my mother the following afternoon, once I'm home from work and changed. She didn't come in today, and I'm hoping it's because she spent the morning making up with my father.

"Any word from Dad?" I try to sound nonchalant, but I can't fool my mother. She can tell.

"No, honey. But everything will be fine. Don't worry about it." But I do worry. I wonder if they'll get a divorce. Still, if she doesn't want to talk about it, I'll keep quiet.

"I had dinner with Mr. and Mrs. Mello last night. Frank invited me."

"Oh, that's very nice, Robin. What did Angie serve?"

"Roast pork. It was a heavy meal for a hot night."

"Oh yes, that's not a summer supper." She clucks her tongue, the woman who loves menu planning.

"Mom, Frank asked me to the house for *dinner*. I mean, we're dating, you know? But he never acted like I was his girlfriend when we were in the house. And he said something in front of his parents about us being just really good friends. We had a fight on the way home." I realize this is the kind of conversation I should be having with one of my girlfriends, but I don't really have anyone I can talk with. My friends from college? Friends write. They call. They check up on you to make sure you're okay. And I suppose I could talk to Kay about it, but I don't know if she could relate. Kay was always the girl everyone wanted to invite to their house for dinner.

"Did he explain why he acted that way?" my mom asks.

"No," I say. "No, he didn't. Or maybe he told his parents about me already and they didn't approve. They're very old-fashioned, you know. I'm sure they want him to meet a nice Portuguese girl and make a lot of babies."

"Robin, you and Speedy have been friends forever. Why wouldn't they approve?" In the minute of silence on the phone, she must have realized that I'd already answered her question, because she says, "Oh, that's just silly. You need to talk to Spee- Frank about it. Find out what the problem is, honey."

"I know. I will. We talk every night. Well, if he calls me tonight," I trail off.

"He'll call, dear. Listen, I need to go, but let me know if you need anything."

"Okay. Bye, Mom."

I wanted to work Mr. Newman into the conversation, but there really wasn't any good way to do that.

I'm still mad at Frank. He should have at least explained to me why he acted so stupid last night. It's only three o'clock, and I need to get out of here for a while, maybe find that ice cream truck. I slip my feet into my sandals and lock my door behind me. I'm walking down the hill toward the harbor when I hear a truck pull up behind me. I'm on the sidewalk, but I turn to look and am disappointed to see it's David.

He leans over to roll down the passenger side window. "Can I give you a lift somewhere, Robin?"

"No thanks, I'm just taking a walk." Memories of his noisy sex from last night shiver inside my head. "I'll see you later." I turn and keep walking. He inches along beside me.

"Can I ask you a question?"

I stop again and lay a hand on my hip.

"Did I do something to piss you off? Or do you just not like me?" He's leaning toward the passenger window, one arm resting on the steering wheel.

I don't want to be a bitch, even if I don't find him the least bit attractive. He's fat and gross, sure, but it's not like I have to date him. He's caught me being mean, plain and simple.

"Sorry, I'm just always tired. You know, from work. And it's hot." I shrug the rest of my explanation away. "Sorry," I repeat, this time looking him in the eye. "You didn't do anything." I manage to smile.

"I know it's hot. Hey, feel like getting an ice cream somewhere? My treat." He leans over and unlatches the passenger-side door.

"Sure, okay," I say. What the heck. He's trying to be nice. I climb in and shut the door. He makes me buckle my seat belt.

I direct David to the place about a mile up the road, across from the drive-in. It's just an outside stand, really, with picnic tables set up in its parking area. We get out and stand in line at the window, then bring our ice cream to one of the empty tables.

"This is nice," he says. I'm not sure if he means the ice cream or eating it with me.

"Thanks again," I say, dipping my little flat wooden paddle into the mound of coffee ice cream. It's melting quickly in this afternoon heat. I glance around but don't recognize anyone. Not that I care; it would be a hoot if Frank's parents drove up right now and saw me eating ice cream with another guy. Hey, Frank and I, we're 'really good friends,' right? So no big whoop.

"So tell me more about yourself," says David, who's just about finished with his ice cream cone. He inhaled that thing, I think. No wonder he's so big. He wipes his mouth with a paper napkin.

I push the ice cream around with my little paddle. "Nothing much to tell," I say with a shrug. I look up and see him staring at me, his eyes locked onto mine. "Okay, truth. I got kicked out of college for selling pot. That's why I'm living back here. And why I work in the diner. My dad was pretty pissed off about the whole thing."

He laughs. "Are you kidding? Wow, Robin. I never would have expected. So, you're smart?"

"I guess I'm not that smart, since I got caught. Look, everyone was either smoking it or selling it. But I can't go back to school unless my father pulls some strings. And unless he lets me go back. I can't pay for college on my own." I push the carton of half-eaten ice cream to the side. I don't want to talk about myself anymore, and as much as I'm not interested in this guy, I'd rather listen to him talk about himself. "What about you? What brought you here?"

"Work. I'm from Washington originally." I don't know if he means Washington state, or Washington, D.C., or some town called Washington, and I don't care enough to ask, so I just nod. "I went to tech school, learned how to do electrical wiring, started out as an apprentice. I always have work."

"Family's back home?" I'm treading into those personal waters I usually steer clear of, unless I'm really interested in someone. But he bought me ice cream, and really, I am trying to be nice.

"My mother's back home. Got two sisters and a brother, coupla nephews. I was married, for less than a year."

I look up. "Less than a year, that's not long."

He looks out across the asphalt parking lot and the sunlight leaves his face. Maybe it's just a cloud passing above. "It was a mistake to begin with." He recovers quickly. "You all set?"

"Yep." I stand up and toss the carton into the trash can next to the building.

He opens the passenger-side door and waits for me to slide onto the seat before closing it. He goes around to the driver's side and hoists himself into position before turning the key in the ignition.

"We should do this again sometime. That is, if your boyfriend doesn't mind. What's his name again?"

"Frank." When I say his name, little pinpricks of guilt stab at my skin. If he's called me, he'll wonder where I am. We need to make up from the fight.

David's sweaty hand on my thigh makes me jump. "Hey!" I yell, pushing it away.

"I wish I'd gotten to you first," he says, staring straight ahead. I inch away from him and stare out the windshield. It needs cleaning.

"Well, tough. I'm with him, David." I take a deep breath. I'm not usually the one doing the rejecting. And I hate to hurt people's feelings. "This was really nice of you, though. Thanks again for the ice cream." Now drive me home, I order him silently.

He shifts into drive and we rumble out of the parking lot.

The Olympics are on television, but my little black-and-white is a piece of crap. And I can't stay up late to watch, anyway, although I'd like to see the gymnastics events. That little gymnast Nadia Comăneci is really good.

I stare at the telephone, willing Frank to call me. He's the one who should call. And when he does, I'll tell him about ice cream with David. Only because I don't want him to find out from someone else and draw the wrong conclusion. I didn't go with David because I was mad at Frank. I went with David because I was trying to be nice.

The telephone rings at quarter to eight.

"Hey," he says.

"Hey. Are you watching the Olympics?"

"No, but I might later. You?"

"Probably not. My TV's no good, too small. Except I want to see Nadia."

Silence.

"I'm sorry, Robina. I was an idiot. I'm really sorry."

"Can I ask you a question? How come you acted so weird last night? Didn't you tell your parents we're going out?"

He lets out a heavy, ragged sigh. "Yeah, I told them. They didn't take it too well. And I didn't want to tell you when I picked you up, because I was hoping we'd just have a nice dinner."

"Well, I knew something was up. So they like me as your 'really good friend,' but I'm not acceptable as your girlfriend."

"You know my folks, Robin. They're traditional. They want me to get married. To a Portuguese girl."

"Well, for crying out loud, Frank, we're not talking about getting married!"

"I know we're not, but that's how they see things. I'm going out with a girl, and they consider the marriage potential right away."

"Oh God. Well, did you explain?"

"It's hard with them. They have their ways."

"*Their* ways. Not your way, Frank."

"I live there. And don't say it, you've already told me I should move out. I just can't do that right now, Robin. Look, give it time."

I stare at the ceiling. It's quiet upstairs, for once. "Give it time? I don't even know what that means, Frank. Your parents aren't going to change. You know, my mother is having an affair with Mr. Newman because she's miserable with my dad. Is that what you want? To marry a girl your parents deem suitable? Then twenty years later, one of you cheats because you've never been happy? You need to figure out what it is you want."

"I want you," he says quietly.

"Then come and get me. Because I'm right here. Good night, Francisco." I hang up before he can tell me he loves me again.

15

I call Kay before dinnertime, before Skip would be home. I don't like to gossip, but I need to talk to someone about my mom. And I don't want to ask Skip. Because if our mother really is having an affair with Mr. Newman, and if Skip doesn't know about it, well, I don't even want to think about that.

I tiptoe around the subject, but she's willing to talk.

"Robin, you know I love your parents equally. But I'm closer to your father, for some reason."

For some reason, yeah. Maybe because he thinks of you as his daughter, I say to myself.

I ask, "Do you think this split is just temporary? I mean, come on, they've been married this long, can't they just stick together?"

"Can you hear me if I whisper? Nancy's still here with the kids." She must have her lips right on the receiver. I tell her yes, I can hear her.

"I'm 99% sure she's having an affair. You know the guy from the shoe store? With the blond hair?"

I feel the drumbeat in my chest, a tympani now. "Mr. Newman." My voice squeaks when I say his name.

"Yeah, yeah, him. He came over last night, late. I was outside near the garage around nine-thirty. Skip had turned in early, and when I looked out the window, I noticed the kids' toys out in the driveway. I went outside to get them. It was so dark, I'm sure he didn't see me."

"He just drove up to the house?" Wow, ballsy, Mr. Newman.

"No, he walked. No car. Doesn't he live a few streets away?" I think she's right. Kay continues. "Anyway, he walked up to the front door and, jeez, Robin, I'm embarrassed to say I hid in the bushes and spied. Your mom opened the door and let him in."

"Well, do you know how long he stayed? Like, did he stay over?" If she let him stay over, I don't know what I'll say.

"I don't know. I'm sure if he stayed over, he didn't leave in the daylight. God, Robin, in your dad's house!

That's nervy. Hold on." I hear her say good night to Nancy.

The idea of Mom entertaining Mr. Newman, it's…well, it rattles me. Especially if she took him upstairs. That doesn't seem fair. Maybe they did it in my old bedroom. Probably not. My parents have a huge bedroom and a very fancy bathroom with a big walk-in shower. Images dance in my head. Ew.

"Do you know where my dad is staying?" Not that I plan to go visit or anything. I'm just wondering.

"Skip said he's at the Royale downtown. Doesn't he belong to their health club? Listen, I really should go. Skip'll be home any minute and I haven't even started dinner."

"Sure. Thanks, Kay. Tell him I said hi." So I still don't know if Skip is aware of this, but he has to be. I mean, he works with Dad, and they have a close relationship. Dad must have said something to him. And as for Kay, if she didn't tell Skip last night what she saw, she'll tell him tonight.

My father doesn't have a lot of friends. It's surprising, because from all the people who show up at the annual Fourth of July barbecue or the Christmas party he hosts, you'd think he had more friends than anyone. But they're just sucking up, hoping for something in return. Hap Fortune hasn't done a lot to cultivate friendships. He's made a lot of money developing tracts of farmland into plats, but not everyone is happy about the town's growth. If you take the hill from Main Street and head west, you'll drive past one of the few remaining dairy farms before reaching Autumn Hollow, his first project. Twenty-six ranch-style homes built in the early sixties, a neighborhood with streets named Foliage Court and October Way. Imaginative. Next to Autumn Hollow is Summerfield Estates. Yep, my father thought of seasons and ran with it. Beyond Summerfield Estates is Spring Meadow Gardens, of course. He hasn't yet developed a winter-themed neighborhood, but it's just a matter of time, and then he'll buy out some poor farmer. So much for the cornfields. You have to drive fifteen miles west to find any open land anymore. So, not everyone likes Hap Fortune.

Still, people must be talking by now. We live in a small town, and in a small town folks tend to know everyone's business, whether they want to or not. Townspeople know he hasn't been home, and who knows, someone besides Kay might have seen Mr. Newman creep up the driveway to the house, and skulk back out before daybreak. But that's a problem for my parents to figure out.

It's the day before the best day of the summer. I'm exhausted, because I didn't have Tuesday off this week, in order to have Friday off.

Frank and I are going through the motions, but it's not the way it was. He came over Tuesday and wanted sex, and I refused. It's not that I'm playing games with him, and I would have liked it, too, but it doesn't work that way. He's got it easy, living at home, his mama making his meals, doing his laundry, probably wiping his nose for him. I need a man, not a little boy. Time for him to make some choices.

Andrew stopped in yesterday morning, and I told him I'd be off on Friday. I also told him why, and he seemed pretty excited for me. He said that Barbara was really enjoying my book, and she would definitely have the whole thing done by the end of August, because school starts up again right after Labor Day. I was surprised it would take that long, but I guess she's really doing it right. I wanted to ask him if she was making a lot of changes; I mean, it's my book, right? Anyway, another month and it'll be ready.

I haven't seen David since we went out for ice cream. He still clomps around upstairs, but I don't think he's had anyone back to his apartment, because it's been relatively quiet, except for the footsteps. He's on the porch when I come home from work this afternoon. Actually, he's sitting on the porch step, reading his mail.

"Hey," I say when I see him.

He looks up from what he's reading. "Hey, Robin, how you doing? Just finished with work?"

I open my mailbox and pull out a catalog from Spencer Gifts. How I got on their mailing list, I have no idea, but it's fun to look at the stuff in there. I sit down next to him on the steps, keeping about a foot between us.

"Yeah, finished now. I've worked nine days straight."

"How come?"

"I'm switching days off with Jenny. She and I work together. She has Fridays off, and we switched, so finally I'm off tomorrow." I'm not sure I want to tell him why.

"Big plans?" He stares at the envelopes in his hands, instead of looking at my face.

"I'm going to an author event." I say it softly and for a few seconds he doesn't react. Then he turns to look at me.

"No shit. Who's the author?"

"Maryana Capture. I've read everything she's ever written. She's coming to the Thousand Words Bookstore in Westham tomorrow. I can't wait." I want to tell him everything, all about her books, how

I felt the first time I read *Somewhere Down the Road*, how much of an inspiration she's been to me. How her books inspired me to write my book. But no one except Andrew and his wife know that I wrote a book. Not even Frank, not even in our most intimate conversations did I mention it, and here I am about to tell this guy who lives upstairs from me.

"Wow, that's cool. I'm not familiar with her books."

"Do you read?"

"When I can find the time. Usually when I'm on vacation."

"Who do you read? What kind of books do you like?" Not many guys I know read. Frank knows who the bestselling authors are, but he doesn't read, although he'll listen to me go on and on about books.

David pulls his shirt away from his chest a few times in a futile attempt to fan himself. It's actually not that hot today, but a big guy like him probably sweats a lot, I think. "Stephen King. I read *Carrie*. Excellent book."

I know about *Carrie*, but never read it. Horror doesn't appeal to me at all.

"They're making it into a movie, you know. Can't wait for that." He fans himself again, this time with the envelopes in his hand.

"Hmm," I say. Yeah, that's one movie I won't be seeing. Not that I ever go to the movies. I'm too tired. "Well, I should go. See ya, David."

"You hungry?" he calls after me. "If you wanted to get a pizza or something."

I stop at my door to consider. I am hungry. And we could go to the Little Italy pizzeria up on Main Street. And maybe it would be good if I'm not home when Frank calls. I'm not the kind of girl who plays it coy with a guy, but I also don't want him to think I'm always there, waiting for him to call me. He could make more of an effort with this relationship. "Sure, okay. But I need to shower and change my clothes. I'm grubby from work."

David rises to his feet. "Great. How about we meet back here in an hour?"

I'm too hungry to wait an hour. "Half an hour?" I grin. "I'm starving!"

"Half an hour, Robin." He starts to walk away, so I shut the door. It'll only take me a few minutes to shower and change.

I'm back out on the porch and waiting for him. He comes around the corner, from his entrance on the side of the house. Jingling his keys in his hand, he says, "Ready?"

"Oh! You know, there's a great place right up on Main Street. Let's walk." I wonder if he can handle a walk up the hill.

He shoves the keys in his pocket. "Sure, that's fine," he mutters.

We take off up the hill and I notice he's not talking. By the time we hit Main Street, he's huffing.

"It's just down here," I say, a little concerned about him. His face is red. "You okay?"

He nods. "Outta shape is all," he says. "Too much driving, not enough walking," he puffs.

"Okay, well, come on." The walk is good for him, I tell myself.

The Little Italy Pizzeria has been a fixture on Main Street for decades, and as we walk through the front door, I realize I'll undoubtedly know some of the people who are here. But it's early for dinner, not even five, and the place is nearly empty.

We sit at a table near the back. It's dim inside, but cool and very clean. A waitress brings us plastic glasses of ice water, and David downs most of his immediately.

"Drinks?" I look at her, but she's unfamiliar. Who are all these people in this town and why don't I know them?

"You like red wine?" David asks.

"Sure." He didn't say that he was paying, but I'm going to assume he is. This is like a date. Wine and pizza. I didn't really plan on it, but hey, Frank's being a dickhead, so I don't really care if he finds out that David and I are out together. And David is polite enough that I bet he'll pay.

The waitress brings a bottle of Chianti. I expected two glasses of cheap red wine. David pours for both of us, then raises his glass to mine. "To the prettiest girl in the place," he says, making me laugh.

"So I beat out the waitress, huh?"

"No contest," he says. When she returns, he orders a large pizza with mushrooms and pepperoni, after checking with me. I can't even remember the last time I had pizza. Probably with my father. I drink more wine.

We drink a lot more wine, apparently. The bottle is empty and he orders two more glasses. I'm sure David can hold his liquor better than I can. I mean, he's got a lot of room for it. I'm definitely feeling it, and I start babbling on about Frank. I can hear the words coming out of my mouth, but I can't seem to stop them. He listens to it all, just like a friend would do. He pats my hand as I complain, and I grip his to make a point.

The pizza is gone, the wine is gone. He picks up the bill and pulls out his wallet.

"We can split it," I say tentatively, hoping he won't agree to my offer. Or at least I think that's what I said, but he waves his hand, laying a ten and a five on the table. Shit. I only have four bucks in my pocket. "Thanks. Again."

"My pleasure, Robin. I don't like to go out by myself, and you're really good company."

"Waitaminnit. You have a girlfriend," I point my finger at him, almost poking him in the eye.

He wraps his fingers around the one I'm pointing with, and squeezes. "What makes you say that?"

I lower my voice to a whisper. "I heard you two the other night." I roll my eyes around in an exaggerated gesture. "All night long. Noisy." I giggle. Jeez, I never giggle. I should drink some coffee.

"Really," he says, releasing my finger and leaning back in his chair. "You listened?"

"I couldn't help it."

"Funny, I've never heard you and...what's his name again, Frank? Yeah, I've never heard you and Frank."

"We're quiet. And respectful."

"And boring."

I laugh out loud, drawing glances from other customers who have filled the small, dim restaurant.

When I settle down, I peek at him. He's staring at me hard, so hard I feel a drunken chill pass over my skin. He leans forward, close to my face. "I'd make you scream."

16

I wake up in my own bed, alone, thank God. My mouth is so dry it might as well be filled with sand. And my head is leaden. I can't even raise it off the pillow. I'm dressed in panties and a tee shirt. What the hell? I don't even remember walking into my apartment.

David. Oh God. What the hell happened after we left the pizza place? I lay still, trying to remember the sequence of events. But it's all a blank. Did I undress myself? Did I let him in? We didn't have sex. I'd know if that had happened. Oh God, I can't drink like that.

I take my wristwatch from the bedside table and hold it close to my face. Seven-forty-five. I think we left the pizza place around nine. How long have I slept? I roll out of bed, carefully, and slide to the bathroom. I turn on the light and squeeze my eyes shut against the harsh glare. But I look in the mirror for any telltale signs that David and I were together. Any hickeys? Not that I can see. I lift my tee shirt. No bruises. I just look like shit.

A shower will help. As I stand under the warm water, I remember. Today is the day. Maryana Capture. And I feel like death warmed over. I need coffee. Maybe even a walk to the beach. Or more sleep.

I gulp down water and set the kettle on the stove so I can make coffee. There's just enough Taster's Choice in the jar for one cup. And one cup isn't going to be enough today.

I push aside the curtain and look out the window at the front yard. His truck is gone. Thank God. I don't want to see him today. As much as I want to know what happened last night, I'm afraid to ask. I know my tongue was loosened with all that wine. God, that was a lot of wine. No wonder I feel like crap today.

I drink my coffee and think back. And I almost drop the cup when I remember what he said to me. "I'd make you scream."

By eleven o'clock, I'm out the door and on my way to catch the bus. I'm going to try and avoid David at all costs for the next few days. First, I don't remember everything that happened last night. Second, I don't know if I want to remember. Third, I need to talk with Frank so he understands that David and I weren't really on a date. Fourth, I should never drink again. And fifth, somehow I need to make sure I didn't send any signals to David that I was interested in him. Of course, I was plastered, so who knows what signals I might have sent? And how did I get undressed?

My head still aches, but I'm focused on meeting Maryana. I have all of her books in my bag, hoping she'll sign them for me. I'm surprised she doesn't have a new book out. Usually authors make the rounds when they have a new novel to sell.

I stop for a quick bite at the McDonald's next to the bus stop. The kid there looks pissed off when I tell him I don't want any pickles on my burger. I glance behind him and see five burgers, wrapped and ready to go, languishing under warm lights. Too bad, kid. Make me a fresh burger. I wait, and watch, and I unwrap it before I walk away.

"Perfect, thank you," I purr at him. He looks past me to the next person in line. Sixteen-year-old robot with pimples and braces.

I bring my burger and fries to a little plastic table and eat slowly. There's plenty of time to waste and it gives me a chance to think again about last night. I wonder if David got me drunk on purpose. If he undressed me and put me to bed. I just remember those eyes, staring so hard into me before he said that line that I can't get out of my throbbing head. I need to stay clear of him.

I'm seated in one of the front-row chairs when I catch a glimpse of Maryana Capture at the back of the store. She gives the evil eye to a girl about my age who's holding a clipboard. The girl nods and hangs her head. Wow, I guess she screwed something up for Maryana to be so mad. But then Maryana strides up to the table, where there are small piles of her books. She grins broadly, showing off dimples in her cheeks.

Dorothy introduces her, and names all of her books. We all clap and I fix my eyes on Maryana. She seems to be looking at something, or someone, at the back of the shop, but I don't want to turn around and look. It's like being in church, all eyes should face forward.

"Thank you! Thank you so much, everyone. Well, I am just *tickled* to be here in Westham, and don't you just love the Thousand Words Bookstore?! Dorothy here is *terrific*. She has a great little bookstore, doesn't she?" We all clap again.

"Well! I guess you're here because you've read one or more of my books. Which one was your favorite?" She looks around the little space where we sit in rows. I raise my arm, but she focuses on an older man behind me. She flutters her long black eyelashes at him and I think those eyelashes have to be false. "Which book did you like best, darlin'?" she asks the man. I twist around to look at him.

He leans forward a little, as if she's a magnet and he's made out of steel.

"I've only read *The Things We Believe*, but I really enjoyed it," he says, not taking his eyes off her. I can't take my eyes off her, either. She's only a few feet away from me, and I've never been this close to a famous person.

"Why, thank you, kind sir," she says, her voice sounding all drippy and gooey. The man looks very pleased. I raise my arm again, but this time she asks an old woman on the opposite side of the room.

"I've read all of your books, Miss Capture, but I just adored *Somewhere Down the Road*. It was your best book ever," the old lady says. That's exactly what I would have said. Now it seems stupid for me to say the same thing. It would be like I was copying the old lady.

"I really loved that book, too, ma'am. Thank you," Maryana says. "Well, all of my books are available here today, and I'm going to sign for the next hour." She looks to the back of the store again, and I twist around in my folding chair to see a nice-looking older man in a gray suit standing against the wall. He has thick white hair and very dark eyes. He nods at her.

Maryana pulls out a chair and seats herself at a square card table. The young girl who must be her assistant places a glass of water on the table and stands to the side. Dorothy steps forward to speak.

"I'll ask you not to take too long with Miss Capture. She has a long line of fans who want their books signed, but she can only stay for a limited time, and we want everyone to have a chance. Let's start with the first row." She gestures with her hand, like the usher does in church when it's time for Holy Communion.

I was hoping to go toward the end, but maybe this is best. At least I'll have a minute with her. If I waited until the end, there might not be any time left.

I'm third in line. The young assistant takes a book from the first person, opens it up, and asks in a quiet voice what the lady's name is. Then she turns to Maryana, sets the book in front of her, and says, "Nancy." I watch as Maryana lifts her eyes to the woman and says, "Nancy! So nice to meet you! Shall I inscribe the book to you?"

Nancy bobs her head, and Maryana signs the book with a flourish. I can see she has a big signature. She closes the book and hands it back to Nancy with a dazzling smile. "Thank you so much for coming." Nancy steps to the side and then walks to the back of the store.

While the person in front of me is waiting for Maryana to sign, the assistant holds out her hand for my book.

"I have all five of them," I say, opening my canvas tote bag. The girl looks alarmed.

"Oh, I don't think you can ask her to sign all five," she whispers.

"Really? I brought all five of them, though. It would mean a lot," I say. I realize I'm now holding up the line. The person in front of me has moved on. I glance to my right and see Maryana trying to signal the man in the back, the good-looking man standing against the wall. She points to her wristwatch.

"Just one," the young girl whispers with urgency.

"Okay," I mumble, pulling out *Somewhere Down the Road* and handing it to her.

"What's your name?" the girl asks, but Maryana has turned her attention to me.

"Hello, sweetheart," she croons, snatching the book from the assistant's hands and opening it to the inside cover page. "What's your name?" She makes eye contact with me and smiles. I notice a lot of wrinkles around her eyes, and she's wearing heavy makeup that fills the cracks in her face. When she lowers her head to start writing, I notice gray in her hair, right at her scalp.

"Robin," I say. "R-O-B-I-N." Then I figure, what the heck, I'm going for it. "I have all of your books, Miss Capture. The other four are here in my bag. Would you sign them as well?"

She regards me, the smile still on her face, but I see a change in the eyes. I don't know what it is, but there's something that's different. "Of course, dear. Which book is your favorite?" Her hand hovers, ready to sign.

"Oh, this one," I say, pointing to the one in front of her. "But I've loved them all." She begins to sign and I pull out the other four books. The young girl looks at me with an expression on her face that I can only say would be the same if she were witnessing a massive fire. Her mouth just hangs open and I feel like cracking a joke about catching flies.

"Well, thank you for being a loyal reader," Maryana says as she signs one book after another.

"I also write," I say quietly, leaning closer to her. I've tossed all trepidation aside. "I've just finished my first novel. You've been such an inspiration."

The man who waits behind me grumbles. "I thought we could only have one book signed," he spouts.

Maryana doesn't react to what I've said. Maybe she didn't hear me? Should I tell her again? She finishes signing the fifth book and pushes the pile of books away from her. Still with the smile on her face, she says, "There you are, Robin. All five of my books, signed. Thank you for coming." And with that, I'm dismissed. She has turned her smiling face to the man on my left. I step to the side, and cast a glance at the young girl, who looks my way once more and shakes her head before asking the next customer her name.

I take my books and slip them back in the tote bag, then sit in one of the empty chairs. The line of people waiting is long. That was my chance. She'll be out of here as soon as she's signed the last book, I can tell. The man in the back is waiting for her.

I stand and lift the canvas bag. It feels heavier now than when I walked in. I snake around the folding chairs and work my way to the back wall, where the man stands like a soldier on guard at a palace.

"Are you her husband?" I ask, leaning against the wall next to him.

He turns to regard me and his lips curl upward. "I'm a good friend," he says, looking at his watch. He keeps his eyes on Maryana, who is still signing and smiling and saying, "Thank you so much for coming."

"She's my favorite author. I want to be just like her," I gush. He's going to think I'm an idiot.

"Is that so. Did you tell her that?" He continues to stare, doesn't turn to me when he speaks.

"Yeah, I told her." I watch the line progress. The assistant still looks scared. "I wish I had that girl's job," I say, pointing with my chin to the assistant.

That remark makes him laugh, a gruff snort, like I told a really bad joke. "No, you don't," is all he says. "Excuse me," he adds, then moves away from me and toward the table. I see Maryana look up as he approaches. It hasn't been an hour yet. It's only been about fifteen minutes, and I count seven people still in line. There are probably more people who will come into the store, too. He stands just behind her, then he bends at the waist and whispers something into her hair. She signs, smiles at the customer, says, "Thank you so much for coming!" and turns her head slightly to him.

"Excuse me for one quick second," she says, standing and stepping off to the side to confer with her good friend. They lean in close to one another while the assistant continues to take names. She doesn't write them down, and I just know that if she messes it up, she'll be in big trouble. I could memorize up to twenty names, I bet.

Maryana sits back down and says to the folks standing next to her table, "I have an emergency, so I'll need to just sign the rest of these books and leave. I'm so very sorry." Dorothy is up at the cash register, so she doesn't know about this piece of news, but I don't think she'll like it much. After all, the sign in the window says Maryana Capture will be here from three to four, and it's only three-twenty-five. Meanwhile, Maryana is scribbling furiously in the books, like a machine.

I watch the scene unfold and wonder what her emergency is, or is the guy just bored with the whole thing. Maybe he's her agent and also her lover. I picture the two of them together, doing the things Frank and I do sometimes, but an image of David trespasses into my mind. David. What the heck happened last night, anyway? I'm so caught up in trying to remember that I don't even see Maryana get up from the table and walk to the back area where she was when I first entered the bookstore.

I glance at Dorothy, who is oblivious to the whole thing, and I wonder if Maryana will even say goodbye. Of course she'll say goodbye. She's been very gracious. An emergency is an emergency. The customers file away. Most of them leave the bookstore, and finally Dorothy turns to the author table. The empty author table. The only thing on the table now is an empty glass. When she looks around and sees me, I gesture with my head that they're in the back. Dorothy turns her palms up and raises her eyebrows, but I just lift my shoulders before dropping them.

Still, I wait around to find out what's going on. I'm intrigued by this trio – Maryana, the man who's her good friend, and the young assistant who trembles like a bird in the shadow of a cat. Maybe Maryana really is a demanding author. I hang out at the end of the military history aisle and try to overhear the conversation as Dorothy approaches them.

"Is everything all right? I thought you'd be here until four," Dorothy says.

"…emergency…so very sorry…customers…appreciative." It's Maryana's voice but I can't make all of it out.

"We really must leave," says the guy. "I'll be in the car." I watch as he exits the back room and hurries past without noticing me.

"I understand, Miss Capture," I hear Dorothy say. "Thank you again for coming." If I were Dorothy, I'd be more peeved that Maryana's leaving, but Dorothy probably figures she'll keep selling more of her books either way. "No, take all the time you need," I hear her say as she walks out of the back room. I stoop low and pretend to examine a book, because I don't want Dorothy to think I'm an eavesdropper, even though I am.

Dorothy returns to the front of the store, but I stay in the stacks and listen. Actually, I'm hoping I might accidentally on purpose bump into Maryana one more time, let her see my face again, maybe tell her (again) that I've written a novel. Maybe she'd want to read it. But all of that splits apart when I hear her yelling at her assistant.

"You're an imbecile! Didn't you understand me when I said one book and one book only? That stupid girl brought all five of my books with her! I don't know why I put up with idiots like you."

My mouth falls open. She's talking about me! I'm not stupid. And I bought all of those books. I watch as she storms out of the back room. She doesn't see me as she marches past, but the young girl trailing behind her does. Her eyes are wide and red, and she scurries to keep up. I watch them exit the store and don't even know what to think.

17

The bus drops me off on Main Street and I have to walk by the Little Italy Pizzeria on my way home. I want to sneak into my house and not see David. Plus I need to talk to Frank before anyone who might have been in the pizza place last night and saw me acting stupid with David and calls Frank to tell him.

Lucky for me, I slip inside my apartment unseen. I pull all the shades and sit quietly with a cup of tea. Even though Frank isn't home from work yet, I pick up the phone and dial his number. His mother answers.

"Hi, Mrs. Mello, how are you?"

"Fine, fine, Robin. Are you looking for my Frank?" She's polite, but clipped. No chatting with Mrs. Mello. And, yeah, I caught it. *Her* Frank.

"Yes. I realize he may not be home from work yet. Would you please ask him to call me when he has a chance?"

"Of course, dear. It probably won't be until after we've had our dinner."

"Sure, that's fine. Thanks, Mrs. Mello." I replace the receiver. I wonder if he'll call. Or if she'll even remember to give him the message.

I stay quiet, listening for noise from upstairs, but there's nothing. I sit at my kitchen table and look at my calendar. Two red circles around today's date. Maryana Capture. Well, that was an interesting afternoon. I pull one of her books from my canvas bag and look at the back cover photo. She's a lot older in real life than she is in this picture. I take all five books out of the bag and lay them on the table, one next to the other, all with the back covers facing up. Same photograph in each one. I pick her first novel, *Somewhere Down the Road*, and open it to find the copyright date. 1966. So this photo of her is at least ten years old. I open the next book, *I Found my Own*. 1968. Then 1970 and 1972. Her most recent book, *The Things We Believe*, was published in 1974. So a book every two years. That means she should have a new book coming out this year. But she didn't say anything about a new book coming out. Wouldn't she have told us? That's weird. I pick up the books and replace them on the shelf in the little bookcase that's in my bedroom.

Frank calls me before six. I smile, because it means he's calling me before dinner, defying his mother.

"Hey," I say. "How're you doing?"

"Why are you whispering?"

"Was I? Sorry. It's so quiet around here I didn't even realize."

"How was the book thing? You went, right?"

He didn't mention the pizza place right away, which might mean he doesn't know. Good. "It was okay, but I can't wait to talk to you about it. Any chance you could swing by after you eat? I miss you," I add.

"You sure? You're not mad at me?"

"Not a chance. Come over. Hurry up." I hang up the phone and my pulse quickens. I press my thumb to the inside of my wrist, the way the nurse did that time in the hospital when I sprained my arm.

I don't want Frank and David to see each other, and David's not home yet. I can only hope to grab Frank as soon as he pulls up in the driveway. I sit at the table and tap my fingers, like I'm playing the piano, only I don't know how.

A vehicle pulls into the front driveway and I tense. Pulling aside an inch of the curtain, I see David's truck. Shit. Shitshitshit. I let the curtain go and stay very still. Frank will be here any minute, if he left right away. I hear David's heavy footsteps on the porch, just outside my door. I stand against the front wall, next to the door, away from the window. I can actually hear him lift the top of the metal mailbox next to the door. Please just walk away with your stupid mail. It's quiet outside. Did he sit on the front steps again? Reading? Waiting? Oh God. I can't stand this. I dare to peek out again and I don't see him. But that doesn't mean he isn't lurking around.

And now here comes Frank. Please, I pray, please let David be back in his apartment. I hear footsteps again, this time light as Frank leaps up the three steps to my front door. He raps twice and I open the door, pulling him inside by the arm. Quickly I shut the door behind him and lock it.

"What's going on?" he asks, but I stop him with a long kiss. It turns into a full make-out session in the kitchen and soon we've crab-walked into my bedroom. We finally pull apart, me gasping for air and Frank with a bemused look on his face.

"Hey, I've missed you, too," he says, grinning. He takes my face in his hands. They're rough against my cheeks, but I don't mind. "You gonna tell me about your day? Or should that wait?"

I unbutton his shirt. "It can wait."

An hour later, we're lying in my bed, covered with a cotton sheet. I've told him all about Maryana, and how she looked a lot older than the photo on her book covers, and that she was mean to her assistant. All leading up to the big story.

"Listen, I want to tell you something," I say, pulling the sheet up around my neck.

He turns on his side to face me, propping himself up on one elbow.

"You want to tell me again how incredible I am?" He smirks and I roll my eyes at him.

"No, I want to tell you something, because I don't want you to hear it from anyone else and get the wrong impression. Last night, my neighbor upstairs, David? He asked me if I wanted to grab a pizza with him. I figured why not, because he knows you and I are together, so it wasn't like a date or anything, just neighbors grabbing a bite. So we walked up the hill to Little Italy."

Frank is watching me intently. "Okay," he says, a big question mark in his voice.

"Well, I had too much to drink. He ordered a bottle of wine. Anyway, I was pretty drunk. Had a big hangover this morning." I laugh and shake my head. That's it, I think. That's the story.

"Was he trying to get you drunk?" Frank fingers the sheet that covers me.

"I doubt it. He's so big, he probably thought a bottle of wine was no big deal. I mean, he ate a lot of pizza, too. I probably should have eaten more, but really, he ate most of the pizza."

"Did he try anything with you?" His fingers travel over the sheet, barely touching me, tracing patterns on the cotton.

I shake my head and feel pressure building behind my eyes. "I just drank too much, that's what I regret. Nothing happened between us, Frank."

He leans in to kiss my mouth. "No worries then. I trust you completely."

I touch his face as I feel tears spill from the outer corners of my eyes. Damn. "I love you, Francisco."

"I love you, too, Robina."

Frank leaves at eight, but I'm restless. Usually I sleep really well after we have sex. I need to sleep, though, because Saturday morning means back to work. He said he trusts me completely. He's a good person, too good for someone like me. What kind of girlfriend would go out and get drunk with another guy? And not even remember how she got undressed, or whether she did it all herself.

I turn from side to side in bed and when my alarm clock rings at four-thirty, I'm dead to the world. I drag myself to the shower and go through the motions of preparing for a long weekend ahead.

Jenny wants to hear all about the author event. I give her the *Reader's Digest* version, keeping it all positive. After all, I do still adore Maryana Capture, and I'm still hoping she might be able to help me get my book published.

We're busy today, both of us hustling to keep coffee mugs filled, breakfast served, customers happy. George seems to be in a good mood, maybe because his wife is working next to him in the kitchen. Doesn't matter why – if George is happy, then I'm happy. And not so tense, waiting for the next eruption.

I'm standing at a table, with my back to the entrance, so I don't see David lumber in and park his butt on a stool at the counter. When I'm in the back at the coffee station, Jenny comes up and says, "There's a guy at the counter asking for you."

I crane my neck to see who it is. "Shit," I mutter to Jenny, who raises her eyebrows.

"That's my upstairs neighbor. I don't like him. Make sure he stays at the counter. I don't have time to talk to him, anyway."

"Don't worry, kiddo. I've got this." She marches back to the counter. Jenny can handle anyone, I know, but at some point I'm going to have to acknowledge his presence. I bring tea and coffee to a couple of tables and take orders. After I clip the paper slips up for George, I turn around and acknowledge David.

"Morning. How you doing?"

"Morning, Robin! I told you I'd be in, and here I am." He looks around and nods his approval – of what, the décor?

God, like I should care.

"Enjoy your breakfast," I say, hurrying off to ask customers if they need anything. The same customers I asked five minutes ago.

Forty-five minutes later, he's still there, even as Jenny tries to move him along, clearing his plate, slapping his bill on the counter in front of him. She meets me back at the coffee station.

"I think he's going to stick around until he can talk to you, Robin," she says. "Want me to tell him to scram?"

Yeah, that would be great, I say to myself. But I need to deal with him. "He needs to understand that I'm not interested in him," I tell her. "Let him sit there. I'm busy. If he wants to hang out on that stool until we close, just make sure he buys something."

David stays until we close. I manage to avoid him for the most part, busying myself with the tables in my area, even taking time to wipe everything down as the customers file out the door, happy and full. He's the last customer in the restaurant, and George notices, casting a wary eye on him but saying nothing.

"David, you're still here. Did you need something?"

He glances away from my gaze and drinks what's probably his tenth cup of coffee. "Listen, Robin, I just wanted to talk to you. About the other night. And apologize. I drank too much…"

"So did I. I wish I hadn't."

"Well, I just really enjoyed being out with you," he says, flipping a sugar packet around on the counter.

"And you know I have a boyfriend. I told him about it last night, because I didn't want him to get the wrong idea. You and I shared a pizza, that's it."

"And way too much wine," he adds with a chuckle.

"And way too much wine, yes," I say carefully. "I don't want it to happen again, and I don't want you, or Frank, to get the wrong impression." I cross my arms over my chest.

He slides off the stool and stands up straight. Then he sticks his big hand out. "Friends?" he asks.

I pause. How can I not shake his hand? I place mine in his. "Neighbors," I reply. Then I feel kind of bad, because it's like I'm saying I don't want to be friends with him. Even though I don't. But I remember how it felt when I was nine and Missy Bornberg said she didn't want to be friends with me.

"You heading back home? I'll wait for ya."

Jenny calls from behind the counter, "Robin, you promised you'd come with me after work!" She gives me a pleading look.

I turn to David and shrug. "Sorry. See you later."

His mouth twists in a kind of smile and he nods. "Yeah, see you later."

As soon as he's out the door and down the street, I embrace her.

"Yeah, he's creepy. Stick with the skinny kid," she says.

18

David must be away. I haven't heard his heavy footsteps above me for almost two weeks. His truck isn't around, either. I welcome the respite, and am much more relaxed when Frank comes over.

Andrew hasn't said a word about my manuscript, but the end of August approaches, and that means Labor Day is coming. And he told me that his wife would be finished with all the correcting and typing by Labor Day. I flip up the calendar page and draw a red circle around September 6. Then I'll have to decide what to do with the finished product.

According to the inside of her books, Maryana Capture is published through Bellest Hapshaw, on Fifth Avenue in New York City. I'd need to get her to read my book first, then maybe she'd recommend it to her publisher. Or maybe, knowing how much of a fan I am, she'd put in a good word for me, even if it's with a different publisher. Maybe she'd even write something I could put on the back cover, like "A brilliant debut novel!" or something like that.

The diner's busy for a Thursday morning, so I don't notice right away when Mr. Newman walks in, alone. It's only when I stop at his table to take his order that I see the thin hair covering his almost-bald head. He looks up at me and smiles, but it's a tentative smile, tight and unsure.

"Good morning, Robin," he says, with his little half-smile and his thin hair. I'm holding a pot of hot coffee in my hand. I haven't spoken with my mother in a few days, but as far as I know, she's still having an affair with him. And my father is still not living in his own house. I'm tempted to spill the coffee in his lap. But I was raised to be polite, and I will be polite. Besides, I can't afford to get fired.

"Good morning, Mr. Newman," I say. "Would you like some coffee? Breakfast?" I lay a folded menu in front of him.

"Well, uh, I'm waiting. For your mother." His eyes dart to the door. The coffee pot is heavy in my hand. He eyes it and says, "Coffee would be great, thanks." I pour some in his cup, careful not to spill any, and walk away from him. He's meeting my mother for breakfast? Here? I'll be waiting on them? Unbelievable.

I'm about to tell Jenny all about it when my mother sashays in, all decked out in a yellow pantsuit. She sways her hips as she walks across the restaurant to Mr. Newman's table, like she wants to be sure everyone sees her. He stands to pull out her chair, like they're at the Waldorf-Astoria restaurant, for crying out loud. I catch Jenny's eye and shake my head before returning to their table.

"Mom," I mutter under my breath, pouring coffee for her. I set another menu at her place.

"Robin, darling," she gushes, as if this is the most normal thing in the world for her to be having breakfast with stupid Mr. Newman and not her husband. I give her a hard look but she doesn't even make eye contact with me. All her attention is on him.

"Do you need a minute?"

"Russell, why don't you order for us?" she purrs, and I feel a wave of nausea course through my stomach and up my throat.

He reddens, all the way up to his shiny scalp, which I can see very well. My father's hair may be gray, but he has a lot of it. At least he did the last time I saw him.

"Well, Ruth, you do enjoy French toast, don't you?" He glances up at her and smiles, not the tight little smile he gave me earlier, but one that's intimate, like there's a secret behind it. I look away while I jot down the order. "So, French toast with fruit for your mother, Robin, and a ham and cheese omelet for me, please." He folds his menu, picks up my mother's, and hands them both to me. He grins, and I notice his bottom teeth are all crooked. Good.

I stomp over to the counter and clip up the order. George turns around, with a bowl of oatmeal in one hand and a plate of ham and eggs in the other. He sets them down, barks, "Jenny!" and I see his eyes linger on the table where my mother sits, her hand in the grasp of Mr. Newman's. George looks at me, his dark eyes magnified behind his eyeglasses. I stare back at him, daring him to say something.

He lowers his voice and leans forward. With a jerk of his head, aimed at the door, he says, "You want to go home? My wife can take over for you. It's okay."

That's about the kindest thing George has ever said to me, and I swallow back the lump forming in my throat.

"I'll stay, George. I'm all right." We share a look, without words, but I know he understands. He takes the slip of paper from me and turns back to the grill.

I busy myself with the remaining customers I have, pouring coffee, making change, wiping tables. At quarter to two, the only customers left in the diner are my mother and Mr. Newman. They've been at their table for nearly two hours. I walk over with the bill and lay it right in the middle of them. He'd better pay for this breakfast, that's all I can say. "Whenever you're ready," I murmur. Wait until I tell Kay about this. And she'll tell Skip, who'll probably tell my dad. Then again, maybe no one would be surprised.

"Robin, wait," Mr. Newman calls out. He pulls his wallet from his back pocket and takes out a twenty-dollar bill, then lays it on top of the bill. He hands both the bill and the money to me.

"Be right back with your change." I take them and turn away.

"It's all set," he says, too loud, as if he's trying to impress people who aren't even there.

Twenty bucks for a seven-dollar tab? I don't think so. I might take money from my mother but I'm not about to accept it from him. I pretend I didn't hear him and go back to the register, where I ring up the sale and pull out the change, twelve dollars and forty cents. I bring it back to the table.

"Oh, Robin, keep it."

I will not meet his eyes. He may be able to charm the pants off my mother, but it won't work on me. I've had the pants charmed off me before.

"It's too much. Please, take your change," I say, then I walk away before he can say anything else. I hide in the back until Jenny tells me they're gone. "Your mom said she'd call you later. I told her you were in the bathroom."

When we both walk back into the restaurant, George's wife is sitting at a table, drinking coffee and eating pancakes. I swipe at the outer corners of my eyes and sit next to her. Jenny hangs a "closed" sign in the door.

George brings plates of pancakes from the kitchen. Mine have blueberries in them.

"Thank you," I say, looking down.

"She make a fool of your father, in his town. Is not right."

"I know, George. I know." On any other day, I'd have argued that this is not my father's town, but today I don't have the energy. I scarf down the pancakes and gulp a glass of milk. George doesn't always hang out with us at the end of the day, but when he and his wife relax, we're all more comfortable. I stand to take the plate and glass back to the kitchen, but he stops me.

"Go home, Robin. We wash up. I see you tomorrow."

"Okay. Thanks, George. Bye, Maria," I say to his wife. "Bye, Jen," I call at the door.

The tips were good today, for a Thursday, even with giving back Mr. Newman's ridiculous overpayment. I head up the street, in the opposite direction of home, to pick up a few things at the market. I wonder if Kay is around.

Nancy the nanny says she's due back shortly from errands and would I like to wait. As long as I don't have to see my mother, I will. Nancy has Kool-Aid for the kids and offers a glass to me.

We're sprawled in lawn chairs, under the shade of a white ash tree. The kids run circles around each other, Happy always teasing Samantha. Her adoration for her big brother trumps any humility. I was that way about Skip. Still am.

Skip arrives home first, parking his pickup truck outside the garage. He looks surprised to see me. Nancy slides her feet into loafers and stands up.

"Kay should be home any minute," she says. "I'm heading out." She gathers up her things and waves goodbye before jumping in her car and driving away.

"How come you're home early?" I ask Skip.

He surveys the yard. "I want to mow the lawn. It could rain tonight." He pulls his tie loose and unbuttons his shirt at the neck. "I gotta change. Keep an eye on those two, will you?" He sprints into the house.

Before he comes out, Kay drives up. I stand guard by the kids while she drives her car, a brand new white Oldsmobile with upholstery that's like sofa cushions. Everything in her car is automatic – the windows, the locks, and she has a remote opener for the garage door so she doesn't have to get out. I guess that's nice for when it's raining.

Once the car is docked, she steps out and calls to me from inside the garage.

"Hey, Robin. Skip's home already?" She reaches in the back seat and pulls out a big shopping bag with "Caterina of Hollywood" written on it. Ha, I know that store. Well, I've never bought anything there. But when we were in high school, Deb and I used to stroll by and stare at the leopard-print nighties and red satin bras on display. I look away from the bag.

"He just went inside to change his clothes. Said he wanted to cut the grass."

Kay sets the bag down on the driveway and wraps the kids in a big hug. I walk away from the happy scene and feel the long grass between my toes. One thing I always loved about summer was this yard. The swimming pool is in back, which makes sense, but there were times, when everyone was sitting around the pool, that I'd wander to the front yard and just lie down in the grass. Just me and my dreams. I used to close my eyes and try to picture my adult life, as a writer or an artist. I can't draw, but I can write. I drop down in the long grass and clasp my fingers behind my head. The light is already shifting. August marks those changes, with later sunrises and earlier sunsets, and there's a melancholy associated with the end of summer that's palpable. Or maybe it's just everything else.

"Hey, lazybones, get up unless you want me to run you over with the mower," Skips yells from just outside the garage. I do a sit-up before standing, then walk to meet him as he pushes the lawnmower out of the garage. "Kay said you can stay for dinner if you want."

"Doesn't Dad have people who come and do this?"

Skip cuts his eyes to the right, toward the house. "I'm taking care of it now."

"Because he's living in the city?"

"Yeah." His curt reply warns me not to ask questions. That's all right, I'll talk to Kay.

He pulls the cord and the mower roars to life. With a raised hand, he pushes away from me. I pick up my sneakers and socks that I'd removed when Nancy and I were sitting together, and put them back on my feet before entering the house.

Kay's in the kitchen, making a salad. She makes her own salad dressing, in a glass cruet with Wesson oil and vinegar. She snips herbs from little plants that line the sunny windowsill above the sink.

"What do you put in the salad dressing?"

"Oh, this one, thyme, and a little of this one, basil." She minces them with a knife and sprinkles the tiny bits into the cruet. Then she adds garlic powder and those red pepper flakes that are hot on the tongue, covers the top and shakes it vigorously. "There!" She looks very proud. I smile and then I think about what I want to tell her, and my smile fades.

"My mom came into the diner today. She and Mr. Newman had breakfast together."

Kay stops what she's doing and looks out the kitchen window. Skip is still mowing, I can hear it.

"Are you kidding me?" Her eyes blaze, dark and beautiful, and I think she's even prettier when she's mad. "Now she's just trying to humiliate him."

"I don't know. It was so weird, Kay. Mr. Newman came in alone, which was creepy enough, but then she came waltzing in, all dolled up, and parked herself right at his table. *My* table! Like it was the most normal thing in the world. Like everyone should know."

Kay lays a hand on my shoulder and rubs, like my mom used to do on my back when I didn't feel good. "I'm sorry, Robin, that must have been hard for you."

"Well, yeah. And then he tried to give me a tip that was twice as much as their stupid bill. I wouldn't take it." I trace a half-circle on the Congoleum floor with the toe of my sneaker.

The kids are in the den, both lying on their stomachs watching an old episode of "The Partridge Family." Kay leans against the counter and takes a deep breath.

"Your mother's going to move in with Mr. Newman. Apparently she told your father last night. He's moving back into the house this weekend."

"Are you serious? How do you know?" How does Kay know and I don't?

"Your mom called your dad last night to tell him. Dad told Skip today, and Skip called me this morning to let me know."

I look out the window at my older brother pushing the lawnmower across the giant front yard. He wants it to look nice for Dad. That's why he's mowing.

"And Skip couldn't tell me that just now? Jeez, Kay, I'm part of this family, too." That really ticks me off.

"I'm sure he was planning to tell you at dinner," she says.

I gnaw at the inside of my cheek. "I can't stay for dinner." At this point, I'd rather eat macaroni and cheese from the box than listen to my brother tell me something I should have already known.

"Robin, it's hard for all of us," Kay murmurs.

"Yeah. Well, I really have to go," I say. I give her a half kiss on the cheek and don't even bother saying goodbye to the kids. I jog down their driveway so I can get as far away from my brother as possible.

19

I walk down Main Street as fast as I can. I don't want to see anyone or talk to anyone. All I want is to barricade myself inside my apartment.

My mother is moving out of the house and in with Mr. Newman?? I still can't believe it. I wonder what my father thinks. Was he furious with her? Man, he must have been. I move along, past the cobbler and the mirror shop, and I actually feel a little bad for my dad. I mean, it's rotten for this to happen. Everyone in town will know, if they don't already, and that's embarrassing for a guy like my father. And I really don't want to speak with my mother right now.

The parking spots in front of the house are empty, thank God, and I check for mail (none) before letting myself inside. I'm sweaty from practically running home and am just about to step into the shower when the phone rings. I pause and stare at the pale green telephone next to my bed. I wish there was a way for me to know who was calling before I picked up. I let it ring and turn on the shower. Eventually it stops.

The phone doesn't ring again until I'm standing at the stove, boiling water for my macaroni and cheese. This time I pick up. It might be Frank.

"Hello."

"Robin, it's your mother." Her voice is subdued, quiet like the way it was when she told me my grandmother had died. Of course, that was six years ago, but I remember like it was this past weekend.

"Yes, Mom." I mimic her tone. I know why she's calling.

"Something tells me you already know what I'm about to tell you." She clears her throat, delicately, and I think she just did it for effect.

"That you're leaving Dad and moving in with Mr. Newman? That?" I empty the box of elbow macaroni into the pot of water and stir.

"Yes, dear. That. I'm sorry you had to hear it from someone else. I assume it was your brother." Her voice takes on a slight edge. Defensive, Mom?

"Actually, it wasn't Skip. But it could have been just about anyone in town, Mom. After that display in the diner, I imagine everyone knows you've been carrying on with Mr. Newman."

"Robin! I'm still your mother and I won't be spoken to that way. You have no idea how difficult a decision this was for me," she says, and I can hear the trembling in her voice.

I stir the macaroni again and twist the wooden spoon between my fingers like it's a baton.

"Mom, I have something in the oven. I, uh, listen, I wish you luck with this." That's not at all what I wanted to say. But it's out there now and I can't take it back.

She laughs, hard and bitter, and it's as if I can see her twenty years from now, at seventy, gray and wrinkled and laughing that bitter laugh. And she's alone, living in a dingy apartment not unlike mine. Perhaps through the benevolence of my now-remarried father and his much-younger wife.

"Someday we'll talk about all of this, dear." She hangs up softly.

I sit at the table, twirling my spoon, the macaroni boiling away on the stove.

It's the Friday before the long Labor Day weekend and I wake to pouring rain. Wonderful. I pull on my work clothes and slip my rain poncho over my head before running out the door. I jog up the hill and am grateful to live just minutes away from where I work.

Inside, George is grumbling about the weather. "They say rain all weekend. Is not good, Robin, not good at all."

"Maybe it will be good, George. If people can't go to the beach, they'll come here!" I try, but it fails. He scowls at me and turns back to his preparations.

I set up the tables and the counter spaces and am just about finished when Jenny comes in. Her face is nearly as gray as the skies outside.

"You okay, Jen? You don't look good." I follow her to the back, where she hangs up her raincoat and sticks her umbrella in a wrought-iron stand that must be a hundred years old. She pulls a small comb from her purse and tries to fix her hair.

"Walt had a rough night. Didn't get much sleep." She exhales loudly, then catches herself. "I'm sorry," she says. "I don't mean to bring my problems in here." She gives me a small smile and my heart hurts for her.

"I'm really sorry, Jen. Let me know if I can help. If we're not busy, you should leave early."

She shakes her head. There's more gray in her hair, I swear it. Maybe that's what happens when you're caring for a dying husband. "We haven't even started yet, kiddo. Come on, let's go face the music." She leads the way back into the restaurant.

I run to the bathroom and when I come back into the restaurant, Andrew is seated at a table. The rain has let up outside, and his raincoat is slung over the empty chair opposite him. Normally, I'd pick it up and hang it on one of the pegs by the door, but it doesn't look too drippy. After bringing food to another table, I scurry over to him.

"Good morning," I say, fixing my eyes on him. He's reading the menu. Since when does Andrew read the menu? But I see the corners of his mouth. He's trying not to smile. Finally he peeks up at me.

"Oh, Robin. Nice to see you. How are you?" His face is serious, but he can't hide the laughter in those eyes.

I keep staring at him. Does he have my manuscript? Did she finish? All questions I have yet to ask.

"I'm fine, thanks. Coffee?" Focus, Robin. Maybe she didn't finish it.

"Coffee, yes. And a grilled blueberry muffin." He folds the menu and hands it to me.

I take it from him and turn away quickly. My stomach is making gurgling noises, and it's not because I'm hungry. The suspense is eating away at my insides. I clip his order and get him some coffee.

"Any plans for the long weekend?" he asks cheerfully.

I set down his coffee hard. It sloshes but doesn't spill over. "Work," I say, giving him the sarcastic look my father always hated.

"Robin," he says softly. "You're not going back to college? This would be the weekend."

No kidding, Andrew. I shake my head. "Not right now," I say. With everything going on between my parents, it was hard to ask my mom about whether or not I'd be going back. As the days passed and no one told me anything, I kind of figured that my father wasn't going to step up and fix things with the dean. Then again, my mother wasn't speaking to my father, and my father wasn't speaking to me. So I asked Skip to find out. He said that my father wanted me to take a year to "regroup," whatever the hell that was supposed to mean. A year waitressing? I look at Andrew. "My father made that decision for me."

As I turn my back to him, I hear him say, "Of course. Well, maybe when you're finished with work and back home this afternoon, you might want to look over your finished manuscript."

I whirl around so fast I almost cover everyone and everything in my radius with hot coffee. He stands up and walks around to the opposite chair. Lifting his raincoat, he picks up what looks like two shirt boxes. Really? I think. My book is that long?

"One box is the typed pages, the other contains your original notebooks," he says by way of explanation. "Barbara really loved it," he adds, and I break into a grin. I want to cover his face with kisses.

"She did? Wow. That means a lot." The first person who read it, and she liked it. No, she loved it. He said she loved it. She loved my book. Screw my father. And screw college.

"I only read a little of it, but it's good, Robin."

I want to sit down across from him, ask him what parts Barbara liked best, but George pounds on his little bell and bellows my name from the kitchen. "Robin! Order up!"

"That must be your muffin," I say, not even caring if George yells at me. Barbara loved my book!

Andrew eats quickly, and says he can't stay, but he wishes me a good weekend. I take the two boxes to the back and stash them in my locker.

Jenny corrals me at the coffee station. "What's in those boxes?" she asks. If she were feeling better, I know she'd give me grief about them, but I can see she's not really into it.

"Some books. His wife thought I might like them," I say with a shrug. The explanation seems to satisfy her, but this morning I think I could have told Jenny the boxes had dirty shirts in them and she would have just nodded and returned to work.

I float through the rest of the shift and George makes me a grilled-cheese sandwich with tomato for lunch. I wrap it in two paper napkins and look up to see a quizzical expression on his face.

"You no eat here?"

"I need to get home," I say.

"Stay. Eat. Is hot."

"Okay," I say, giving in. It won't take long to eat. I pull a carton of chocolate milk from the refrigerator and pull apart the top to make a spout, then take a long drink without even pouring it into a glass.

"Jenny, you go," says George. "Go home."

"Go, Jen," I chime in. "I'll clean up." George raises his eyebrows at me. After all, I just said I needed to go home.

"Thanks," she says wearily. "His sister is coming to stay with us. She should be at our house by now," she adds, looking at her wristwatch. "I'll see you tomorrow."

We watch her leave, then sit in silence for a couple of minutes.

"Her husband is sick," I say softly.

"I know. Is bad." George stabs at his salad, attacking it with ferocity.

20

Back in my apartment, I open the shirt box and stare at the manuscript. I lift the pages carefully from the box and feel the weight of the paper. Holding the sheets in my hands, I turn and lift the last page. There it is, "THE END" typed about two inches from the bottom. And the last page is numbered "304." Three hundred and four pages! Wow. I place the sheets back in the box, then fit the cover over the top. In the other box, I find my spiral notebooks, the genesis of my novel. I place that box on the floor next to my dresser.

I know what I need to do next.

Jenny's husband passed away last night. He went peacefully, she told us when she stopped in, on her day off, to let George know. He instructed her to take the week off, and later, after she'd gone, he wondered aloud if she'd be back at all. I think she will be, because Jenny needs to work. She also needs to be busy. She'll be back.

A few days later, George and Maria pick me up at my apartment and we drive to the funeral home for the evening calling hours. I wear my one black skirt and a dark gray top. Jenny's very appreciative that we came, I can tell. Her eyes are red-rimmed and puffy, but she smiles when she sees us walk in.

Jenny's husband is in his polished casket, dressed in a fine suit that's too big for him and there are rosary beads entwined in his hands. Last time I saw him was right after I started working in the diner, when he came to take Jenny home after her shift.

I try not to stare at his face. He looks awful, but I hear people telling Jenny how good he looks. I'm not going to say that to her. She'd know I was lying. George says they fix up dead people at the funeral parlors to make them look better than they looked when they were alive. I don't know about that in this case. Anyway, we get in line to tell Jenny how sorry we are that her husband died. She sobs a little when we hug, and I rub her back the way my mom did when I used to cry. Then we sit in the room for about twenty minutes, until George says it's time to leave. After all, we have to get up early.

Maria covers for Jenny while she's out. We get along okay, but it isn't the same. When Andrew comes in, I let him know about Jenny's husband. And I hand him a small box, wrapped up in yellow paper and tied with a light green ribbon. That was Kay's idea. A gift for their baby, in what she called neutral colors. It's a set of three bibs, one red with hearts, one yellow with ducks, and one green with a turtle on it.

"This is just to say thanks for everything. Your wife really helped me."

"Is this for the baby?" he asks, smiling.

I nod. "I know it's early, so you can wait to open it until it's closer."

"That's very sweet, Robin. Barb will be tickled." He finishes his muffin and wipes his mouth, even though there weren't any crumbs that I could see. "So what's the plan now?"

Oh, the book. "Well, I'm going to see if Maryana Capture is interested in it. I know who her publisher is, but I think I'd rather give it to her to read."

Andrew nods. He looks like he wants to say something, but then he shakes his head, like he decided against it. "Good thinking," he says, so I guess he agrees with my plan.

My father is back in his house, rattling around all alone. Kay tells me he eats dinner with them every night, unless he's out for a business meeting.

"He's just so sad, Robin. My heart breaks for him." It's Monday afternoon. I hear David's truck crunch on the gravel driveway, then his heavy footsteps on the porch as he checks his mail. I'm sitting at my kitchen table and can see his bulky shadow through the curtain that covers my front door window. We've only seen each other twice since he returned from what he said was a business trip. It was fine, I guess. We're cordial and friendly, but I maintain my distance with him. And no more pizza together.

"Yeah, I feel bad for Dad, too, Kay. Just because it's embarrassing. I mean, in this town, everybody knows your business, so they all know that Mom was cheating on him, and now she's living with Mr. Newman and they couldn't even move to another town?"

I'm ticked off at my mother, which puts me on the side of my dad. Isn't that ironic. My dad's no prize, that's for sure, but he didn't deserve this. I'm actually surprised he didn't punch Mr. Newman's lights out when he had a chance. But Skip said he'd never do something so stupid, risk being arrested for assault, that kind of thing.

"Listen, Robin, why don't you come for dinner tonight? He'd be happy to see you," Kay says.

"No, I don't think so," I answer immediately. "It would be awkward. We'd need to smooth things over first, just him and me. I don't want it to be in front of everybody. But…thanks anyway, Kay."

I don't tell her about my plans for tomorrow. I haven't even told Frank, who's coming over after he gets off work. I know I should clue him in about the book, but, I don't know, I want to wait until I have some good news. I'm keeping this to myself, just in case it turns out to be a big flop. I know Barbara liked the book. No, she loved the book, but she's only one person. And maybe she was just being nice.

My plan tomorrow is to bring the manuscript to the publisher. I checked the bus schedules and if I leave early enough, I can do it in a day. I'm used to getting up early anyway.

The telephone rings and I pick up, expecting Frank. But it's David and my heart drops a little inside my chest.

"Hi Robin, how ya doing?" he asks. "You been hiding away? I haven't seen ya for a while."

I want him off the line, in case Frank is trying to call. "No, I'm not hiding. Working a lot, you know."

"Yeah, well." He coughs. "Interested in grabbing a pizza or something? No wine, I promise."

"Oh, sorry. Frank's taking me out tonight." Remember, my boyfriend? I will never go for pizza with David again. And Frank doesn't know it yet, but he is taking me out tonight.

There's silence on the other end. "You still there, David?"

"Yeah. Sure. I'm sorry, Robin. I wasn't thinking. Just missed your company, that's all." His voice gets all quiet and low, like he's depressed or something. I picture him sitting in a chair upstairs, all sad, with an empty refrigerator.

"Some other time then, okay?" I bite my tongue. Jeez, I shouldn't have said that. Now he's going to call me again, and probably soon.

"Absolutely. You have a good night." The line goes dead.

When Frank arrives, I run out to the car. Before he's even shut off the engine, I've slid into the front seat.

"You're taking me out tonight," I say, buckling my seat belt.

He laughs. "I guess I am! Where to?" He backs out of the driveway and onto the street. I wonder if David is watching us from his window upstairs, but I don't dare look.

"Anywhere. The Chinese place in Westham," I say.

"You don't like the Wokery? It's right here, next to the drugstore. Why go all the way to Westham?"

"I just want to go somewhere else. Somewhere away from this small town." I stare out the window. "It's ten minutes' drive, big deal," I mutter.

"Robin, I'll drive an hour if you want. But why don't you tell me what's really bothering you?"

Where do I begin. My mother, acting like an old fool. My father, unwilling to make the first move. David, the creep. My book, and is it any good. Maryana, and will she help me. My job, and will I ever be able to do something else. So many things, I don't even know where to begin.

"I'm hungry, that's all. You know how I get when I'm hungry."

"All right, honey. I'll take care of you." He lays his hand on my thigh and it reminds me of David.

When Frank drives me back home, I let him come in, even though I'm not in the mood. Too much on my mind about tomorrow, but I go through the motions. I don't think he even notices, which is pretty sad. But it's easier than making up an excuse.

We're lying in my bed, both of us on our backs. I pull the sheet up to my neck.

"Got any plans for your day off tomorrow?" he asks in a sleepy voice. For once, I'm glad he won't spend the night. I don't even ask anymore.

"Yeah, I'm going to the bookstore in the morning and Kay and I are meeting up for lunch." He'll never know I'm lying.

"Sounds good," he says, yawning. "Well, I guess I should head home." He rolls toward me. "Sorry I can't stay the night."

I turn my head to his. "I understand. You need to sleep." I kiss him lightly, but he turns it into a bigger kiss, and for a second I'm afraid he'll be ready to go again, but he ends it with the kiss and rolls out of bed to get dressed.

I know I have to get up, too. Otherwise the front door will stay unlocked, and I've become a fanatic about locking my door. You just can't trust anyone these days.

Once he's gone, though, I pull the box from under my bed and open it. I touch my fingertips to the front page. THE WAY TO REMEMBER in all caps, and underneath it, 'a novel by Robin Fortune.' I close my eyes and say a prayer, all the time feeling guilty that I never pray except to ask for something.

If this is meant to happen for me, please let it happen. And if it isn't meant to happen, please don't let it hurt too much.

I replace the top on the box and slip it into my book bag. I check my alarm clock again, turn out the light, and wait for sleep.

21

I hear the roar of water gushing through the pipes just as I'm about to head out the door. David is taking a shower, and that means I can leave the house without running into him. Good.

I walk halfway up Main Street in the dark. It's nearly fall and I feel the morning chill through my light jacket. There's no rain in the forecast, though, so once the sun is up it should be warmer. The bus station is busy at this hour, filled with men in dark suits carrying briefcases. Everybody's going somewhere. I purchase a round-trip ticket at the counter and walk out the back to where four different buses are idling. I find the one that has "NYC Express" lit up over the windshield and climb on board, handing half of my ticket to the driver. I find a seat next to a window and lower myself into it. The shirt box, wrapped in a plastic bag, sits flat on my lap inside my canvas book bag. I'm so excited I can't stand it.

The bus rolls into the Port Authority two hours later and I wait for everyone else to exit before I pick up my bag and sling it over my shoulder, crossways, so it hangs down in front. I step off and breathe in. The strong diesel smell is choking and I walk through the bus loading platform as fast as I can. There's time for breakfast, and I'm starving, so I enter a little coffee shop on 42nd Street and get a bagel with cream cheese, feeling like a native. People move really fast around me; everyone's in a hurry. That's New York, I guess. I could be like them, if I lived here. I wonder if I'd move here to write. Or maybe just outside the city, since I probably couldn't afford to live in Manhattan unless I sold a million books. I sit at a little table and watch the women who come in the deli. One wears way too much makeup and her hair looks like Wonder Woman's. Another wears a navy blue dress and a pearl necklace. She's very skinny and orders just coffee, no bagel or anything. She never smiles, not once. Gonna be a long day for her.

After a half hour, I figure I should get going. Now I'm nervous about the whole thing. I have this plan, and I've rehearsed it plenty of times, but I don't know if it'll work. Well, I have to try.

I want to see Times Square, so I walk up 42nd Street, past the Follies Burlesk, featuring "the most beautiful showgirls in the world," which sits above a Howard Johnson's. There's a sign advertising peep shows for a quarter, and a marquee screaming about a "dominatrix fantasy." It's dirty and gritty and fascinating and reminds me of *Looking for Mr. Goodbar.* One of the movie houses is showing "He and She" and "The Animal," both films I've never heard of. And something tells me they probably won't come around to the two-screen cinema at the mall.

Twenty minutes later I arrive at the address. A brass plaque on the outside of the building says "Bellest Hapshaw & Co." and I take a deep breath. I pull the box from my book bag and unwrap it from the plastic bag, which I stuff back into the canvas tote. I enter the building and look at the directory on the wall. Sixteenth floor. I walk to the elevator and an old man in a uniform stands inside waiting. He nods to me and says, "What floor, miss?" Oh. He runs the elevator. Cool.

"Sixteen, please," I say, feeling rather important. Then I laugh at myself. He's the elevator operator, Robin, he's not *your* elevator operator.

The doors open and I smile at the old man, knowing I'll see him again on my way down. I pull open the heavy glass door with gold lettering that says "Bellest Hapshaw" and walk up to the reception desk. A young woman, probably about my age, is on the telephone.

"Yes, sir. One moment, please, I'll see if she's in." She presses a button on the telephone and starts to look for something on her desk. I wait. She glances up at me and says, "One moment." I nod and give her a big smile, then step back a couple of paces, because I don't want her to think I'm one of those impatient or demanding kinds of people.

The woman presses a button on the phone and says, "Miss Thomas? Alexander Fletcher for you. Yes, ma'am. Yes, I'll connect you now." She hesitates, takes a breath, then punches another button on the phone.

"I'll connect you with Miss Thomas now," she says, hitting yet another button before replacing the receiver.

Finally, she exhales and looks up at me. "I'm sorry," she says. "May I help you?"

Before I can answer, a middle-aged woman with a helmet of brown hair marches out of her office down the hall and up to the reception desk.

"You disconnected him! Alexander Fletcher! You hung up on him! Do you not know how to use a goddamn telephone?" She glares at the receptionist, who looks like she'd rather melt under the desk. When the girl tries to speak, the older woman holds up her hand. "Forget it, I'll call him myself." She pivots and storms back down the corridor.

I'm transfixed by what just happened, but steel myself for what I have to do. The young woman turns shimmering eyes to me.

"I'm new here," she says, as if an explanation is necessary. I'd figured that out already.

"Then I won't take up much of your time," I say quickly. "And I have a really simple request." I lean on the reception desk so I can speak to her in a lower voice. "My aunt is Maryana Capture. You know, the author? Well, I know this is her publisher, but I'm supposed to be at her apartment today, and I lost the one piece of paper that has her address and phone number on it. Could you please just give me her address?"

The young woman eyes me warily. "I don't know. I'm probably not supposed to do that," she says carefully.

I sigh. "Look, I don't want you to get in any trouble. But I'm supposed to be there this morning, and I don't want her to worry about me. You won't get in trouble. I'm her niece Carolyn. Please." I smile again and tilt my head, my best begging look.

Her face brightens. "My name's Carolyn, too," she says.

"Come on! What are the chances?" Really, that was a coincidence. I look at my wristwatch and back at her.

"I just don't know," she says with a nervous glance down the corridor.

"Would you like to ask Miss Thomas?" Now that's a gamble, I know.

"No! God, no," she says. She makes a face, like she's trying to do a complicated math problem, then she looks up. "Okay, you look trustworthy," she says. She pulls a Rolodex toward her and begins to flip the small cards until she finds "C." "Capture, here it is." She pulls the card free and shows it to me.

I memorize the address. "Yes, now I remember. But if I didn't see it, I'd have been walking forever. Thank you so much," I say, touching her forearm for emphasis.

Carolyn looks much more relaxed now. "You're welcome. I'm glad I could help."

I really hope she doesn't get fired because of this. But I push the thought from my mind and wave goodbye. When the elevator doors open, I step inside and say, "Ground level, please."

It's a thirty-minute walk to Maryana's apartment building, which is just outside Central Park. She lives in a big building with a brown canopy that runs from the front door to the curb. A doorman dressed in a dark blue uniform with gold buttons opens the front door for me.

"Thank you," I murmur and enter the lobby. Wow, it's huge. Everything is black and white marble.

"Miss? How may I assist you?" Another man, dressed in a black suit, stands behind a podium. He's tall and balding and has one of those skinny mustaches you see on movie actors from fifty years ago.

"Hi, I have something…a package, for Miss Capture. Miss Maryana Capture," I say. "If you could just direct me to her apartment?"

He sucks in his cheeks and his nearly non-existent lips point out, and I almost laugh because he looks so funny. He makes a noise in his throat.

"Whatever you have for Miss Capture, I'll be happy to take it and deliver it to her," he says with no inflection in his voice. He stands tall behind that little desk, as if he's about to give a speech or something.

"Oh, well, I really need to give it to her myself. It's very important." I sense I'm in the middle of a losing battle here.

"I'm sorry, then, miss. The only way to deliver your package to Miss Capture is via me." He says 'via' like vy-uh, all pretentious and smarmy. I hate him.

I lay the box on the high shelf between us. Raising my eyes to his, I say, "Do you have a piece of paper? I'd just like to include a note for her."

"Most certainly," he replies, and reaches into whatever is hidden in that desk. He produces a crisp sheet of cream-colored stationery and an envelope. At the top of the paper it has "Westmore Arms" stamped in gold letters with a little drawing of the building underneath. Fancy. Then he steps away, presumably to give me a bit of privacy. I'm flummoxed as to what I should write.

Dear Miss Capture, We met in July. This is the manuscript of my first book. I would be so grateful if you would read it. Was that lame? I'd already written it, in my best penmanship, and I was afraid to ask Sir Smarmypants for another sheet of paper. *I would love to be published by Bellest Hapshaw. Thank you. Robin Fortune.* I write my telephone number at the very bottom, so she'll have a way to contact me, even though both my address and my telephone number are on the extra page in the back that Andrew's wife had typed up. I fold the sheet of paper and slide it into the envelope, then write "Maryana Capture" on the front of the envelope.

"Okay," I say. "Since this is the only way to get my book to her, here."

He steps back into place behind his podium-desk and takes the envelope. He lays it on top of the shirt box, which now I wish was a better box than something made out of flimsy cardboard.

"I'll see that it's delivered to Miss Capture today," he says, in a voice that's clearly meant to end our conversation.

"It's really important." I plead with my eyes, but he's already dismissed me, I can tell. "Okay, well, thank you very much," I add, figuring I still need to be polite. If I tell him what I think of him, she'll never get that box.

"Have a good day, miss," he says.

I look at the lobby one more time before turning to leave. Everything is pinned on this, on the hope that Maryana Capture will actually read my manuscript. That she'll like it (hey, Andrew's wife loved it, and she's smart). That she'll see fit to help a young author out by showing it to her publisher. I find a bench at the edge of Central Park and sit, letting my mind wander toward the fantasy that my favorite author would be willing to launch my writing career. I know it's foolish, and improbable, but I hang onto it because I can't bear the thought of aimlessly stumbling through life. I can't work in the Liberty Diner for another year, either, waiting for my father to decide whether it's worth sending me back to college or not.

The bus ride back home takes forever. By the time I step off the bus at the station, it's nearly six and I'm starving. There isn't much food in my apartment, so I stop in at Little Italy and order a meatball sandwich to go. It's the first time I've been in here since the night with David. That's the table where we sat. Where I drank all that wine. He said he would make me scream. I think I know what he meant by that, and even thinking about it makes my cheeks burn. I mean, I'm not a prude, but David? Why can't Frank ever say things like that? Why can't Frank ever make me scream? Maybe I need to spice things up with Frank. If he won't do it, I'll have to.

I pick up my sandwich and walk home. There's one piece of mail in my box, an advertisement for a secretarial school in the city. I tear it up and toss it in the garbage.

There's a can of Fresca in the fridge, so I pull off the top and set it next to my sandwich. I'm just about to take a bite when the phone rings. It's either Frank or my mother, but my mother doesn't call much these days, now that she's with Mr. Newman. I guess he's keeping her busy. I grab the phone from the table next to the bed. It has a long extension cord, and I pull the phone into the kitchen and sit down again.

"Hello?"

"Robin, where have you been?" It's Frank.

"It was my day off, remember?"

"Yeah, I know, and you said you were going to the bookstore, but it's after six o'clock!"

"So?" I take a big bite of my sandwich. It tastes so good.

"Well, I got worried, that's all."

I chew and swallow, and take a sip of Fresca before responding. "You don't have to worry, but thanks."

"Listen, my mom's putting supper on the table, so I can't talk long. You want me to come over later?"

"Nah, that's okay. I'm beat. You can call me to say good night, though."

He's quiet for a few seconds. I count to myself and reach five before he speaks. "Of course I will. I always do."

"Okay. Well, go eat and I'll talk to you later." My sandwich is getting cold.

"Sure," he says before hanging up.

22

I wake with a start. My clock says it's just after three. It wasn't a nightmare that woke me, but I suppose you could call it that.

I realized that I handed over the only typed copy of my novel to Maryana Capture's guard. I actually hit myself on the side of my head when I understand what an idiot I am. Why didn't I take that box of paper to the copy store and have them make a copy? I pound my fists and my heels on the bed. After my silent tantrum (I'm not about to scream, it's the middle of the night), I get up and make a cup of coffee. There'll be no going back to sleep now. I sit at my kitchen table and say yet another prayer.

If she doesn't like it, please let her be nice enough to send it back to me. Please.

Frank comes over the following night and I make American Chop Suey. It's easy, really. I chop up a small onion and cook it in butter in my big frying pan, then I add a package of hamburger and cook it. I scoop everything out and pour the grease into a coffee can that I keep in the refrigerator. Then I put the onion and meat back in and add a big can of crushed tomatoes. Meanwhile, I cook some elbow macaroni in a pot of boiling water, and when it's cooked, I drain it and add it. See? Easy. The first time I made it for Frank, he said it wasn't spicy enough, and the next time he came over, he brought a little jar of red pepper flakes. Now I let him add as much as he wants.

We're eating supper and not saying too much, but it's comfortable, not awkward like it is sometimes when two people don't talk. At least I think it's not awkward. That is, until he clears his throat and speaks.

"So, anyway, my cousin Lillian just got engaged," he says, shoving a big forkful of chop suey into his mouth.

I look up. I met his cousin Lillian once. I think she's a couple of years older than we are. "Oh, that's nice. When's she getting married?"

"I dunno. Next spring, I think. They're having an engagement party for her on Saturday."

I nod and chew. "Where?"

"The Azorean Club. Of course." He smiles and shrugs.

"Of course." I wipe my plate with a small piece of bread. "What should I wear? I mean, is it dressy?"

He pushes the last of his food around on his plate without eating it. Then he sets down his fork and rubs the side of his head. When he looks up, finally, to see me staring at him, he looks away quickly.

"Frank? Am I not invited? I thought that's why you told me about it." Hey, I don't really care, because I couldn't stay late anyway, not on a Saturday night. And I'd have to find something to wear. And probably buy her a present. But if he's going, wouldn't he bring me?

He actually squirms in his chair. What the hell is going on? I cross my arms over my chest and wait it out.

"It's very Portuguese, Robin. I know you wouldn't like it."

"It's not about whether I'd like it or not! Why the hell did you tell me about this party? To let me know that I'm not invited?" I stare at him hard. "Oh, wait," I say slowly, as it dawns on me. "Do your parents still not see us as a couple?" I haven't been back to his house since that night in July, so I have no idea whether his parents know we're still together. I work so much, it's not like I have time for a social life, anyway, outside of Frank coming over here to share a meal and screw me. Because that's pretty much what our relationship is.

"Robin, you know how they are. They're traditional. They think ethnic groups should stick together." He still won't look at me.

"So…they would rather see you with a Portuguese girl. Of course. And will there be a single Portuguese girl at this engagement party?" I draw out my words, as if he's stupid. Moronic. Idiotic.

He spreads his hands. "Robin, I…look…this is something I have to do."

I pick up the plates and bring them to the sink, only because I'm not the kind of person who breaks things on purpose. With my back to him, I say, "What you have to do, Frank, is leave. Now." I turn on the faucet and start washing the dishes.

"Robin, come on. Don't be like that. It's just a stupid party."

I shut off the faucet and throw the wet sponge at him. Smack! Right on the forehead. See? Sponges aren't breakable, so it's okay. Besides, I had to throw *something* at him.

"Hey!" He picks up the sponge from the floor and tosses it into the sink.

"Get out," I spit. "You're weak, Frank. You tell me you love me? But you're so weak you can't tell your parents? You know what? I don't need this crap. Go to your little Portuguese party and maybe you'll meet your wife there. Now just get the hell out." I stomp over to the door and open it. The air outside is chilly. "Out!"

"Fine," he says, using his shirtsleeve to wipe his forehead. "But you don't understand." He walks past me and out to his car.

"I understand plenty!" I'm yelling now. "You're a little boy! I don't want a little boy, I want a man!"

Oh shit. And there's David, witness to our shouting match. Well, my shouting. He stands, frozen, at the corner of the house. I don't think Frank sees him there. I shake my head and slam the door, then turn back to the sink and resume washing the dishes.

"Robin." He's opened the door. Sure, because I didn't lock it. I whirl around to face David.

"What the hell, David? You can't just walk in here."

He stands on the threshold. I can see behind him that Frank is gone, and David's presence in my apartment unnerves me. I don't want him here.

"You're so upset, and I was worried. I'm sorry, but I heard it all." He stands in place, not moving toward me. "I want to help."

"Help? Help would be leaving. Next time you want to visit, you knock first." I wave my hand to shoo him back out onto the porch.

He backs up, slowly, his eyes on me the whole time. "I'd be good to you, Robin. You know that."

"David, please," I say with a heavy sigh. I shake my head and close the door, this time turning the lock in place. I have to remember to always lock that door. But even as I turn back to the sink, I sense him still there, waiting. I leave the dishes in the sink and shut off the kitchen light.

In my bedroom, I check that my windows are shut and locked, the shades drawn all the way down. Still, I change out of my clothes in the pitch dark. And at only seven-thirty, I'm lying in bed.

Frank and I are as good as broken up. I just can't see us continuing this way. It's bad enough that my own family is fractured, but his parents won't acknowledge me as his girlfriend, and Frank has never stood up to them on this. Like he's embarrassed by me? Ashamed? If I'm going to be with a guy, I want to know that his family at least accepts me.

And David? God, that's the last thing I need right now. I get that he's lonely, but I don't take on charity cases. Now that he knows Frank and I broke up, he'll be around me like a honeybee. And I can't let him think I want it. I don't. Not from him.

Everything hinges on Maryana Capture, I realize that. Her nod, her recommendation could be my ticket out of here. Even if I have to wait tables in New York while I write books in my spare time, I'd do it. Get away from my father, my mother, stupid Frank. There's nothing for me in this little town anyway. And I don't need to go back to college. That's what I wish my dad knew. He thinks he's holding this over me, waiting for me to go crawling to him on my knees, begging forgiveness for messing up, for maligning the holy Fortune name. Well, screw it. I don't need any of them.

When I see Andrew in the diner, I let him know that I delivered the manuscript to Maryana, and he seems impressed that I just took the bus to New York and did it, all on my own. But there isn't any time to chat. I'm swamped and he's in a rush.

"I'll be away on business for the next week, Robin, so I won't see you for a bit," he says, handing me a ten-dollar bill.

I dig in my pockets for change and he waves it away. "Andrew, you give me too much money. Every time," I say. "Really, you don't have to."

"I know I don't," he says. "Just let me do this, please. I'll see you in a couple of weeks." He puts on his coat and heads outside.

I'll miss seeing him. Wednesdays and Fridays are the bright spots in my week, knowing Andrew will be here. I clean his table so it's ready for the next customer.

On Saturday afternoon, there's a knock on my front door. I'm cleaning the bathroom and pull off rubber gloves before peeking through the curtain to see my mother standing on the porch.

"Mom! What are you doing here?" The only other time my mom came to this apartment was to pick me up for my birthday. She looks like she'd rather be anywhere else than on my front porch. Maybe because my dad owns this building, or maybe because it's "below Main." Anyway, I'm relieved the kitchen's clean.

"Robin, I've been trying to call you for days. I was worried," she adds in a smaller voice. She steps inside and touches the back of a chair. "May I?"

"Of course," I say. So she's the one who's been calling? Not Frank. And not David.

"Have you not been home, dear? I called three days in a row. This morning I telephoned the restaurant and George said you're fine but he wouldn't call you to the phone." She made her I-just-bit-into-a-lemon face. "I should think you could spare five minutes to speak to your mother."

"You called the diner? He never told me," I say. "Mom, you want a cup of tea or something? I have Tab, too."

"Nothing, dear." She examines her fingernails. They're painted bright red, as usual. "Robin, this isn't easy, but it shouldn't come as a surprise, either. Your father and I are divorcing."

I count to five silently before answering. "Well, of course I'm not surprised. You've been with Mr. Newman for months now. When is the divorce official?"

"Soon," she says, then looks up at me. "Robin, Russell makes me very happy. I hadn't been happy with your father for years. I tried to hide it, and we had agreed to stick it out, at least until you were grown, but there's no use pretending anymore. Our marriage was over a long time ago."

I get up and open the refrigerator. There are two cans of Tab on the shelf and I pull one out. "You want to split this with me?" I hold up the bright pink can until she nods wearily. Opening the cupboard, I take down two glasses and pull the top from the can, then split the contents evenly between us. I place one glass in front of her and take a gulp from mine.

"We're going to move."

I set the glass down on the table, but keep my fingers around it, feeling the wet coldness and wondering what to say. "Far?"

"No, not far. Just over the line in Westham. But neither of us wants to live in this town anymore." She lowers her eyes and I imagine she's heard the gossip.

"I understand." I want to tell her about the book. I want to tell her so badly, but I don't. This is her thing right now, and I need to let her express her feelings. Telling her about the book might not cheer her up, although my mom's always been very encouraging about everything.

"How's Speedy?" she asks. Well, I can tell her about that.

"Frank and I broke up," I say dully. Without looking at her, I continue. "We had a big fight, Mom. Actually, he's at a party tonight. His cousin got engaged. And he didn't want me there with him."

"Oh, Robin. What are you talking about?"

"I'm not Portuguese, Mom. His parents have known me all my life, and they liked me fine until I started going out with their son. And Frank? Frank lives at home, he won't move out." I shake my head as if I could clear the images in it, like my brain is some kind of Etch-a-Sketch. "He comes by, for dinner and sex. That's pretty much it, though. I don't think I meant any more to him than that." I look up, wary of her reaction.

She's not embarrassed. Thank God. Someone I can talk to. I keep going, telling her about David upstairs, about the night at the pizza place, about how he creeps me out. It's like someone opened a faucet in my mouth and I can't stop talking. But my mom, she listens to it all. No faces, no smirks, no eye rolls. She sips her Tab and listens. And when I finally shut up, she takes a moment before speaking.

"Sounds like you've been wanting to talk for a long time, dear. I'm sorry I haven't been around more. And I am sorry about you and Spee...Frank. He's a nice boy, honey. But maybe not what you need. And neither is this David, from what you tell me. Best to steer clear of him and not let him think you're interested. Do you feel safe here?" She glances around the kitchen and past me, into the bedroom.

"Yeah, I feel safe. I don't think he'd ever hurt me, Mom. He just has the wrong idea, and you're right, I don't want to give him any sign that I'm interested. If I had someone I could fix him up with, I would." I'd play matchmaker, the way Frank's parents are doing with him. "I want to go back to college, Mom. I can't wait tables in a diner for the rest of my life." I think again about telling her about the book, but something holds me back. Even if the book is accepted for publication, I should still finish school.

"Honey, I'll try to speak to your father about it, but he isn't much for listening to anything I have to say these days. Your brother might be a better option."

I bend my elbow and make a fist, and let my cheek rest against it. Begging to Skip would be better than begging to my father, although I can't even imagine how it would go when I finally have to talk to my dad.

228

I've already missed out on this semester, but maybe I'd be able to get back in for January. Maybe.

"I should go, Robin." She pushes her chair back and stands. I see my mother differently, not just as my mom, but as a fifty-year-old woman who looks renewed. She doesn't look like a grandmother. She's vibrant and healthy. She's pretty. And I can understand why Mr. Newman would find her sexy. Hey, at least she looks happier.

I stand, too, and give my mother a quick hug. She was never one for long embraces, but she holds my face in her soft hands and makes me look in her eyes.

"Everything will work out for the best, Robin. Don't settle."

"Okay, Mom," I say, opening the door to let her out. I stand there, in the cold, and wave as she backs the car out of the driveway. Then I shut my door and lock it.

23

I trudge into autumn as if I'm carrying a thirty-pound load on my back. Every step I take, up the hill to work, back down to my apartment, is an effort. My job is tedious, George yells all the time, Jenny never laughs anymore, and even Andrew, my Wednesday and Friday bright spot, seems down. One Friday in the middle of October I ask him about it.

"Is everything all right with you? You haven't been your usual happy self lately," I say.

"Is it obvious?" he asks, then shrugs, like he doesn't care about anything. "Just busy at work. I have to travel more, and I don't like leaving Barbara alone. She's over the morning sickness, but everyone in our family lives across the country." He pours cream into his coffee and stirs, longer than necessary, I notice. It doesn't take that long to mix the cream into the coffee, but he just keeps stirring, rattling his spoon against the cup. "Her mother's coming to stay when the baby's born, but that's not until January."

"What about neighbors? Friends?" They must have friends. I imagine the two of them at cocktail parties, galas, even library things. He's young, smart, very handsome, how could they not have a big group of friends?

"Our neighbors keep to themselves. Believe me, we've tried. When we first moved here, we invited everyone in the neighborhood over for a barbecue. And out of a dozen or so families, only three responded to the invitation! And out of the three, only one actually showed up." He runs a hand over the top of his head, messing up his hair. I so want to smooth it out for him.

"And Barbara doesn't like the cold," he adds with a hard laugh. "It's only October! We took a drive to see the foliage, and it was pretty, but she didn't want to get out of the car. I know this winter's going to be rough for her."

"But she'll have the baby and she can stay home, right?"

"Right," he says, and his voice is somewhere else, far away.

I don't want to stay too long at his table. George was really mad at me the other day when I didn't pick up an order on time and the eggs got cold. He had to make a whole new plate for the customer and he threatened to take the cost of it out of my wages.

"I gotta go," I say, turning away with the coffee pot in my hand.

"Robin," he calls after me. "Have you heard anything?"

I shake my head and hurry away.

I saw Frank today. Of course, I looked like shit, coming off an eight-hour shift. But I had just gotten paid, and needed food, so I walked to the supermarket after work. Now that the weather is colder, and it gets dark so much earlier, I'm making a lot of soups and casseroles. So, I blew a lot of money and there I was, pushing my grocery cart full of chicken and hamburger and vegetables, all kinds of good food, and on impulse I'd just picked out a frozen cheesecake, so that was on top of the other stuff. I rounded a corner and almost rammed my cart right into him.

And he wasn't alone. Nope. He was with a girl, probably the one he was fixed up with last month at his cousin's party. She's pretty. And he looked really happy. Well, until he saw me.

"Robin! Hey." His ears turned red.

"Hey." I turned to the girl. "Hi." I bet her name is Maria.

"Oh! This is Melanie. Mel, this is Robin, an old friend."

She stuck her hand out and gave me this big grin. Her teeth sparkled white like a movie star's. She had perfect skin, a cute little nose, huge eyes. Perfect. I shook her hand, and her skin was probably the softest I'd ever felt, not that I shake hands that often. I knew what mine felt like to her – burlap. Burlap hands.

"Yeah, I'm Frank's *oldest* friend." I wouldn't even look at him. "And I'm actually running late. Nice to meet you," I said to Melanie in my kindest voice and pushed my cart toward the cash registers at the front of the store.

And sure enough, I was standing behind a woman with a screaming toddler, who was buying enough food for a month. They rolled up right behind me.

"Hi again, Robin!" Melanie is one of those people who's perpetually happy, apparently. Or else Frank makes her that way. I wonder if he gave her a silver bracelet. I wish I was wearing mine, I'd shove it in his face. Or aim it at his eye.

"Hi again," I mumbled. I unloaded my cart, aware that they were watching, because what else do you do when you're waiting in line, right? You look at what the person in front of you has in their cart. I was glad I didn't have all junk food, like some pathetic girl who sits home on Saturday nights eating Funyuns and watching *Sanford and Son*.

"Ooh, cheesecake! Robin, is that one any good?" Melanie turned to Frank. "Honey, would you get us a frozen cheesecake?" She scrunched her shoulders up around her ears as he loped off toward the frozen food section.

I shrugged. "I've never had it. But my boyfriend is coming over for dinner, and he loves cheesecake." I made a face, like she and I were in on a big secret about boys.

The cashier rang up my food and a boy with long stringy hair packed everything into two brown paper bags. I handed over some money and waited for my change.

"Well, see ya," I said, hoisting the bags in my arms.

"Maybe we could double date some time," she called to me, just as Frank reappeared with a box in his hand. He stared at Melanie, then at me.

I pretended I didn't hear her and walked out of the grocery store as fast as I could.

Back in my apartment, I dump the bags on the kitchen table, relieved to have them out of my arms. It's a long walk from the market to my house with two heavy bags of groceries to carry. I'm going to make a giant pot of chicken soup. Tomorrow.

As I slide the cheesecake into the freezer, I look at the picture on the box. Next to it, it says, "Eight Pre-Cut Slices." All for me. No one to share it with. I'll eat one slice every night.

I hear heavy footsteps on the floor above me. I stand in the kitchen and listen, feeling the rough brown paper of the grocery bag between my fingers.

The refrigerator is packed with food. Tomorrow I'll make a chicken soup with barley, and a big pan of lasagna. Plenty for me to eat.

Frank's parents must be very pleased with Melanie. She and Frank look like they belong together. A perfectly-matched couple. Stupid Frank.

Without stopping to think, I open my door and march around the house to the side, and press the doorbell. I wait, shivering in the damp October evening air. I hear him clomp down the stairs before I see him, and when he opens the door, I see the surprise on his face.

"Robin! Are you all right? Did you lock yourself out?" He's wearing a dark green sweatshirt and gray sweatpants.

"No," I say, wrapping my arms around myself. "Um, I just wanted to invite you over for dinner tomorrow. If you're not busy. I have a ton of food, way too much to eat by myself."

He doesn't answer right away. He just stares at me.

"Well? I'm freezing out here, David."

"Sure. Yeah, sure, thanks. I'll bring wine. What time?"

I almost tell him not to bring wine, but then I figure I'm gonna need it. "Six-thirty okay?"

"See you then."

I run back to my place, my heart pounding against my chest.

I check the time before dialing Skip's number. He picks up on the first ring.

"Hey," I say into the receiver.

"Hey, Rob. What's going on?"

"Nothing. You guys done with dinner and everything?"

"Yeah. Kay's giving Sammy a bath. Everything all right?"

"I guess. Well, kind of. Mom told me about the divorce and everything. And they're moving. Um, is Dad okay?"

"Ah, you know. It's been rough on him. All the gossip. Let's put it this way, we won't be having both Mom and Dad in the same room anytime soon."

"It makes me sad. I mean, Mom and Dad! I don't know, Skip, maybe I was just naïve about it all, but I never knew their marriage was this bad. And for so long. Was I that stupid not to notice?"

"Nah. Robin, they hid it. I knew it was over, but they put on a pretty good show. It's just too bad it had to end like this. You know, Mom could have asked for a divorce *before* she took up with Russ Newman."

"Yeah, I know." I need to get to the point. "Listen, Skip, I really want to know if Dad is ever gonna let me go back to college. I can't be a waitress for the rest of my life. And I know it's not good between us right now, so I was wondering if maybe you could talk to him. Let him know I want to go back."

Skip is silent. I wait it out. I know he's turning this over in his head. My older brother has always been methodical. He weighs his options before making any decisions. I think he test-drove a dozen cars before he bought Kay that new Oldsmobile.

"I'll talk to him, Robin, but this is something for the two of you to work out. You know he expects you to apologize. You should take the first step toward mending your relationship with him."

"Yeah, okay. I know. But he should be sorry, too, Skip. What I did was not a big deal. He's the one who made it into a federal case."

"You broke the *law*, Robin. Okay? I don't care if everyone else was doing it, you got caught. And you embarrassed him. He did everything he could to keep you in school. You're the one who owes him an apology. A big one."

"All right, well, just pave the way for me, will you?"

"He's in Texas right now on business. I'll talk to him next week."

I guess that's the best I can hope for at this point. "Okay, thanks. Say hi to Kay."

"Good night, Robin." I hear the click as he lays the receiver down.

24

For once, my day at work goes by fast. I try not to think about my hasty decision to invite David for dinner, and I don't have time to dwell on it because I'm so busy. But when the shift ends and I run back home, I realize he'll be knocking on my door in a few hours.

Why am I nervous? We're just neighbors. It's not as if I'm looking for anything from him. I'm just trying to be nice. So first I get the chicken soup started. There's good music on the radio to keep me company. An hour for the soup, and hour for the lasagna, an hour to clean up and shower. I'll be fine.

The soup simmers on the stove. I lift the lid and see the barley has plumped up nicely, adding thickness. The lasagna is in the oven, covered with foil to keep it from drying out. Kay taught me that trick. She said a half hour before you serve it, take the foil off, add a ton of cheese and turn up the heat. That way the cheese is all melted and browned on top. I pull the cheesecake from the freezer and open the box. An image of Frank and Melanie feeding each other cake flashes through my mind, but I shake my head to dismiss it. The pieces are already cut, so all I have to do is take out two and let them thaw. I bought a can of cherries to spoon over the top. This will be a great dinner. Screw you, Frank, you don't get any of it.

I clean the kitchen and set the table. In my bedroom, I take off my clothes and throw them in the laundry basket, then shove the basket into my closet. After a quick shower, I pull on black jeans and a hooded sweatshirt, and slip socks onto my feet.

I leave the radio on. It'll help fill any awkward moments of silence. And a few minutes before six-thirty, I have a panic attack. *What am I doing?* Of course he'll think this is a date. And is it? Or am I just reacting to seeing Frank with his girlfriend? I'm using David. Yes, that's exactly what I'm doing. I've invited him over for dinner and cheesecake, in my apartment. Oh my God, I'm sending signals. He's definitely going to think there's something there. I consider

turning off the oven and sneaking out of the
apartment, maybe hiding up at Skip's house for the
night.

But he knocks. Five minutes early. I can't leave. So I
open the door and paste a friendly, unsexy smile on
my face. "Hey! Oh, what's this?"

I step aside to let David enter my kitchen. In one
hand he holds a bottle of wine, in the other a bouquet
of flowers wrapped in green tissue paper. I see yellow
and orange and rust-colored mums, all fall colors.
Very thoughtful.

"For you," he says. "And just one bottle." He sets the
bottle of wine on the table. It's Portuguese wine,
dammit. Mateus, in the low, squat bottle, the kind you
stick a candle in after the bottle is empty.

"Thank you," I murmur, feeling my throat constrict,
as if there's a giant piece of unchewed lasagna lodged
there.

"Smells great in here," he says, shrugging out of his
jacket. I take it from him and lay it on the bed. I wish
I had a coatrack or something. I close the door to the
bedroom. My little apartment, a bedroom and a
kitchen. It's fine when it's just me, and it was fine for
Frank. But with David, I wish I had a living room. He
pulls out a chair at the table and sits. He looks like

he's lost some weight, but I don't think I should mention it. It would mean I noticed.

"I just have to put the cheese on the lasagna," I say, opening the oven door. A rush of warmth hits me and I'm dizzy for a second. I take the bag of shredded mozzarella cheese from the fridge and open it. I lift the foil from the pan and lay handfuls over the bubbling lasagna. Then I turn the heat up to 400 and close the oven door.

"I'll open the wine," David says. He reaches in his pocket and pulls out a combination bottle-opener and corkscrew. "I grabbed mine in case you didn't have one of these," he says. He removes the cork with ease and fills both glasses.

"We have soup to start," I say, ladling thick soup into small, shallow bowls. I remember buying these dishes with my mom, right after I came back home in the spring. I blink hard against the memory. So much has changed since then. "Anyway," I say, partly to myself to dispel the thought. I sit opposite David and wait for him to try the soup. "There's salt and pepper if you need it."

He lifts a spoonful to his lips and I think about how that mustache probably picks up whatever he's eating. I wonder what he'd look like without it. He eats and nods and doesn't pick up the salt or the pepper.

"It's great, Robin. Doesn't need a thing."

I smile, pleased with my soup. He doesn't slurp or make noise, and he eats his soup the way my mother taught me when I was younger. He scoops it from the middle to the back, and he doesn't lean over the bowl. He sits straight and brings the spoon to his mouth, and eats noiselessly. I'm mesmerized by this, and have to make an effort not to stare.

I raise my glass to drink and he sets down his spoon to raise his as well. "Here's to good friends," he says, looking at me directly. "Thanks for the invite."

"Sure," I say before taking a big gulp. I don't want to get drunk tonight, I just want to lose this edginess. He refills my glass, even though it's not empty, and I take another long drink. There's only this one bottle, so that's good. I guess.

I ask him about his family, school, childhood. Trivial questions that serve as filler, and he answers them in a gentle, friendly way. But it's not a conversation. He responds to the questions I pose, but doesn't offer anything more. Still, he seems sincere.

"What about you, Robin?" We've finished the soup and I put the bowls in the sink, then run water in them. I take the lasagna from the oven, nearly burning my hand. I use my spatula to lift a piece from the casserole and it falls apart, so I put that one on my plate. I cut David a bigger piece and it stays together, for the most part. I think he'd eat it however it looked.

"What about me?" I know it sounds coy, and that's not what I intended. I don't want to be coy around him.

"What are your dreams? Something tells me you're not satisfied working as a waitress in a diner. You're too smart."

I set our plates on the table and sit down. Then I get up again and find the canister of Parmesan cheese in the refrigerator. I'm stalling, I know, because I do not want to talk about my writing with David. Man, I didn't even tell Frank and he was...well, he was special. I look across at David and wish like hell it was Frank sitting here, enjoying my lasagna.

"Well, Robin? Don't you have dreams? Aspirations?"

"Sure, everyone has dreams. But I'm a realist. I don't think about things happening that have no chance of ever happening."

"Like what?" he asks. "By the way, this is really good." A tiny bit of melted cheese is stuck to his mustache and he doesn't seem to even know it. "Some people want to be a rock star, or a famous actress. What were you studying in college, before you got thrown out?"

I look up sharply. That's right, I told him about that, when we went out for ice cream. "English. I was majoring in English."

"You wanna teach? Write?" His eyes look darker and bigger. Looking at him makes me nervous for some reason. Like he can see into me and know the things I'm afraid to tell anyone else.

"Not sure." I will not tell him anything about this book. And why the hell haven't I heard anything from Maryana Capture, anyway? Tomorrow I'm going to try and find out. I look up. "Yeah, teach, I guess."

"Well, I'm sure you'd be a great teacher." David wipes his mouth and drinks from his glass. The bottle of wine is empty. Just as well, I think, because I'd drink more if there was another. He must see me staring at the bottle, because he pushes his chair back. "Hang on a sec," he says, then opens the door and leaves. What the heck? I hear him open his truck door and slam it, then he walks back in with another bottle of the same wine. Uh-oh.

"Oh, I don't know if I can drink any more wine," I say with a nervous laugh. I'm feeling pleasantly buzzed right now, and I'm glad I ate, but another bottle might do me in. I have that feeling, the one I get when I drink wine. Like I'm sexier than I really am. And David is handsomer than I realized.

"Then I'll drink it," he says, laughing. "I can handle it. You're a wuss, Robin." He laughs, showing his teeth. They're straight and white. Good teeth. He pours himself a glass and holds the bottle up to me. "One more?"

"Half," I say, staring at his neck. How bad would it be to go to bed with this guy? I know he likes me. But if I do, I'd be crossing a line, over to a different place. I wouldn't want Frank to find out, even if he's in love with Melanie. I'd be embarrassed if he found out, that's the truth. And it's not like I can be with David and pretend it's Frank. They're so different.

David fills my glass anyway. So he's trying to get me drunk. Like the last time, and I still don't know how I got home or undressed, and if he had anything to do with it.

"Hey, remember the night we went to the pizza place? And drank too much?"

"Of course I remember," he says steadily. He doesn't even seem buzzed. Man, he really can drink. "Do you remember?"

"No, not everything. I had a lot to drink that night. I don't even remember getting home." I chew my bottom lip before asking. "Did you help me?"

"Of course I helped you. You could barely walk."

I stare at his hands, his long fingers. Clean fingernails.

"I mean, did you help me get undressed and into bed?" I feel my heart racing. Did he?

He drinks before answering me. "Robin, you were in rough shape. I felt bad that I'd allowed you to get so drunk you couldn't function. And I was worried about you, that you might get up in the middle of the night and fall or something. So yes, I helped you inside and I put you to bed. That was it."

I exhale. He could have had me that night, and I wouldn't have known the difference. "Thanks for that." I place my hand over my glass, then push it away. "I don't want to get like that again."

He runs his fingertip around the rim of his glass before looking up at me. "Robin, I'm not sure why you asked me here tonight. I get that you're not interested in me, not the way I'm interested in you. I know you just broke up with your boyfriend, so I guess I'm the rebound guy. I'm usually the rebound guy. I'm the guy girls have one date with." He swallows hard. "But if you asked me here for a one-night stand, it's not gonna happen. I really like you. You're smart and you're sexy, and I'd want more from you than just a roll in the sack."

I don't know what to say. It's like he knew I invited him over as a reaction to seeing Frank with Melanie, like he knew I was thinking about having one night of sex with him, with no emotional investment. I might as well be naked in front of him right now. And I don't want him to know that he was right.

"I'm not looking for a one-night stand." I pick up the plates and put them in the sink with the bowls, then add more water to the sink. "I have cheesecake," I say, with my back to him. I didn't expect him to make me feel so weird. I start to scrub the plates, just so the food won't be like cement in the morning. And then I feel him standing behind me, close. His belly is up against my back and I catch my breath.

"Robin," he whispers. "The dishes can wait."

I can't turn around, and he takes a step forward, closer. I feel him against me. He reaches around to take my hands from the soapy water. It's like I'm powerless, and I don't like it. But I *do* like it. I like the sensation of all of this. He moves slowly, methodically, and each touch is sensory overload. When he lowers his mouth to my neck, and I feel the tickle of his mustache against my skin, I almost scream.

"David…"

"Yes," he says against my skin. His arms move down to encircle my waist and he squeezes, forcing air from my lungs as I gasp.

"Oh God," I groan. This can't happen, my mind keeps telling me. But my body is responding to everything he does, and I don't want him to stop. He has me in his grip. I wonder for a second if he'd ever hurt me, then he slips his hand down the front of my jeans and I don't even care.

25

He must have left while I was still asleep, because I wake up alone. I squint at the clock next to the bed. Almost seven-thirty. I never sleep that late, but then again, I drank a lot of wine last night. Not so much that I don't remember everything. I remember it all.

I roll out of bed and pull a long tee shirt over my head. I walk into the kitchen and see that all my dishes are washed, dried and stacked on the counter. The flowers are back in the center of the table. No note. I thought he might have left a note or something. I pull aside the curtain at the door. His truck is gone. Of course, it might be my day off but it's not his.

I'm glad to be alone, because I wouldn't have wanted him to see regret in my eyes this morning. I need to process this series of events. And with no one to talk to about what happened, I need to be away from here.

When I was in high school, I had a few close friends. Jayne, Laura, and Deb. The four of us had known each other since first grade. We had occasional fights, and sometimes it was Deb and me versus Laura and Jayne, but we stayed close all the way up to graduation. Then Jayne went to college in Minnesota, where her grandparents lived. Laura's family moved to Georgia after her dad lost his job. And Deb and I had a huge fight the day after graduation and that was it for us. It was a stupid fight, over nothing important, but we were both too proud to admit any fault and that was that. She's down in DC now, from what I hear. Laura and I wrote letters for a while, but eventually we stopped. I'm sure she made new friends in Georgia. And I saw Jayne last summer when she came home, but she told me she was planning to stay up in Minnesota during summer breaks. She got a job at one of the hospitals, and she works part-time during the school year and full-time in the summer.

The girls I met at college scattered when I was busted. Yeah, they bought plenty of pot from me when I was selling, but as soon as I was caught, they weren't my friends anymore. I guess that's the true test of friendship – who stands up next to you when you're bruised and bloodied. They didn't, that's for sure. I wonder how my high school friends would have reacted.

When I first came back home, Frank was there for me. He'd always been there for me, and now I don't know if we'll ever be friends again. Although Melanie sure seemed friendly at the market the other day. If he's with her now, I can't see that we'll ever be the same. And maybe that's why I went running to David. Dammit. He's not a one-night stand kind of guy, he said. So that means he expects us to have a relationship now. I don't see that happening, and I'm going to have to tell him before this gets out of hand. I mean, last night was unbelievable, like nothing I'd ever experienced in my thin sexual past. But I just don't see myself with David. I don't even know his last name or anything about him, which only makes the guilt heavier.

I dress for the day, gray and raw. There's fog hanging over the harbor at the bottom of the hill, and no blue in the sky. I guess I'll go to the bookstore. Maybe Dorothy would have some information about the whole publishing business. I'd sure like to know what my next step is.

An hour later, I step into the Thousand Words Bookstore and poke around while Dorothy waits on a customer. I feel kind of bad that I hardly ever buy books from her. Mostly I borrow them from the library, because my budget just doesn't allow for new books all the time. Except for Maryana. Her books I'll buy.

Once Dorothy is free, I walk up to the counter. She smiles in recognition when she sees me.

"Hi there, Robin! Nice to see you. Today's your day off, isn't it?" Her hair is twisted into a long braid, and today she's wearing light pink lipstick. Dorothy isn't one to wear makeup, but she looks nice with a little color on her lips.

I nod. "Yep, my one day off. And there's no other place I'd rather be than here." I should really buy a paperback today. "Listen, I have a question for you. If someone writes a book, how long does it take before it's published and in your store?"

Dorothy fixes her eyes on a far corner of the bookstore as she considers my question. "Well, I think it depends. If the story is well-written, and doesn't need too much editing, I suppose it could be ready in six months or so. Book production takes time, Robin, but publishers also want their best books out there as soon as possible." She cocks her head, reminding me of an old seagull on the beach. Wearing pink lipstick.

"Don't worry, dear, I'm sure Maryana Capture will have a new book out soon," she adds.

"Yeah, hope so," I reply. "She puts out a book every two years. I noticed. So she's due for one." I spot a couple of customers browsing the rack of paperback books, so I lean forward and lower my voice. "I mean, let's say *I* wanted to write a book. Not that I have time," I add with a chuckle, "but maybe someday. How long would it take for *me* to get published?"

She pats my hand, and it reminds me of my mother. "I think it might be a long time, Robin. You would have to write the book, and that takes a lot longer than you think. Then you'd have to check it for errors, probably have a professional look it over. Then you'd send the manuscript to one of the big publishers in New York and cross your fingers."

So she really doesn't have an answer for me. Great. I let out a big breath.

"Robin, you're young. Plenty of time to write lots of books!" She notices someone looking for help and pats my hand again. "I'll let you know when Maryana's new book comes out."

"Okay, thanks," I say. I meander down an aisle and pull out a biography of Judy Garland. So I don't really know any more than when I came in, and Maryana Capture has had my manuscript for over two months. I can't afford to go back to New York right now, and I can't even be sure that snooty concierge delivered the manuscript to her. I kick myself again for not making a copy of the whole thing.

There's a mall across the street from the bookstore, so I might as well waste time there. I don't want to go home, even though I know I'm going to have to have that conversation with David. My father is still in Texas, so there's no news on that front, and pretty soon it'll be too late to register for the spring semester, even if he does let me go back to school. And I have no money. Ever since my mom moved in with Mr. Newman, I don't see her very much. I miss our shopping trips, and the extra twenties she used to slip to me.

I work six days a week and have practically nothing to show for it. My bank account has a balance of two hundred bucks, and right now there's a ten and two ones in my jeans pocket. Maybe I could get a job in one of these mall stores. But doing what? Selling bras to old ladies? I'd rather bring them bacon and eggs. Besides, I'd miss Andrew. And Jenny. And, once in a while, George, too.

The burger place is busy at lunchtime. I order a cheeseburger and fries, and a Tab, and sit at a small table near the front, so I can watch people walk by. Here's a woman who probably works in one of the stores, maybe Worthington's. She's got a lot of makeup on, so she either sells cosmetics or perfume. I can spot them a mile away. Now here are two old ladies wearing polyester pantsuits and sneakers. They swing their arms when they walk. And...oh crap, it's Mrs. Mello. And I'm sitting here in plain sight. Crap! I don't want to see her.

"Well, hello, Robin, what a pleasant surprise!" She's such a liar. She doesn't want to see me any more than I want to see her. But I wipe my mouth and smile up at her. I will not invite her to sit with me. No way.

"Hi, Mrs. Mello." I sip Tab through a straw so I don't have to talk to her.

"How's everything, dear? The job?"

"Job's fine, same as always." I'll be polite, because I was raised to be nice to adults.

"I was so sorry to hear about your parents, Robin." She lays a hand on my shoulder and squeezes lightly. "Very sorry about that."

I stick the straw in my mouth again and try to keep the threatening tears back behind my eyeballs. I just have nothing to say to her. She removes her hand from my shoulder.

"Well, I'll be sure to let Frank know I saw you," she says.

I raise my head and set down the cup. "Tell him I hope he's happy. Really. I want him to be happy." I blink hard and press my tongue to the roof of my mouth. I read somewhere that helps keep you from crying.

She can't say anything to that, so she just pats my shoulder and walks away, her heels clicking on the floor until I can't hear them anymore.

Because today wasn't bad enough, David pulls his truck into the driveway before I can barricade myself in my apartment. I wait on the front porch, wondering how in the world I'm going to get out of this situation I put myself in. He steps out of the truck and comes toward me, grinning.

"Hey, beautiful." He opens his arms as he steps up onto the porch. I allow myself to be embraced but I keep my arms at my sides.

As we pull apart, he leans in for a kiss. At least he keeps his mouth closed. And his breath is minty.

"Hey," I say. "How was your day?"

He laughs. "It was crummy until this moment. Now? It's fantastic." He must see the panic in my eyes because he pulls back. "Actually, my day was fine. How was yours?"

"Okay," I say. Here comes the lie. "I spent the day with my mom, and boy, can she shop! I'm so tired from walking all over the mall."

"Come on up and I'll give you a foot massage. Besides, I should cook dinner for you. Unless you want that cheesecake. We never did get to it last night," he says, wiggling his eyebrows.

Do it, I tell myself. Do it.

"Come in for a minute, David. We need to talk," I say, pushing my door open and walking in ahead of him. He shuts the door behind him.

"What's going on?" I can tell by the inflection in his voice that he's already on the defensive. Oh boy. This will not go easily.

I pull out a chair and sit. After all, I have tired feet. "Look, last night was a mistake."

He remains standing, but he grips the back of the chair and I can see his knuckles are white.

"No, it wasn't, Robin. It wasn't a mistake at all."

"Yes, it was, David. It shouldn't have happened. I had too much to drink."

He bends forward and lays his palms on my table. Those hands. I remember those hands and my face warms with the memory.

"Robin, I've seen you drunk. Remember? That night we went to the pizza place, you were drunk. You couldn't walk. I brought you home and I put you to bed. I could have easily taken advantage of you that night. But I didn't." He takes a deep breath. "Last night you might have been buzzed, but you weren't drunk. And you were *very* willing." His face darkens, like one of those clouds in the sky dropped down and passed right over him.

"I'm sorry," I say, surprised at how small my voice sounds.

"I told you I wasn't into a one-night stand. I even asked you again before we…" He swipes his hand across his mouth. "You said it wouldn't be." He stares me down and I'm caught. He's right. I remember. "Let me take care of you, Robin."

No. I want him gone, now. How do I tell him to get the hell away from me? That this will never work?

My telephone rings. Oh! I really understand that phrase 'saved by the bell' now. 'Saved by the knock' would have been better, but I'll take it. I hurry to the bedroom to answer the phone. It's someone trying to sell me a newspaper subscription, but David doesn't know that.

"Good evening, ma'am. I'm calling from the Gazette. How are you this evening?"

"Hi, Skip! You sound upset."

"Excuse me? No, my name is William and I'm calling from the Gazette. We're running a special deal on six-month subscriptions to the morning edition, and it includes the Sunday paper as well."

"Oh my God! I'll be up as soon as I can. Tell Kay I can handle everything. Bye."

I hang up and walk back to the kitchen to find David leaning against the table.

"What's wrong?" he asks.

"My brother's kid had an accident and he's at the hospital. My sister-in-law wants to be there, but I need to watch the little one. I'm sorry, David," I add, giving him my sincerest look.

"I'll drive you there," he says, pulling his keys from his pocket. "Come on, let's go."

No!! Crap. I don't want him to know where they live. "No, it's okay, they're not far." I grab my coat from the chair where I tossed it.

"Don't be ridiculous, Robin. It's cold out. And dark. I'll drive you to their house." He opens the door and I don't have any ammunition left for this one. I lock my front door and trudge behind him to the truck. He opens the door for me. Oh God, he'd better not walk me to Skip's door. Shit.

He pulls out of the driveway and starts up the hill. "Just direct me to their house."

I tell him where to go, and he pulls into the side driveway leading to Skip's house. As soon as he stops the truck, I open the door.

"Thanks," I say, then I stop and lean in to kiss his cheek, hoping it'll keep him in his place. "Listen, I'll call you later to let you know how everything is."

"You sure you don't want me to help you? I'm great with kids," he says.

"I'd rather introduce you on a different day. Okay?" I touch my fingertips to the spot on his cheek where my lips had just been. "Thanks."

David spreads his fingers through my hair. "Anything for you, Robin."

I jump out of the truck and run to the door, leaning on the bell. Please pull away, I pray. Wait! Please don't let Skip answer the door and show himself to this guy.

Kay opens the door, thankfully, and I push my way in.

26

I stay the night with Skip and Kay. Skip's reading in the den when I barge in, and doesn't ask any questions when Kay tells him I'm sleeping over. She lends me a nightgown and gives me a new toothbrush.

"I always keep extras of everything here," she explains, pointing to the closet just outside the bathroom. "You don't mind sleeping with Sammy, do you?"

"No, of course not," I tell her. It's taken me almost an hour to explain why I'm here, about Frank and Melanie, and David. I don't give her all the details, obviously, but I think she gets my drift. "Thanks for letting me crash here. I was so sure David was going to catch me in that lie."

She shakes her head. "You have to tell him, Robin. Just tell him it isn't working. He'll understand."

No, he won't. I want to explain about David, but then I'd have to explain about myself, too. About what a hypocrite I am. How I used him. No, it's easier to make him the bad guy in all of this. At the same time, I can't live with Skip and Kay forever.

"I should look for another apartment," I say as she hands me a clean towel. It's so thick and soft, more like a blanket than a towel, and I wonder if I'll ever own stuff like this.

"You can't run away, and besides, isn't that apartment practically free?" She smiles at me, like a mother would smile at a child.

"Yeah." So I'll deal with David tomorrow. Tonight I need to sleep. "Is there an alarm clock in there? I need to get up early for work."

"Skip's up at five, and he'll drive you. I'll let him know." She gives me a hug and I hate to let go.

"Thanks, Kay. For this." I clutch my thick towel to my chest and go into the bathroom, closing the door behind me.

Skip wakes me at five past five, gently shaking my shoulder. I was dead to the world and could have slept for hours. Without speaking, I get up and discover that Kay has set out some of her clothes for me to wear. Her jeans are snug, but I can get through the day with them, and at least I have clean underwear and a clean shirt.

I drink a cup of really good coffee with Skip and think my next purchase should be a Mr. Coffee maker.

"English muffin?" he asks, holding up the package.

"Is there time?" I'm out of my element in their kitchen. I want to be home, but now I'll anticipate David on the porch at every moment. And if not on my porch, then leading me into my bedroom.

"Of course there's time," he says, and there's a sharpness in his voice as he places two halves in the toaster. He drinks coffee standing up, so I do the same. When he sets down his mug, I feel his eyes on me.

"Kay told me, Robin. That's not a good situation."

"Yeah, I agree. I'll handle it."

"What happened with Speedy? I thought you two were together."

I rest my chin in my upturned hand. "We were. But his parents fixed him up with a Portuguese girl. I guess I'm good enough to be his pal but not good enough to be his girlfriend. They want to marry him off."

"Well, I'm sorry about that. Spee…Frank's a good guy. But you can't live in fear of your upstairs neighbor. If you want me to step in, I will."

"No, I can handle it." And I'm not living in fear. What did Kay tell him, anyway?

I accept the toasted English muffin from him and slather butter on each half. I eat hungrily and don't speak again until I'm finished, in record time. "But please talk to Dad about me going back to college, okay?"

"Okay. He flies in tonight. Give it a day or two, let him settle back in. Come on, let's go." He picks up his coat and briefcase and we head out the door into the garage.

He drives down a deserted Main Street. No one is up at this hour, and I have a feeling Skip wouldn't be up this early, either. Kay made him do it. Just before I get out of his truck, he grips my arm. "No more lying to this guy, Robin. And if you need my help, call me."

Jeez, Kay told him everything then. I'm glad I didn't spill my guts to her.

"Thanks for the ride. I'll be fine." I jump out of the truck and run into the diner.

Andrew steps into the restaurant and I feel my heart expand inside my chest. He waves at me before sitting at his regular table. I bring the coffeepot.

"Good morning, Sunshine," he says, his eyes shiny and bright.

"Good cold morning to you," I say in return, smiling because my day is so much better when I see him. "The usual?"

"Sure. So, what's new?" He glances around the diner, but it's mostly empty this morning. Which is good, because I need his opinion.

"Andrew, I need to know what's going on with the manuscript I delivered to Maryana Capture. How can I find out? She never wrote to me, or called. What do I do now?"

"The process can take time, Robin. I'll talk with Barb tonight, but I wouldn't expect anything so soon. Look, if she hated it and didn't think it could be published, I'm sure she'd have sent you a nice little note, thanking you for the submission with the usual blah blah blah. Even if she sent it to her publisher and *they* hated it, you'd probably have received a rejection letter. Not hearing from them may be a very good sign."

"It's so hard to be patient. I don't know where my life is going right now, and I need to know. I need to have a plan to get out of here."

"What's going on, Robin? You sound worried," he says, narrowing his eyes. "Is everything okay?"

"No, everything's all messed up." It just comes out, and he raises his eyebrows. "I mean, it'll be okay. I'm handling things." I refill his cup and look over to see if George is ready to scream at me.

Andrew laughs. "That's my girl. You're strong and powerful, you know that?" He gives me a funny look, like he's proud of me or something, although I don't know what in the world I've done to make anyone proud.

Everything feels as though it's suspended, like I'm not moving forward, in spite of the days passing quickly. Skip thinks I'm afraid of David, which isn't true. What's true is that I don't have the guts to tell him how I feel. That I don't see myself with him, that he's not the man I had in mind. Still, I can't deny that he knows how to get to me. He brings me flowers, he massages my tired feet, he treats me like a queen. And I feel like crap for letting him.

He orders a pizza tonight, so at least I don't have to cook. Less than ten minutes after he called the order in, there's a knock on the door. Wow, I think, that's fast. I open the door to find my father standing there and my breath is sucked right out of my lungs. He fills the entire door frame. It's been so long since I've seen him, I just stand there with my mouth open, aware of David sitting at my kitchen table. But my dad doesn't notice him. His eyes are red and puffy and his voice is hoarse, as if he'd just spent the past hour cheering for the football team.

"Robin, your mother's been in an accident. It's bad."

My hand flies to cover my mouth and I step back. My dad's eyes go to David, who stands up fast, almost knocking his chair over.

"Who are you?" he asks.

"David, sir. I live upstairs." David sticks his hand out. My father ignores it, but maybe not on purpose.

"I need to be with my daughter. Would you leave us, please?"

"Well, I'm her boyfriend, sir. She might need me…"

"Get the hell out of here!" my father barks, and David scurries out the door like a scolded puppy. I throw my arms around my dad's barrel chest and feel his arms encircle me. I don't want to let go.

"I'm so sorry, Dad," I sob against his chest and he hugs me tighter.

When we finally pull apart, he looks down at me and says, "Grab a few things, Robin. I want you to stay with me. We'll go to the hospital and I'll explain everything on the way."

David is completely forgotten as I pull my suitcase from under my bed, swipe the dust off it, and toss in some clean underwear, tee shirts, pants, socks, and a sweater. I grab what I need from the bathroom and toss those things in on top of my clothes, then I close the lid and fasten the hinges. My dad takes the suitcase from my hand.

"You can always come back and get whatever else you need," he says. "Let's go."

We walk out to the driveway where his Cadillac is parked next to David's truck. He opens the trunk and lays my suitcase inside, and I slide into the passenger seat just as the pizza delivery guy drives up. I pop out long enough to say to him, "Ring the bell on the side for the second floor. He ordered it." The kid nods and walks around the side of the house as my father starts the car.

On the way to the hospital, he tells me that my mom and Mr. Newman were driving on one of the back roads last night when apparently Mr. Newman lost control of the car and it went off the highway and down an embankment. It hit a tree and Mr. Newman died. My mom is in really bad shape. She was able to crawl out of the car but she was on the ground all night, until someone found them this morning. His voice breaks as he tells me about her injuries.

"Will she make it?" I ask, afraid of the answer.

"I don't know. Pray for her."

"Dad, I'm so sorry. About everything." I choke it out, and it doesn't matter that I apologized first. "I embarrassed you, and I'm so sorry."

He takes his hand from the steering wheel and holds mine. We stay like that until we reach the hospital.

27

A week after my mother's accident, she's still hooked up to a bunch of tubes, and a machine is breathing for her. My father told me there was some swelling in her brain, but she looks better than she did seven days ago. I took some time away from work, and asked Jenny to let Andrew know what happened. She's brought her niece in to help, and George sent flowers, which was very thoughtful.

I've been staying in my dad's house, back in the bedroom I lived in for eighteen years. We've talked a lot, and although it's too late for me to get back to college for the spring semester, he does agree that I should return. I've apologized so much he finally told me to stop, then *he* apologized, and I promised I wouldn't be selling (or smoking) pot again. And I meant it. It doesn't hold any appeal to me anymore. In some ways, being back home is like it used to be, but mostly it's all different. I realize there's no going back in time, as much as I want to, and it's just one of those hard truths I imagine adults have to deal with all the time.

So my days consist of visiting with my mom, sometimes for hours, just sitting next to her bed and reading, then returning home to clean the house, do laundry, make dinner for my dad and me. Some nights we eat with Skip and Kay, but just because they live next door doesn't mean we see them all the time. Skip and my dad work together every day, so I'm sure they both appreciate some time apart.

And David? Well, he sent flowers, too, but for me, not for my mom, which ticked me off. I brought the flowers to the hospital and put them in my mom's room. He called once, and my dad picked up the phone. I heard him say, "Who the hell is this?" and then "Listen, we're going through a lot right now, maybe she'll be up for a conversation later." After he hung up, I thanked him.

"Is this guy bothering you, Robin?"

"No, Dad. He just likes me more than I like him."

"That's usually the way it is," he said quietly.

Today I'm going back to work. My dad and I agreed that he'll drive me to work, I'll work my shift, and then we'll go to the hospital together after dinner. He drives me to the diner every morning, even though I can walk. But he's like Skip and doesn't want me walking the length of Main Street in the cold and dark.

We had a little snow last night, not much, but it looks like angel dust on the front lawn. The streets are just wet, because it melted when it hit the pavement.

When he arrives in front of the Liberty Diner, he shifts the car into park. I give him a kiss goodbye before leaving.

"If this job is too much, Robin, you let me know. You don't have to work here." My dad pushes my hair back from my forehead, the way he did when I was little. He hasn't been this affectionate with me in years. Not that I mind.

"It's fine, Dad, really. It'll be good for me to be busy. I'll see you when you get home."

George gives me a hug when I walk in and asks about my mother. His black eyes, magnified behind his thick glasses, are shiny. His wife Maria hugs me, too, and says everyone was asking for me. The only one I care about is Andrew. And today's not his day.

But apparently today is David's day. Not ten minutes after we open, he walks in. I gesture to Jenny and pull her into the back room.

"Has he been coming in every day?" I hiss.

She nods. "Yep, every day. He always asks me when you'll be back, if you'll be back, and I always say the same thing. That I don't know." She gives me a sad smile. "Can't keep him from coming in, kiddo."

"I know," I grumble. "But at least he's at the counter. He's your customer." I roll my eyes. There are empty tables available.

I haven't seen David since that night my dad showed up at my door. I know he tried to call me at the house, but we haven't spoken, and I can only hope he'll let this thing between us go. Yeah, right.

"Robin." He stands with open arms as I approach. I raise my palm and shake my head.

"Come on, not here, David." There's only one other customer in the diner this early, but I'm not going to have him hugging and kissing me in my restaurant. I mean, come on.

"I've missed you. How's your mother?"

I shrug. "Pretty much the same. She's still in a coma. The doctors induced it. She had swelling on her brain." I glance over at my one customer, reading the menu. "I have a customer," I say, pulling away. He grabs my forearm.

"I need you. And I think you need me. Can I see you tonight?" His face is inches from mine and I can smell him. It's a clean smell, though, not unpleasant, although having him grip me is. I tug my arm away.

"David, I go to the hospital every night. My dad needs me, too. Please try to understand." I walk away from him and tend to the man at a table on the other side of the room. I spend extra time with him, mentioning practically every item on the menu. After he orders, I walk toward the pass-through, where I clip his order up for George. I know David is staring at me the whole time, but I won't look at him.

A few more people come in, and they keep me busy. Eventually David has to leave to go to work, but he walks over to me before he leaves.

"Don't stay away from me, Robin. I know you're hurting. I want to be a part of your life, no matter how sad it is. If this is the only way I can see you, then I'll be in here every morning. And tomorrow I'll sit at a table." He presses his lips against my cheek and I feel the scratch of his mustache on my skin. At least he didn't try and kiss my mouth.

I don't say anything. I just watch him leave. Tomorrow's my day off, and I want to move my stuff out of the apartment. I'm not going back there. My father and I are doing better, and there's no reason for me to stay there. In my dad's house, David can't smother me. I'll tell my dad tonight.

Tuesday morning, I wake up at eight o'clock, a true luxury. My dad's already left for work, so I have the house to myself. Last night I told him that I wanted to move back in here for good, and he was all for it.

"I love having you here, Robin," he'd said over dinner. I made spaghetti and meatballs with salad and garlic bread, and we both had a glass of red wine. "I'll send one of the guys down with a van to pack up your things. And don't worry about cleaning, we have a service for that."

"Great," I'd said. No more David! He'll get over it eventually.

So now, after breakfast and a shower, I head down the street toward my apartment. It's brisk but sunny and the walk feels good. Christmas is weeks away, and with my focus on my mother, I haven't had time to think about Maryana Capture. Or Frank. Although his parents sent a lovely card and a plant to the hospital for my mom, he couldn't bother calling to see how I'm doing. Too wrapped up in Melanie's arms, I guess. Well, that's how it is when you move on. He could have called, though. Unless he called my apartment and doesn't know I've been living with my dad. That's a possibility.

I turn the corner and start walking downhill to the house and there's a van already in the front drive. But it's not there to help me move my stuff. It has "All-Star Cleaning and Damage Service" printed on the side. Were the movers here already? I wanted to pack up my own stuff, dammit.

My front door is open and I run to it. I almost hit one of the guys who's walking out.

"What's going on?" I ask.

"You live here?" He pulls a cigarette out of his mouth and grinds it out on the front step.

"Yeah. But I haven't been here for a couple of weeks."

"Well, you've got a broken water supply line and major damage to the apartment. Started upstairs. That apartment's ruined, too." He shakes his head in disgust.

"*What?* What are you talking about?" I heard the words, but I can't make sense of them.

Oh, my notebooks! I push past him and enter the apartment, against his protests. The notebooks were in a cardboard box on the floor next to my dresser. Oh God.

And there's the box, sitting in water. The flimsy cardboard comes apart when I try to lift the lid. The paper was like a sponge, and each notebook is bloated, like I suppose a body would be if it was left in water. Everything is ruined.

"Miss, come back out, please. You shouldn't be inside. We'll try to salvage what we can."

I walk backwards out of the bedroom and into the kitchen. I don't care about the furniture, it wasn't mine to begin with. It was just some second-hand stuff my father bought for the apartment. The clothes in my closet might be okay. But who cares? My notebooks are wrecked. Everything is gone. It's all gone. Two years of work. All gone. And my only other copy is God knows where.

28

David was relocated to another apartment because of the water damage. And it's not near the diner. He came in to tell me where he's living now.

"I want us to be together for Christmas," he says. Christmas is a week away. My mother has regained consciousness, although she has no memory of the accident. And when she opened her eyes and saw my father, she thought they were still married. The doctors say that's not unheard of, but eventually she may remember that they divorced and she had married Mr. Newman, and then my dad will have to explain. She has a lot of rehabilitation ahead of her, so she won't be home for Christmas, but her condition is improving, and for that I'm grateful. It's also given me strength to do what I should have done a long time ago.

"No, David. I don't want to be with you. I don't have the same feelings for you that you apparently have for me, and for that, I'm sorry. But there is no 'us.' If you want to think of us as broken up, fine." I stand in front of him, a coffeepot in my right hand. And if he gives me any trouble, I swear I'll dump it over his head.

But he doesn't say anything. He drops his chin and stares at his feet. I see a vein pulsating in his neck. Finally he raises his eyes to mine.

"I love you, Robin. I'll always love you. And I'll be here when you change your mind." He says all of it quietly, in a monotone, like someone pulled a string in his back to make him talk. Then he lowers his eyes again and walks away from me.

I wait until he's gone, then run to tell Jenny.

"Something tells me you haven't seen the last of him," she says, eyeing the door. "But he's gone for now!"

Yeah, he's gone for now. I stare at the door until I hear George's voice from the kitchen.

Our family is together for Christmas. Back in June, I didn't think it was possible, but here we are, on

Christmas Eve. My mom is in a rehab facility one town over, and we're all there to visit. The kids are full of excitement and can't stop bouncing around. All that sugar hasn't helped, either, I'm sure, but seeing my mother laugh is the best Christmas present. She still thinks this is the way it's always been and hasn't mentioned Mr. Newman once. I wonder if she's blocked all of it out, you know, subconsciously. I think my dad knows the proverbial other shoe could drop at any moment, and he tries to prepare himself for it, but today, he's genuinely happy.

We have supper with my mom, in the dining room. The food is soft and bland, and a nurse helps my mother eat, because her right arm is in a sling. She looks old today. Her hair is all gray (she hasn't been able to withstand a color treatment) and without any makeup, she looks older than fifty, but she's still my mom, and I'm happy to see my father so attentive to her. Maybe their life will be better, once she heals.

Tomorrow my dad and I will go to church. He asked me to go with him, and even though neither of us has been to church in a long time, I agreed. Seemed like a good thing to do, to give thanks for the blessings this past year. I'm trying to be positive about my life. Yes, my notebooks were destroyed in the water damage, and I don't know whether Maryana Capture tossed my manuscript in the garbage, or whether she brought it to her publisher and said it would be a good book. But I try not to dwell on it, because it's out of my hands. I'm just glad I never told anyone else about it. Even my father would have lectured me about taking care of what's mine.

And my dad and I are getting along. He's caring for my mom, as if everything she did to him, all the embarrassment, is forgiven. It made me think about Frank. If I care about him, truly care about him, then I should be happy for him, if he's in love with Melanie.

Once we're back in our house, after we said good-night to Skip and Kay and kissed the kids, I go up to my bedroom and pick up the phone. It's only nine-thirty, and I want to wish Frank a Merry Christmas. His dad picks up on the second ring.

"Ho ho ho, Merry Christmas!" he booms into the phone. I wonder if he's drunk.

"Hi, Mr. Mello. This is Robin. Robin Fortune. Merry Christmas!"

"Merry Christmas, Robin! You wanna talk to Francisco?"

"Yes, please. If he's there."

"Hold on." I hear a muffled yell and imagine Mr. Mello, with his big hand over the receiver, yelling at Frank, who's probably on the other side of the house.

And then I hear a click, and dead air. Mr. Mello hung up on me. Oh, for crying out loud. Should I call back? Or will he tell Frank it was me? And if he did tell him, will Frank even call me? I decide to wait for a minute.

After ten minutes of silence, I decide not to call back. What if Frank was with Melanie? I'd only be an intrusion, unwelcome, especially on Christmas Eve.

I walk back downstairs and find my father in the den, sipping whiskey. "Merry Christmas, Dad." He sets down his drink and gestures to me. I climb onto his lap and bury my face in his neck so he won't see the tears in my eyes. Because he won't understand. I'm not crying for Mom.

"Merry Christmas, little girl. You'd better get to sleep before Santa comes down the chimney." I hug him harder before running up the stairs to my room.

I don't think I've ever been sadder. Or felt more alone. I didn't buy Frank a Christmas present. Well, with my mom and everything, I hadn't thought much about it, but honestly, he's out of my life. Only he isn't. I throw off the blanket and turn on the light at my desk, the same desk where I did my homework for so many years. I open a drawer and find stationery, pale yellow sheets of paper decorated at the bottom with blades of grass and tiny butterflies. I start writing.

Dear Frank,

Merry Christmas! I plan to hand-deliver this letter to you on Christmas Day. I didn't buy you a present this year – it didn't seem appropriate, since you're with Melanie now. I don't want to do anything to make her think I'm trying to get between you two, because I'm not.

But you're still my friend, Francisco. I hope that hasn't changed. I want you to be happy, and if Melanie can give you the happiness you deserve, then I'll be your biggest cheerleader.

It's been a difficult few months, for a lot of reasons. You know about my mom, I'm sure. And I'm back living with my dad. We've reconciled and everything is really good, and he's happy to have me home again.

I hope 1977 brings better days. And I hope it brings you everything you want, my friend.

Lots of love always,

Robin

I read it over and hope I said it right. I fold the paper in half and slide it into a similarly-decorated envelope, then write Frank's name on the front in my pretty handwriting. I leave the envelope on my desk so I won't forget it tomorrow and get back into bed. And as I try to imagine what sugarplums would look like dancing in my head, I let sleep overtake me.

29

I wake to the smell of bacon. It's enough to rouse me at six-thirty on Christmas morning. Wrapping a terrycloth bathrobe around my long tee shirt, I pad downstairs to the kitchen, where my father is hard at work playing cook.

"You know how to wake me up right! Merry Christmas, Dad." I rise up on my toes to kiss his cheek and pour myself a cup of coffee.

"I'd have kept these warm for you, kiddo. But I'm glad you're up. I figured we could eat something before heading next door. We have to see the kids' faces when they get a load of all the loot under the tree." He grins like a seven-year-old. "Come on, grub's ready."

We sit on stools at the counter and scarf down scrambled eggs and bacon. I manage to have a second cup of coffee before we walk next door.

We drive to church just before ten. I have Frank's letter with me, and I tell my Dad that I'll walk home. He doesn't ask me why, just nods and takes my arm as we walk into the church together.

After services, my father stands outside shaking hands with people who wish him "a better '77" and tell him he's "a decent man." I catch his eye and he holds up four fingers, reminding me that Kay's serving dinner at four. I stroll away from the crowds and head in the direction of Frank's house. By now there could be a ton of people there, but I'm not going to sneak up. I want to wish my friend a Merry Christmas in person. Still, my hand shakes as I point out my index finger to press the doorbell.

It's a gift that Frank, not his mother, opens the door. I watch his face register surprise, then joy as he opens his arms to hug me.

"Merry Christmas," I say into his flannel shirt.

"Where the hell have you been?" he asks, looking very angry.

I back away. "Why are you mad at me?"

"I called and called. You never called me back," he says, but he's smiling big, so I know he isn't really mad.

"I had all this damage in my apartment. Water from upstairs," I add, making a face, like it was all David's fault.

"No kidding. So where are you living?" He ushers me inside and shuts the door. We stand in the front hall. I hear voices from the other end of the house.

"With my dad. You know about my mother, right?"

He nodded. "I'm sorry. I called after I heard about it. I just figured you were so mad you wouldn't even talk to me."

"Really? I'm not mad at you. I want you to be happy." I remember the letter and pull it out. "Actually, I say all that in this letter. I wrote it to you last night. Sorry I didn't buy you a Christmas present." I offer the letter to him and he takes it, but sticks it in his shirt pocket without opening it.

"Is Melanie here?" I ask in a subdued voice.

"No," he says and I stand a little taller until he adds, "She's coming over soon, though."

I slump against the wall, so tired I feel I might fall to the floor. Not that I'm being dramatic, I just don't have any energy left. Everything's been sucked out of me.

"I guess she's the one for you, Frank," I say, feeling my throat swell until I can barely swallow. My mouth is so dry anyway, there's nothing to swallow.

"I don't know if she's the one for me. But she's good enough for now."

I don't know what to say to that. I want to slap his face hard, and I want to tell Melanie that he's using her, but how can I? Because what he said makes me feel better. And I hate myself for that.

"Don't use her, Frank. You wouldn't want someone to do that to you." I brush by him as I open the door. "Have a nice Christmas," I say and leave.

It's a cold walk back home, but I don't hurry. Eventually I find my way to Little Beach, deserted on this Christmas Day. I lower myself to the cold sand and lay on my back, staring up at a milky sky. An airplane passes overhead, so high that it's only a speck, and I wonder where it's headed. Wherever it is, I wish I was on that plane. Never before have I felt such a longing to go away from this town. I'd miss my family, sure, but I can't stay here. Too many reminders of Frank, too many chances to run into him. And David, too.

Dad gave me cash for Christmas, along with some stuff I know Kay picked out, and I think I'll go back to New York, right after New Year's. I have to try and find out what happened to my manuscript. Even with going back to finish college, I want to know. And if Maryana hated it, maybe I could get it back, shop it around somewhere else. After I make multiple copies of it. I'm sure Andrew's wife would help me find another publisher, after she has her baby.

I sit up and brush sand from my hair. There's a rowboat out on the bay. I squint to see it better. Looks like one guy, out for a Christmas excursion. Good for him, brave soul. If I had a boat, I'd be out there, too, where no one could bother me. Surrounded by water, the winter sun warming my face, I could stay out for hours.

At a little before three, I head back to the house. I open the front door and it's quiet inside. My dad must be next door. I run upstairs to change my clothes and brush my hair, then walk across the lawn to Skip's. It's only when I step inside their house and breathe in the aromas from the kitchen that I realize how hungry I am.

Skip and my dad are seated in front of the big color television. The kids are on the carpet, watching an animated Christmas movie. There's a snowman talking to a rabbit. I turn to Kay.

"Can I help?" I lift the lid off one the pots on the stove.

"We're almost ready," she says. "Could've used you about an hour ago." She looks beat, and I feel guilty for lazing on the beach when I could have offered my assistance to her today.

"I'm sorry. I went over to see Frank, and it didn't go well. Then I took a walk down to the beach because I felt sad. I should have come over here instead."

"Don't worry about it," she says, but I can tell she's tired. She's done this whole meal herself. Because in this family, the men don't help when there's a woman in the kitchen.

"Sorry," I say again, as if repeating it will help.

"There's a package for you. I think your dad has it."

A package? I walk into the den and approach my father, who looks to be dozing in his chair. I touch his shoulder and he wakes with a start.

"Oh! Robin, there you are." He rubs his chin and sits up straighter.

"Hi. Kay said there's a package for me?"

"Yeah, it was on the front step this afternoon." He looks around. "Where is it, Skip?"

Skip reaches for a box, wrapped in Christmas paper with a red bow stuck on it. I prefer ribbon myself. Bows are too easy. You just peel back the paper and slap them on the box. What next? Pre-wrapped gifts? Bags?

"Who's it from?" I ask, holding the box in my hand. It's not too heavy. My skin tingles.

"No idea," says my dad. "I almost didn't see it when I stepped out earlier. Open it up."

I tear off the paper, knowing somehow that I should open this box away from everyone. It's the perfect size and shape to hold a watch or bracelet. Frank gave me a bangle bracelet for my birthday. I don't think this is from Frank, though. In fact, I'm sure of it.

It's a watch. A fancy, expensive watch with a silver link bracelet. "It's a watch," I say.

"Well, let's see it!" Skip leans forward in his chair. Even the kids turn from the television to look at the present.

I hold it up. Kay walks in from the kitchen to see. The watch is now front and center.

"That's pretty," she says. "I like the bracelet part."

My father holds out his hand to inspect it. I give it to him and he peers at it. "Longines. That's Swiss. You got yourself a good watch here, kiddo. Who's your secret admirer?" He turns it over.

And before I can make something up, he reads an inscription on the back. "Love, David?" He turns his face up to me. "Who the hell is David?"

Skip cuts in. "The guy who lived upstairs from you? I thought you hated him."

"I don't hate him," I retort. "And we're not together. He's a weirdo."

"Yeah, but he *loves* you, Robbie," Skip says, chuckling with my dad.

I rub my nose with my middle finger and give him a hard look. He raises his eyebrows and continues to laugh as I storm away.

I'm not going to wear that watch, are you kidding me? I wish I could return it, but the creep had it engraved. And he delivered it to the house. Ugh. I haven't seen David since that morning in the diner, when I told him, in no uncertain terms, that we were broken up. Not that we were ever together, but it's how I had to phrase it for him to understand. Only he didn't, obviously. And I'm on pins and needles waiting for him to show up again. He won't stay away, not after giving me an expensive gift like that. Maybe I'll lie and tell him I don't know what he's talking about, that I never got a present from him. Let him think it was stolen or something. No, because then he'd probably go out and buy me another one. And deliver it personally.

My dad wrote a letter to the college. With any luck, they'll let me back in come September. It's not like they banned me for life, anyway. It was my dad's choice to decide whether I would go back or not. Then with my mother's accident, his focus shifted. Hey, I know, it wasn't her fault, or anyone's fault, and even though I didn't like him, I'm sorry Mr. Newman died. And I'm glad she didn't.

My dad told me yesterday that when he went to visit her the day after Christmas, my mother called him Russell. I think it freaked him out, but she kept right on talking and the next time she called him anything, it was Hap. He never brought it up, didn't call her out on it, and he did not tell her that Russell Newman is dead. I think he should have told her.

Anyway, my dad was invited to a New Year's Eve party at the Mellos' house. I didn't get an invitation, so either it's just for the parents, or Frank didn't want me there. I don't care, I'll spend New Year's Eve watching television and eating take-out food from the Chinese restaurant. Skip and Kay are going to some fancy thing in the city, and they're staying overnight. I offered to babysit the kids, but Kay said Nancy the nanny was coming over. Sometimes I wonder if Kay doesn't trust me with her kids. What, because of the pot? I don't do that anymore. I hardly ever drink, either. Well, except those two times with David. And since then, hardly ever. Still, if she wants Nancy to stay with the kids, fine. I don't mind being alone.

Andrew didn't come in this morning. I guess with the holiday week and all, he isn't working, but it felt weird not to see him. I so look forward to Wednesdays and Fridays. And since he isn't in today, he won't be in on Friday, either, most likely. Not on New Year's Eve day. I wanted to go back to New York next week, maybe see if I can find Maryana, or talk to someone at her publishing company, but maybe I should talk to Andrew first, since he and his wife are the only ones who even know about this book. I thought about telling my dad, but I stopped short, because if I tell him I wrote a book and I'm trying to get it published, he'll ask about college. He wants me to go back, and I want to as well, even if I'll be behind my friends, who aren't really my friends anymore. Not one word from the girls I shared a dorm room with, nothing from the kids who regularly bought a dime bag. Yeah, I should have known.

30

On Friday after my shift, I stop by the Chinese restaurant and look at their take-out menu. Maybe I should buy the food now, and reheat it later. I don't want to go back out once I'm home.

"You order food?" A middle-aged woman, probably the owner, waits at the counter.

"Yeah. Sweet and sour pork, fried rice, and…" I want more. "And an order of those little dumplings." I point it out on the menu and she nods. "Five dollar, eighty cent." She holds out her hand as I dig in my pocket and hand her a five and a one. "Ten minute, you wait," she instructs, so I sit in a chair with a torn vinyl cushion. Fifteen minutes later, she hands me a big brown bag.

I walk along Main Street, carrying my bag by the handles. The smell of my food drifts up through the crisp air and I'm hungry. Maybe I'll eat a little and save the rest for later. I'm so caught up in the food that I don't see him. He blocks my path on the sidewalk and I nearly walk right into him.

"Robin." His voice is soft and caressing, but when I look up at his face, I don't see anything soft and caressing. I don't get scared often, but the way he looks at me is unsettling.

"David. Happy New Year." I step to the right and he steps to his left. I know he can't do anything to me here, not right on Main Street. Shops are still open and there are people around.

He brushes his hand along my arm, down to the wrist. His fingers reach under my coat sleeve and a puzzled look comes over his face. "Didn't you get the Christmas present I delivered to you?"

I jerk my arm away from him. "Oh, the watch? The very expensive watch that was a completely inappropriate gift? The one you had engraved? Yeah, I got it."

"You didn't like it?"

I won't run away from him. No, he needs to understand.

"What don't you understand, David? We are *not* a couple. I haven't seen you since that morning in the diner, when I thought I made it crystal clear that if you had any delusions about us, you shouldn't. The watch was inappropriate. I'll get it back to you."

"I bought it for you."

"Well, it was a waste of money," I say, skirting around him and walking away. I pick up my pace, even though I'm certain he's following me. I whirl around to face him, but he's standing in the same place, just standing there staring.

My dad looks nice in a sports jacket and slacks. But it's sad that he's alone on New Year's Eve. We're spending the day tomorrow with my mom, who, by the way, might come home next month. We'll see.

"Don't stay out all night," I say to make him laugh.

"I'd rather stay here with you and eat that fried rice."

"I'll save some for you. Come home early."

He leans down to kiss me and lets himself out the front door. I wait a minute, then get up and lock it. Who knows, David could be watching the house. At this point, I wouldn't put anything past him.

I heat up my Chinese food, only taking half of everything so there will be some left for my dad. Settling in to watch television, I try to concentrate, but find myself listening for noises. Nancy the nanny is next door with the kids, but I don't want to go over there. The whole idea was to have a quiet night to myself. Still, I turn off the TV and sit in the near-darkness.

I pace the floors of the house all night. Definitely not relaxing. I peek out the window, but you can't see the street from the front windows, because our yard is so big, and there are evergreens lined up along the street, for privacy. Ha. He could hide there.

Damn. David is doing exactly what I said I'd refuse to let him do. Make me nervous. And scared. I can't shake that look he gave me this afternoon, just standing there on the sidewalk. I never gave him any reason to think we were a couple. Flashing back to that night in October when I invited him over for dinner, okay, maybe he took that to mean I liked him. And he was pretty clear about not wanting casual sex. I remember him whispering in my ear that sex symbolized something special between two people. And I agreed. Well, it wasn't like I could just sit up in bed then and tell him I was horny for a man and he was available. And yes, I played along for a while after that night. It was easier. But I thought I'd made it clear to him recently that it wasn't going to work out. He has to accept that.

I wait up for my father, not even watching the big sparkly ball drop in Times Square, but standing in the darkened kitchen, my eye on the clock. I hear his key in the lock at quarter to one, and rush to open the door for him.

"Hi, sweetheart," he says, taking off his coat. "Happy 1977!" His eyes are clear. I don't think he's drunk at all.

"Happy New Year, Dad. I waited up for you."

"I can see that. Did you have a good night?"

"Yeah, it was great. Very relaxing." What a crock. "I saved you some food." I'm not even sleepy now.

"Oh, I ate a lot at the Mellos'. What a spread." He pats his belly.

I don't look at him when I ask if Frank was there.

"He showed up for a bit. With that girlfriend of his. She asked for you. Melissa?" He scrunches up his brow, trying to remember her name.

"Melanie. I only met her once." So she asked for me, but Frank didn't? "She's nice."

My dad moves toward me and lays his big hands on my shoulders.

"Honey, they got engaged tonight. I thought you should know from me before you hear it from someone else." He watches me for my reaction.

I heard the word 'engaged,' but little else. Frank and Melanie? She's-just-the-one-right-now Melanie?

"I bet she's pregnant." That has to be it.

"Now, Robin. You don't know that. Anyway, they didn't stay for long. And to tell you the truth, I'm beat. You must be, too. We'll go see your mother tomorrow." He starts up the stairs.

"I'll be up, Dad. Just wanted to have a cup of tea first."

"Okay, kiddo. Well, have a good night's sleep." He climbs the rest of the stairs and I hear him close his bedroom door.

This doesn't make any sense. One week ago I walked up to Frank's house and spoke with him. He told me, very clearly, that Melanie was not the girl for him. And now they're engaged? She has to be pregnant. The only other explanation would be that his parents made him propose to her. It's true that Frank has no backbone, but would he marry this girl because his parents told him to?

Engaged. At twenty-one. So now he'll be stuck working for his father. Wow. I'll have to be sure I'm nowhere near this town when they get married. Which could be soon, if she really is pregnant. Well, good luck, I say. And glad it isn't me. No wonder his parents didn't approve of me. They could probably tell I wouldn't ever agree to get married this young. Mrs. Mello must really want grandchildren.

So, my plan to return to New York City and find Maryana Capture somehow (even if I have to camp on the street outside her building and ambush her when she comes out) is on hold. I think I should wait another week. I'll see Andrew on Wednesday, maybe have some of my questions answered. Maryana has had my manuscript for four months now, and I think I have a right to know what she thinks of it.

31

Andrew stops in late on Wednesday morning, but he isn't dressed for the office. He says he's meeting a client in town, and would I like to have coffee with him when I get off work? Yes, of course I would. He says he'll meet me at the sandwich shop up the street.

So as soon as my shift ends, I gather up my things and hurry out the door with just a wave to George and Jenny. I rush up the street and find Andrew sitting at a table, writing on a long yellow pad of paper.

"Coffee, Robin? You want some ice cream? Or a sandwich?" He drums his fingers on the white Formica table.

"Coffee's fine," I say. It's too cold for ice cream. I'd really like a grilled cheese, but I just feel weird ordering, because I know he's going to pay, and he's already had lunch with his client, so I'd be eating alone. I think of all of that before I say that coffee's fine.

"How was Christmas?"

"It was okay," I say.

"Just okay?" His voice is like balm, like aloe after a sunburn, or a cool cloth when your forehead is burning up. I wish I could make a tape of him talking and play it at night before I go to sleep.

I shake my head. "No, everything's awful." I add cream to my coffee and sip. He's waiting patiently, smiling. "Okay, well, you know about my mom. So there's that. She's making progress, but it's slow. My dad's been great, and we're fine now, and maybe next month my mom will come home, and I hope my parents can work everything out."

"What about you, Robin?"

"Well, okay. So I had this upstairs neighbor, David. You might have seen him in the diner. He comes in sometimes." I take a deep breath. "He likes me. Wait. He loves me. Kind of creepy love. Like obsessed love. He gave me a very expensive watch for Christmas, totally inappropriate, and I saw him on New Year's Eve day and he just stared at me, weird, you know?" I realize I'm babbling but I can't stop. "He really creeps me out. I'm living in my dad's house now, and I feel better there." I stop and swallow. Andrew's gonna think I've gone off the deep end.

"Does this guy – David – does he have any reason to think you feel the same way about him that he feels about you?" He asks the question gently, and I imagine he's a really good lawyer.

"You know, I tried to be nice to him in the beginning, so I went out with him a couple of times. After Frank and I broke up." I realize he probably doesn't know who Frank is, but I keep going. "I felt bad for David, he seemed kind of like a loser." A loser I was willing to take into my bed. "And I think he got the wrong idea." Because I said I wasn't into one-night-stands. My coffee is cold by now.

"That happens sometimes. But if you're afraid of this man, that's serious. Does your father know about this?"

I shake my head. "I've been trying to repair our relationship, so, no. Look, I just want to get back to college in the fall." That's when I remember about the manuscript. "Andrew, I have a question. Back in September, I delivered a copy of my manuscript to Maryana Capture in New York. This guy inside her building took it from me and said he'd deliver it. And I still haven't heard anything from her. What do you think I should do?"

He traces his index finger along his jawline, to the middle of his chin and back up to his ear. I watch him, fascinated, and have an image of the two of us together. I drop my spoon on the table and it pops the fantasy bubble above my head.

"I know it's hard to be patient, Robin, but try. It's just after the holidays, and everyone's getting back to work now. Maybe she gave your manuscript to someone to read. Maybe that person has lots of other manuscripts to read." He pushes his shirt cuff up to glance at his watch. "That reminds me, I should really get going." He pulls his wallet from his back pocket and tosses a dollar on the table. "Robin, if you have genuine concerns about this guy, I'd urge you first to tell your father, then go to the police. If you need to get a restraining order against him, do it." He grasps my hand, not gently, more like how Skip would when he's trying to make me pay attention to him. "You haven't done anything wrong."

Right, I think. If Andrew knew the truth, I bet he'd be on David's side. But I nod and thank him for the coffee.

My mother is home. The rehabilitation facility released her yesterday, and my dad brought her home.

She seems happy to be in the house. Most of her memory has returned, so she knows that she was badly hurt in a car accident, and that Mr. Newman died. She doesn't remember anything from that night, and she doesn't smile very much. But my dad is attentive and loving, and it's very sweet to see them together. He hired a nurse named Virginia to stay with my mom during the day. And I'm living in the house for the foreseeable future.

Andrew's wife had a baby girl. He stopped in last week to let us all know, but said he'd probably only come in once in a while now. They named her Helen Marie, after his mother and her mother, he said. I miss seeing him in the diner on a regular basis. It feels like everything is changing.

This afternoon I receive a letter from college saying I'm welcome to return in September to begin my junior year, as long as I finish the classes from my sophomore year. And now I'm having second thoughts. I know, it sounds crazy, and I still want to finish college, but maybe somewhere closer to home. At first I thought I wanted to go away, to be far from David, but I haven't seen him and he hasn't tried to contact me. The state college is only twenty minutes away, and there's even a bus, so maybe I'll go there. I don't know, I just think it's important to be close to my family right now.

I never did go to New York. After talking with Andrew that day, I figured it wasn't worth the expense. I've started writing another story, still using notebooks for the initial draft. I'll type it up on the Olivetti when I'm ready. And I bought a plastic bin with a tight lid to hold all my writing. Not that I'm expecting any water damage here on the second floor of my parents' house, but hey, you never know. And I can always recreate my original story, *The Way to Remember*. But right now it feels good to be writing something different.

Winter finally releases its icy grip on our town and gives way to spring. I feel it one day in mid-March, when the sun feels warmer and there are tiny green shoots poking out of the earth around the shrubs in front of the house. Crocuses will come first. Forsythia, daffodils, tulips. Bursts of color.

32

David came into the diner a couple of weeks ago. He's really lost weight, I can tell. I was in the back by the coffee station and saw him take a stool at the counter. Jenny poured a cup of coffee for him, then I watched as she leaned over the counter to say something to him, close to his face. He turned and looked right at me, but he didn't wave or anything. I thought he'd come over to talk to me, but after he drank his coffee and put money on the counter, he just slipped off his stool and walked out. Jenny told me that she let him know he wasn't welcome in the restaurant, and he'd better not go near me or she'd call the cops on him. She told him her brother's best friend was the police chief, which was a lie.

"Well, I didn't mean that he couldn't come in here. I mean, come on, Jenny, it's a free country. Even you said we can't keep him from coming in." I opened the door and looked down the street, but he was gone.

"Robin, this guy was bothering you, right? Right?"

"Yeah, I guess." I walked away and took care of my customers.

I messed up three orders.

This afternoon I walk home, shedding the jacket I needed this morning. I tie it around my waist and practically jog the entire length of Main Street. I stop at the mailbox and pull out a pile of stuff. Two magazines for my mom. Glamour and Redbook. A bunch of stuff for my dad. And a fancy envelope with curlicue writing on it, addressed to 'Mr. & Mrs. Harold Fortune' on one line and 'Miss Robin Fortune' on the line underneath it. Looks like a wedding invitation. I'd been waiting to hear about the wedding for weeks. When my father told me at New Year's that Frank and Melanie were engaged, I was positive she was pregnant and we'd be hearing about a wedding within the month.

But months passed and now, apparently, here it is. I slip my finger under the flap before I enter the house. I just want to know what's in there so I don't look too surprised. The envelope has another envelope in it and a piece of tissue paper. I open the inside envelope and pull out an invitation along with a little card and yet another envelope.

The invitation is printed on heavy, cream-colored paper. Mr. and Mrs. John Viveiros request the honor of my presence. I scan ahead to find the date. The seventh of May. About six weeks from today. So she's definitely not pregnant. I'll have to plan a trip that gets me away from here that weekend. Something, anything. I can't go to Frank's wedding.

I show the invitation to my mother and she bursts into tears. Something tells me it's not because she thought Frank and I should have ended up together. I look at Virginia and she pulls me aside.

"Certain things will bring up memories for your mom, Robin. A song, a scent, and in this case, a wedding invitation. She'll be all right." Virginia has a motherly way about her, which I suppose is good if you're a nurse. But when she's here, taking care of my mom, I tend to get out of her way. And since she's here until four, I tell her I'm going for a walk.

I head down the hill to the beach and plop on the sand. It's still too cold to put my feet in the water, but with a warm sun, I'm tempted to slip off my shoes and socks and pretend it's July. I lay back, not caring if the sand gets in my hair. There are plenty of other people who had the same idea this afternoon, even a couple of kids who stick their bare feet in the placid water, then shriek because it's so cold. I could have told them that.

Maybe my mother won't want to go to the wedding. I'll make sure to tell my dad about her reaction to the invitation and he might think it's best not to go at all. That would serve Frank right – none of us attending his stupid wedding. We'll still have to give them a gift though. And I'll probably be invited to her bridal shower. But since I work weekends, maybe I can avoid it. I don't want to think about it anymore, anyway.

What am I going to do with my life? I've decided on the state college, and most of my credits will transfer. I still want a degree in English, and I still want to move away when I'm done with school, because for one thing, there's nothing here for me, and for another thing, I can't stand the idea of running into Frank and Melanie and their eight kids. Yeah, I'm betting on a brood for those two. Whatever Mrs. Mello wants.

"Robin?" Oh, crap. I scramble to my feet and turn to face David. Wow, he looks like a completely different person. Half the man he used to be. He's wearing slim khakis and a rugby shirt with yellow and blue stripes. On the old David, those horizontal stripes would have looked ridiculous, but he looks…I don't know…good. Healthy. He gives me a big smile.

Those straight white teeth I noticed the first time. And something else is different.

"You shaved your mustache," I say. His fingers go to his lips.

"Yeah, how does it look?"

I'm surprised he's even talking to me. Guess he didn't believe Jenny when she tried to scare him away from me. Well, good. It's nice to see him. He sticks his hands in his pockets.

"It looks good. Plus you've lost a lot of weight," I say. "Good for you." I can't stop staring at him. I have a hard time remembering him the old way.

He shifts, scuffs his sneaker in the sand. "Look, Robin, I'm sorry for…for being too much. For calling, for showing up at the diner. Obviously you didn't want anything to do with me and I couldn't see that. Well, maybe I could, but I didn't want to believe it. I was unhappy, I hated myself the way I was. And because you were nice to me, I guess I hoped it was something more between us."

Nice to him? I wasn't nice to him. "You started to scare me, David. The stalking, the expensive watch." I never did give that watch back to him. I remember that now. It's upstairs in my jewelry box.

"I know, I know. I'm sorry. I realized I'd taken it too far, and then when I went into the restaurant a few weeks back? Your friend Jenny said she'd call the cops on me if I touched you? Jesus, Robin. I would never do anything to hurt you." He spreads his palms, and it reminds me of church. "Anyway, I'm glad I ran into you. I've wanted to apologize for a long time, but I didn't want to bother you."

Wow. He's not a freak. He's a guy who was awkward and creepy and fat, and now he's thin and handsome and confident. He's normal. And I'm the loser.

"Look, I'm sorry, too. It was too much, David, and it did freak me out." I can't see his eyes behind his sunglasses. "I hope we can still be friends."

"Sure we can," he says. He sticks his hand out and I take it. Even his hand is thinner, not so squishy. It's dry and his grip is strong. Those long fingers. "Again, I'm sorry." He releases his hand and starts to walk away, waving as he heads back up to the street. Now it's my turn to stare after him.

33

Melanie's shower is Saturday. At four. Dammit. I thought I could get out of it if it was a morning event. Plus Kay is invited, too. So we're going together. We bought her a crock pot at the department store in the mall, and Kay picked up a few utensils. She said it's fun to tie them on the box. I really wish I would get sick or something, but I can't get out of it.

And we're all going to the wedding. My parents, Skip and Kay, and me. And I can bring a guest if I want, it said so on the invitation. My mother wants to go, says she's so excited for little Frankie Mello.

I'm thinking maybe I could ask David to go with me. I mean, look at him. He's really cute now, and he's cool. I haven't seen him since that afternoon on the beach, but I've been hoping he'd come into the diner. I even told Jenny we were okay now, that it must have been all that weight that had him acting weird. I can relate, even though I've never been fat. He felt like an outcast. He could never get a date, so when I went out with him a couple of times (yeah, and slept with him), he got the wrong idea. And I'll keep telling myself that it was all David, that I played no (or little) part in the whole thing. Even though I know it's a lie.

I look up his number in the phone book and dial. Funny how my heart feels like it's about to beat itself right out of my chest. After ten rings, I hang up. I'll try again later. We have to get the response card back in the mail soon, and if I can't reach David, I'll tell my parents to include him anyway. He'll go with me.

I now have Thursdays off. Jenny has Mondays and Tuesdays, which doesn't seem fair, but she told George she needed two days off to take care of things at home. And George said okay, which made me wish I'd asked for two days off first. So now George is going to hire another waitress for part-time, because Jenny also has to leave by ten on the five days she does work.

I finally reached David by phone last night. He sounded happy to hear from me, and I was encouraged by that to ask him to go to Frank's wedding with me. He was silent for a moment.

"Oh…Robin. I'm kind of seeing someone. Sorry."

"Oh! I didn't know. Gee, I feel stupid now asking you." I was tempted to disconnect the phone, pretend it just happened, but I stayed on the line, with the receiver stuck to my ear, waiting.

"Don't feel stupid. I'm flattered that you asked me," he said in that creamy voice.

After we hung up, I took the watch from my jewelry box and turned it over in my hand. I guess when he had 'Love, David' engraved on it, he didn't mean it. But I wasn't going to throw that in his face. Of course the girls flock to him now. He's really cute, and he acts different, more sure of himself. And I was the one who told him to leave me alone. He's only doing what I asked.

On Thursday I take the bus to the Thousand Words bookstore and stop in front of the window to look at the display of new books. There's a sequel to Love Story called *Oliver's Story* and *Trinity* by Leon Uris. John Cheever, Erica Jong, and Robert Ludlum.

Nothing from Maryana yet. I open the door and step inside.

"Hi, Dorothy," I say when I see her.

"Robin! It's been ages. How's everything?" Her hair is twisted up into a knot at the back of her head and I think those are chopsticks stuck through the bun.

"Fine, thanks. I know I haven't been in for a long time. So busy," I say, although that's not really true. I haven't been busy at all, except at my stupid job.

"Well," she says, "you'll be thrilled to know that your favorite author is about to release a new book!" She clasps her hands to her chest, obviously pleased to impart this news.

"About time," I say, immediately regretting the bitchiness in my voice. "I mean, I'm glad and all. It seems like this one took forever."

"Well, I'm sure it'll be worth it, Robin." She takes reading glasses from a beaded chain around her neck and sets them on her nose, then looks down at a sheet of paper on the counter in front of her. "May seventh. That's when we should have it."

The day of the wedding. Great. "Could you set aside a copy for me, Dorothy? I have to go to a wedding that day." I wrinkle my nose but she seems not to notice.

"Will do, dear." She makes a mark on the paper and takes off her glasses. They bounce against her chest. "I have another author, someone you might like, coming in next week. Her name is Felicia Frye. Would you like to come back for her visit?"

"Um, I'll let you know, okay?"

"Sure, dear." The telephone rings and Dorothy excuses herself to answer it.

I wander the store and look at all the books. So Maryana has a new book coming out. Well, good for her. I guess she was so damn busy with her own book that she couldn't give mine any time. I say good-bye to Dorothy and walk out into the sunshine.

I need to find something to be happy about. What the hell is wrong with me, anyway? I can't be happy for Frank and Melanie, even though I know for certain that Frank's not the guy for me. I'm jealous of David and his new girlfriend, and upset at myself for treating him badly, when all he really did was show an interest in me that I encouraged. I'm bored with waitressing and feel that I served my punishment for the recklessness I displayed at college last year. And I'm mad at Maryana Capture because…because why? She didn't owe me anything. Sure, she could have sent a note to me saying my book wasn't up to the standards of her publisher. She probably should have, since I hand-delivered a manuscript to her. But maybe she

receives hundreds of manuscripts each month. Who
knows? I went about it all wrong. And unless I can
get the manuscript back from her, I'll just have to
start over again. I remember most of what I wrote,
and I can just start again. I walk down the street to
the bus stop and tell myself to stop wallowing.

So, I'll dress up and attend Frank's wedding, without
a date. I'll hold my head up and toast the bride and
groom. And I'll wish them a lifetime of happiness.
For whatever reason Frank has now decided that
Melanie is the girl for him, fine. It's time for me to
move on.

I'll also be happy for David. I'm the one who missed
out, because all I could see was the person on the
outside. He never was anything other than honest
with me. If I run into him around town, I'll be
friendly and kind. Even if he's holding hands with *her*.

The bus doesn't come for another half hour, so I sit
on a bench at a park across the street and watch kids
play on a jungle gym. Their mothers stand by and
chat with each other. If I've been disappointed by the
men in my life, well, I've also let them down. My dad,
definitely, although we're doing okay now. Frank. I
couldn't be the girl he wanted (or his parents wanted),
and he couldn't be the man I was looking for. David.
I failed to see the real guy within until he lost the
weight, then it was too late. Andrew. Married! He was
just a romance in my mind, but now it's like he's

drifting out to sea, with his wife and daughter, all of them waving good-bye to me as I stand on the shore. I get a feeling we may not see each other again, especially once I go back to school.

Soon I'll turn twenty-one. Some girls my age are already married, and a couple of friends from high school already have a kid or two. It's not what I want, not right now, anyway. I make a promise to myself that when I start at the new college, I'll try to make new friends. Girlfriends. Guy friends, too.

34

Kay and I take my mom shopping before the wedding. She can walk now, unassisted, which is a big deal, so Kay drives to the mall, taking the long way so she doesn't go past the house where Mom and Mr. Newman used to live. We're making a day of it. I need a new dress and shoes, Kay needs shoes, and my mom doesn't really need anything, but we knew she'd enjoy a day out.

She gets tired, though, so we end up taking a lot of breaks on the benches around the mall. I find a dress, light blue with little pink flowers. My mom says it suits me. And some ballet slippers to go with it, because I refuse to wear high heels. Kay is going to wear a pantsuit, in spite of my mom's objections (not to the pantsuit, but she said Kay should show off her legs).

We stop for lunch at the same place where my mom and I ate last year to celebrate my birthday, only this time without the drinks. My mother doesn't drink alcohol anymore, not since the accident. And in deference to her, Kay asks the waiter to bring a pitcher of ice water for the table.

"I've never been to the Estrela restaurant, have you, Ruth?" Kay asks my mom.

"Never. I wonder if they'll serve Portuguese food at the reception."

"They might," I say. "They probably figure everyone expects it, plus most of the people going to the wedding are Portuguese, right?"

"Well, I can't eat that spicy sausage," my mother says, shaking her head at the thought of linguiça.

"I'm sure it'll be fine, Mom. And anyway, we'll all look gorgeous." I make her smile, which is kind of all I aim for these days with her. Sometimes I catch her staring out the window with a look of such sadness on her face, it makes me tear up. Because she remembers. How Mr. Newman made her ecstatically happy, so different from the life she'd had with my father. Of course, my dad still dotes on her, and she knows he's trying to make up for everything, for the neglect and the apathy, but she's still sad. I know she tries to hide it from him, but I see it. So my goal is to make her smile every now and then.

"As long as we don't outshine the bride. You can't do that, you know. That's not proper." She pats her hair.

"Melanie's very pretty," Kay says, glancing sideways at me. Kay and I attended Melanie's shower, but my mother wasn't able to go at the time, so she's never even met Frank's fiancée. I remember at the shower, Melanie ran up to me and hugged me so hard I thought I'd fall over.

"I'm so glad you came!" she'd gushed. I'd turned to Kay and introduced her, and hoped the hot flush on my face wasn't too obvious. We met Melanie's mother, aunts, sister, and cousins. There were a few girls Melanie knew in school, too. And no one called her Mel. It was Melanie, only Melanie. Glad I picked up on that, not that I'd ever be close enough to her to call her Mel, but still.

Her cousins and sister bought her some sexy lingerie, and when Melanie opened the boxes and held them up for us to see, I clapped along with everyone else.

"Oh, he'll like that one!" "You won't have that on for long!" "He might have a heart attack when he sees you in that!" Their words were like little bee stings, so I'm still not immune, I guess.

And here we are, two days before the wedding, crunching on salad and drinking water.

The wedding of Francisco Manuel Mello and Melanie Josefina Viveiros is about to begin, and there's a rumble of thunder just before the organist plays The Wedding March. The writer in me smiles at that bit of foreshadowing. George let me off work today, but it means I have to work on Thursday.

Four bridesmaids in pink satin dresses precede the bride down the aisle. I keep my eyes on Frank, who's standing up front with his pal Bryan next to him. Bryan grins and Frank looks like he might throw up. But he does look handsome in his tuxedo, even with a gray-green complexion.

Nearly an hour later, we're standing outside Our Lady of Sorrows Church. I stand behind a bunch of people who press forward to greet the happy couple. I'd rather just watch from the back, but Melanie sees me.

"Robin! Robin!" She waves from the top step and clutches Frank's arm, pointing at me. He finally makes eye contact with me and raises a hand in greeting. I smile back and approach, weaving through the throng of family members intent on touching them.

MARTHA REYNOLDS

"You look like a fairy princess," I say, and Melanie beams. She really does look beautiful. We may live in a time when the natural look rules, but she's defied convention, covered in ruffles and rhinestones. The light blue eye shadow is a bit much, but it's her wedding day, and there will be plenty of photographs, so she can regret that decision for years to come.

"Frank," I say, leaning over Melanie to kiss his cheek. "You don't look like a fairy princess, but you're definitely a prince. Congratulations."

"Thanks, Robin," he says. We're Frank and Robin now. No more Francisco and Robina. I'm relieved he didn't call me Robina. "Glad you could be here." He looks behind me. "Did you bring a date?"

"Nope," I say as cheerily as I can manage. "One of those ushers must be single."

"Do you want us to fix you up?" Melanie stage-whispers. Her eyes bug out with the thought that she could be a matchmaker for her husband's ex-girlfriend. I pat her arm through layers of puffy satin.

"I'm fine, really," I answer with a big, face-splitting grin. "See you at the reception!" I ease away from them as others press in to kiss and hug.

Skip and Kay seem to be reliving their own wedding day, so I hop in the back seat of my dad's car. My mother dabs at her eyes, but I know it's not the wedding that's gotten to her. My dad probably knows it, too, but he doesn't say anything.

"That was a lovely service," my mother murmurs from the front seat. "Beautiful music."

We make our way through neighborhoods lined with sidewalks and flowering magnolias, past stately two-story homes and small bicycles left in driveways, into the city and then away from it, until we reach the Estrela do Mar restaurant, perched on a hill overlooking the ocean. Its whitewashed exterior gleams bright against a still-dark sky, and for a moment I think we could be in Lisbon.

Inside, we meet up with Skip and Kay, and stand in front of a table set with small place cards. Each card has a guest's name and a table number written in fancy script. Naturally, the five of us sit together. There's a couple at the table already, friends of the bride, and we introduce ourselves. After we're seated, there's one seat left open. In the back of my mind, I wonder if Melanie decided to seat a single man next to me.

No such luck. I spot a big woman wearing a pink and orange tent dress, peering at her place card, then at our table. She makes a beeline toward us, holding her card aloft.

"Table fourteen! That's me! Howdy, everyone, I'm Nadine Winchell, Melanie's old piano teacher." She pulls out the empty chair next to me and says in a loud voice, "You and me are the old maids, darlin.' I guess I'm your date!" Her laugh booms across the table, and Skip pushes my thigh with his. I reach under the tablecloth and pinch him, hard. On the other side of me, Nadine's hip is jammed up against mine.

She turns to me. Her dark hair is piled high on her head and she's wearing a ton of makeup. It settles into the lines around her eyes. "What's your name, honey?"

"I'm Robin. A childhood friend of the groom. This is my brother Skip, his wife Kay, and my parents, Hap and Ruth Fortune." I can't remember the names of the other couple, so I don't say anything about them. Nadine will ask them herself, I figure.

"Fortune! Helluva name, huh? Are you loaded, Hap?" Booming laugh again. Her generous bosom swells and bounces with each breath. She fans her face with a manicured hand and picks up a glass of water. Holding it against her cheek, she looks around the table. "Is it hot in here, or is it just me? Woo-hoo! I get these hot flashes all the time." She sets her gaze on my poor mother and adds, "Miz Fortune, you know what I'm talkin' about." I think my mom is wishing for a trap door to open in the parquet floor so she can drop into the basement and have her dinner there.

Teenagers dressed in black pants and white shirts serve us. Everyone gets the same plate: a poached chicken breast with mushrooms, some wild rice, and overcooked green beans with little bits of bacon. Or Bac-Os. Nadine reaches for the basket of bread and takes a roll before passing it to me. I figure I should eat whatever I can; after all, Melanie's dad sprang for this thing. Makes me think about what kind of wedding reception I might have one day. Hard to think about that when I don't even know who the groom would be.

"So, Robin, what's your story? Pretty girl like you and no date?" Nadine manages to talk and eat at the same time, and she's fixed her attention on me. Well, that's because everyone else at the table is a couple.

I'm not about to tell Nadine my "story." So I simply say, "I'm in college." I sneak a look at my dad, but he's standing up, talking to someone he knows. Because he knows everybody.

"Whaddaya studyin'? Or ya just there to find a husband?" She cackles at her joke, and when she opens her mouth, I notice she has a lot of fillings.

"My major is English," I say. "But I'm not sure what I'll do with it." Because Nadine is about the last person I'd ever tell about writing. She'd probably tell me she has a great idea for a book.

"Huh," she says, giving me the once-over. "I'da figured you more for business, you look so serious."

"I look serious?"

"You just never smile, Robin. Hey, it's a wedding! Everyone should either be laughin' or cryin', know what I mean?" She uses a piece of her bread to sop up the rest of the mushroom sauce on her plate. I'm pretty sure my mother would reprimand me if I did that here, and sure enough, she's giving Nadine a hard look, which Nadine doesn't see at all.

I smile at my mom, and try to remember to keep a smile pasted on my face for the rest of the reception. The last thing I want is for Frank, or his parents, to think I might be upset about this wedding.

After dinner, a band starts to play, and Frank and Melanie dance to "Evergreen." I watch as Frank leads his bride around the dance floor. He's a good dancer, very smooth, and I wonder if he took lessons before today. He and I never danced.

Then Frank dances with his mother and Melanie dances with her father, then they dance with the in-laws. We all sit at our tables and watch, and I dread the time that everyone gets up to dance, because I don't have anyone to dance with. And I'm tired of listening to Nadine yammer on about Melanie and the piano lessons.

Around the time I'm planning an escape to the ladies' room, my father brushes his hand over my hair and asks me to dance. I push back in my chair, eager to leave the table, but stop to whisper, "What about Mom?"

He says, "I already asked her. She said she'll have the next dance. You first." He winks at me and I almost cry. He walks me out onto the dance floor and leads me around to "As Time Goes By." My dad is a really good dancer, of course.

"We'd better practice, kiddo. This'll be you and me some day."

I smile against his jacket. Someday, maybe.

Frank and I have a dance, eventually. I think his parents were hoping it wouldn't happen, but it was Melanie who kind of pushed him toward me as she accepted an invitation from one of the ushers.

"Hey," he says, holding out his hand.

The last time I spoke with him was Christmas Day, and words elude me for once.

"Congratulations. You look nice." I lay my left hand on his shoulder and let him lead the way. I don't recognize the song, but it's old and we just kind of move around with no particular steps.

"I hope we'll always be friends," he says into my hair, and I know this isn't the time or the place for a conversation. Me telling him that he's made a big mistake. Because maybe he hasn't. Maybe this is exactly what Frank needs. To get married, move out, start a family, be a man. It wasn't meant to be with me, anyway.

So I give him my biggest smile and say, "I think you made an excellent choice. Melanie is wonderful and I'm really happy for both of you." Will we always be friends? No, probably not. Well, maybe in thirty years when old hurts are less defined, blurred around the edges. When we've each found our own way to contentment. When other, joy-filled moments push aside the sadder memories. When my own life is so complete that I don't need to be envious of anyone else's.

35

On Wednesday after work I take the bus out to the Thousand Words bookstore so I can pick up my copy of Maryana Capture's new novel. It's funny, in the past I looked forward to each new release. Now I just sit quietly and enjoy the ride. Sure, I'm looking forward to reading it, because I've always enjoyed her books, but I don't idolize her the way I used to. She's just a writer who writes good books. Someone who's a lot older than the photo on the back of her novel, and someone who isn't always very nice to her assistant. So she's human.

The bus stops and I hop down to the sidewalk. It's cold for May, and I zip up my windbreaker. I stop in front of the bookstore window to look at the display and suddenly I can't move. The chill wind blows my hair into my face as I stare. Maryana's book is stacked in full view. And it's called *The Road to Remembrance*.

Shaking off the initial shock, I rush into the store and pick up a copy. *This is my book.* I open to the first page and read the words it had taken me so long to write. Page after page after page. My book. *The Way to Remember* and all she did was change the title.

My knees might give way. This can't be true. I hold out my hand, palm straight, and it won't stay still. I drop into a chair next to the window and flip the pages to the acknowledgments section. There, Maryana praises her editor and cites her dead parents and a dead sister, and someone named Sam, who I think might be the tall guy with the white hair who accompanied her to the bookstore last year. But no mention of Robin Fortune, who wrote the damn story!

"Oh, Robin! You've come to pick up your book, I see." Dorothy's pleasant voice sounds like chalk on a blackboard. I jump up from the chair with the book in my hand. She points to it and says, "I think she's got a best-seller there. I finished it the other night and it's so good!"

I stare at her, then at the book. What do I say to Dorothy? Tell her *I* wrote this book? She'll think I'm crazy. She knows Maryana is my favorite author. Oh my God, what am I going to do?

"Let me ring you up," she says and moves behind the counter. "You know, we're offering a ten-percent discount on this book until the end of the month. So, let's see. Seven ninety-five less ten percent makes it seven fifteen. Plus six percent tax…" she punches numbers on her little calculator. "Seven fifty-eight total." She beams at me.

I pull a ten-dollar bill from my front pocket and hand it to her. She makes change and places the book in a paper bag that has the bookstore's name and logo printed on it. I've just paid for my own book.

"Now don't stay up all night reading, Robin!" She gives me one more giant smile before turning to assist another customer. I take the bag and exit the store.

Once I'm outside, I run around the side, where Dorothy keeps trash cans in an alley, and I retch. There's no food to throw up, but spasms wrack my body and I'm doubled over with dry heaves. No wonder I never heard back from her.

When I'm able to walk without spazzing out, I head over to the mall. I need to sit and think about this. With a slice of pizza and a Fresca, I sit in a corner of the little café, where no one passing by will see me. I don't want to pull the book from the bag with greasy fingers, so I eat and drink and then wipe my hands on multiple napkins.

I slowly take the book out and stare at the cover. It's nothing special, not what I would've envisioned for my book. *My book.* It's a winding road, leading into a sunset. And there's a car driving away, its red taillights visible. Big deal. And on the back cover, there she is, using that photograph that's got to be at least ten years old, because I saw her in real life and she doesn't look nearly as good as this picture.

Why would she do this? She can't write her own book? For crying out loud, she's written five books, all of them really good, and now she has to steal a story from a twenty year old? Wow. Unless she stole all the other stories, too. I wouldn't put it past her.

My dad. How am I going to tell my dad? I don't have the notebooks anymore, to prove I wrote the story. They were destroyed when the pipes burst in David's apartment. I never told Frank, or David, or Jenny. I snap my fingers, and the man next to me raises his eyebrows.

Andrew! And Barbara. They'd vouch for me. And Andrew's a lawyer. He'll know what to do. He hasn't come into the diner for a long time, now that they have the baby. My shoulders sag with the realization I don't even know his last name. Or where they live. Or where he works.

Panic threatens to suffocate me and I find myself gulping air as my chest constricts. The man next to me asks if I'm okay and I nod yes, trying to breathe more normally. What if Andrew never comes back to the diner? I have to find him. Andrew is my only hope.

By the time I return home, I'm acting more like a regular person. I decide not to tell my mother any of this, because she's making great progress since the accident and I really don't want to upset her. But I know I have to have a talk with my dad.

"Hello, dear," my mom calls from the kitchen. "How was your day?"

This is pretty much the depth of our conversations. Some residual brain damage – not enough to render her incompetent – results in her inability to hold a conversation for more than a few minutes, and the chats we do have are pretty vapid.

"Fine, Mom. Can I help you?" I lean against the refrigerator and watch her tear lettuce with her hands. Virginia doesn't come to the house anymore, but my dad hired another woman, Melba, who helps with meal preparation. Melba does most of the work in the afternoon, and leaves instructions for my mother. Today, Melba stuffed three chicken breasts and put them in a baking dish, then covered it all with foil.

The index card on the counter says to preheat the oven to 350 degrees, put the dish in for thirty minutes, then remove the foil and cook another five to ten minutes. There are potatoes, already baked, wrapped in foil. They'll go in the oven, too, to warm. And Melba already cut up vegetables for the salad, but left the lettuce for my mom.

My mother picks up the index card and concentrates on the written words. I stand close behind her, pretending to read it for the first time.

"We can wait for Dad if you like."

She continues to stare at the card. "Okay." She sets it back on the counter, "Robin, am I a different person?"

"Not to me, Mom. You're as beautiful as you've always been." I tense, waiting for what might follow.

"No, I mean, since the accident." She turns her eyes to me, eyes that used to sparkle. "I know things changed after that."

"Mom, things were different even before the accident."

She uses her forearm to push hair from her forehead. When Virginia used to come to the house, she'd do my mother's hair and makeup, but these days Mom looks old without any enhancements. And I leave the house too early to help.

"I had left your father for Russell." This she says without emotion, as if she were telling me that today is Wednesday.

"Yes. Have you said that to Dad, Mom?"

She shakes her head and gives me a guilty smile. "I'm not stupid, honey. I just have trouble concentrating sometimes." She lowers her voice, even though we're the only ones in the house. "I know I'm lucky that he took me back. I know that." But there still isn't any light in those eyes.

I wait until after dinner to speak with my dad. He helps Mom to bed, where she usually reads a magazine for a half-hour or so before turning out the light. When he comes back down, I'm waiting for him.

"Dad, we need to talk." I hold up a bottle of whiskey I found in the liquor cabinet. "Want some?"

"Good Lord, Robin, do I need this?" He takes the bottle from my hand and sets it on the counter. Then he takes a short glass from the cupboard, fills it with ice, and pours a double shot for himself. Before even taking a sip, he steps in front of me. "Please don't tell me you're pregnant."

I flinch. "I'm not pregnant." So that would be the worst thing I could tell him?

He exhales loudly, then drinks half of the whiskey down. "Let's go in the den," he says, leading the way.

By the time I finish telling him all about the book, and Maryana, he's had another drink, and pounded his fist on the table twice, and said a ton of curse words (and apologized, saying they weren't directed at me).

"Dad, Andrew and his wife are the only people who know that it's my book. I really need to find him."

"What kind of a lawyer is he?"

"I don't know."

"He works in the city?"

"I don't know, I think so. Don't they all work in the city?"

"No, Robin, not all lawyers work in the city. And you don't know where he lives?"

I shake my head. "Probably near here somewhere, since he'd come into the restaurant twice a week."

"And when's the last time you saw him?"

I chew my lower lip. "It was after his wife had the baby, because he stopped in to tell us all."

"When, Robin?"

"I don't know, a couple of months ago?" Has it been that long? I've been so caught up in everything – the shower, the wedding, seeing David - that I guess I haven't thought about Andrew very much. Which surprises me.

My father uncrosses his legs and stands up, flexing his shoulders. "All right, let me sleep on this and tomorrow I'll see what I can do."

"Thanks, Dad." He turns to go upstairs, and I add, "Dad? I'm really sorry about all this."

"You don't have to be sorry, honey, you didn't do anything wrong. I just wish you'd have told me you wrote a book." He chuckled softly and shakes his head. "My daughter wrote a book."

I straighten my posture and stand taller. "A good book, Dad."

"A good book, Robin."

36

Today I gave notice at the diner. With my father's concurrence, I told George I would work until the following Wednesday, but then I'd be done. I'll try to find something else for the summer, something with better hours, but I'm finished slinging bacon and eggs every morning.

George didn't take it well. In fact, he yelled at me all morning after I'd told him. But I didn't care, because I only have five more days after today. I was as nice as I could be, and even stayed late to help clean up.

"How do I get a new waitress in a week?" he lamented as we sat together, enjoying some of the day's leftovers.

"You will, George. Lots of college kids looking for summer jobs."

"Eh, Robin. I am very sorry to lose you." He patted my hand and I threw my arm around his shoulders, kissing him loudly on the cheek.

"Okay, okay, you sweet on me now. Maria, she find out and she kill you."

"I'll take my chances, George. You're all mine." He laughed and I knew we'd be all right.

My dad comes home from work early and we sit together at the dining room table, with the Yellow Pages open in front of us. He reads the name of a law firm out loud and I copy it down along with the company's address and telephone number. This is step one, he says. There are nineteen law firms listed, and fourteen more individuals in practice, but none of the individuals has the first name Andrew.

"I'm pretty sure he doesn't work alone anyway," I say, scribbling down the last of them.

"We cover all the bases, Robin."

"Yes, sir."

Step two happens tomorrow. The phone calls. My dad is making me write out a kind of script, something to ask the receptionist or secretary who

answers the phone. I hope this works. I should have
at least asked him his last name. But we were a
waitress/customer couple. You don't need to know
last names.

I wonder how much money Maryana Capture has
made off my book so far. A lot, I bet. There was a
review in our Sunday paper, saying it was her best
effort yet. The reviewer mentioned that her writing
style was very different from her previous works. No
kidding. I picked up *The New York Times* at our
drugstore and there she was, number four on their
best-seller list.

I didn't tell my dad that I knew where she lived,
because I could say with one hundred percent
certainty that he'd have driven to New York City and
waited in that cavernous lobby until she either walked
in or walked out. Or he'd have punched that
sanctimonious concierge and barged up to her
apartment. So I didn't mention anything about going
there.

I've written to the girls I shared a room with at
college. I know they never kept in touch after I was
kicked out, but I thought I should write to them
anyway. So I did. I kept the letters light and breezy,

and maintained a positive attitude about my situation. Hey, I'm not upset about going to the state college. It's my choice, and I know everything will be fine. Probably better to leave the memories of my first two years up in Boston where they belong. And of course I didn't say a word about the whole book thing. I still don't know how this is all going to turn out. But I'll admit, I dream about a day when everyone finds out that I'm the one who wrote Maryana's best-selling novel. I dream about that day a lot.

But whether it works in my favor or not, there's another friendship I need to fix. I don't know if I can call it a friendship anymore, but I want to try once more with David. Not to be his girlfriend, because he already has one, but to be his friend. I used him, even though I knew he had stronger feelings for me than I had for him. I ignored that fact, and played it to my advantage. He'd made it clear to me that he wasn't looking for a casual relationship, but that's exactly how I treated it. Then I bad-mouthed him to Andrew and Jenny so that I wouldn't look like the one who'd led him on. I don't expect that he'll ever want anything to do with me, but at least I can try. I can be kinder.

Tonight after my parents have gone upstairs, I dial his number. I'm more nervous than I've ever been. He's moved on, and who knows, maybe he's engaged now, too.

"Hello?"

My mouth is as dry as a desert. "David. It's Robin."

"Robin! It didn't sound like you at all. Are you sick?"

I clear my throat. "No," I say. "I'm fine. I think it's just nerves."

There's silence before he says, "Nervous to talk to me?"

"Yeah. Because...I've been...listen, is there any way we could meet in person? I have some things I need to say to you. Not bad things. But I'd rather not do it over the phone."

"Okay, sure. Um, I don't really want to come into the diner." He doesn't chuckle, and I bet he's probably still hurt from the last time, when Jenny said she'd call the cops on him.

"How about tomorrow, after you get off work? The new Mexican place on Mill Street? Next to the laundromat?"

"Yeah, okay. Five-thirty?"

"Five-thirty. I'll see you then. David?"

"Hmm?"

"Thanks," I say softly before hanging up.

37

I called all nineteen law firms this afternoon, and no one had a lawyer named Andrew on staff who fit my Andrew's description. Tomorrow I'll call the sole practitioners, even though it doesn't make sense that he'd be there.

I'm finished with the calls by five, and let my mother know I'm heading out.

"Honey, your father will be home soon, and then we'll have dinner. There's lasagna in the oven." She's seated at the kitchen counter, sipping water through a straw. She must have gone to the beauty parlor today.

"Your hair looks pretty, Mom. And I'm meeting a friend for a quick bite, so you and Dad can enjoy dinner alone together."

She frowns at me. "What friend? Boyfriend?"

"No, just a friend who's also a guy. Not a boyfriend. I won't be late." I dash upstairs before she can ask another question.

I spend a lot of time picking the right shirt, fixing my hair, putting on lip gloss. When I head downstairs, I hear my mother telling my father that I have a new boyfriend. He catches me before I can slip out the front door.

"Robin? You're heading out?"

"Yeah. I called all nineteen of the law firms on the list this afternoon, gave an accurate description, and no one has Andrew on staff. I'll try the individuals listed tomorrow, okay?"

"Sure, hon. So, your mother tells me you're meeting a new boyfriend?" He cocks his head, waiting for an explanation, but his eyes are smiling down on me.

"She just wants to think that. He's a friend, Dad." I can't tell him it's David, the watch-giver. "I'll be at the Mexican place on Mill." I have my hand on the doorknob. "And I won't be late. We're just getting tacos."

"Okay, kiddo, have fun."

Main Street comes alive on summer nights. The shops usually stay open until at least eight, the movie theatre has films for teenagers, and the little walk-up ice cream stand has dozens of people milling about with cones in hand.

I head up Main and hang a left on Mill Street. Rosalita's Cantina sits just behind Main Street, a tacky little Mexican place with a neon cactus sign and excellent tacos. Or so I heard from Jenny. I walk inside and see David sitting in a booth, his back against the wall. He lifts his hand when he sees me and I walk back to meet him.

"Hi," I say, sliding onto the bench seat opposite him.

"Hey, Robin." He looks even better than he did when I saw him on the beach. He's tan.

"Thanks for meeting me." Before I can say anything else, a waitress appears with a couple of menus and two glasses of water.

"Anything to drink besides water?" she asks.

We both say 'no' at the same time and laugh about it. Like either of us would drink in the other's presence, ever again. Well, maybe I'm exaggerating, but I need a clear head.

"You look good, David." Man, he really does.

"I started jogging, can you believe it? Me, jogging!"
He laughs, showing off those straight, white teeth. He
reminds me of President Kennedy, all teeth and hair.

I pretend to be absorbed in my menu, but I'm
blinking furiously and can hardly see what's written.

"Your girlfriend must be happy about the new you," I
mumble, in a voice so low I think he hasn't heard.

I look up when I hear him laugh.

"I never had a girlfriend, Robin. I dated a few
women, but it wasn't anything serious. I just wasn't
ready to see you again."

I try to process that bit of information, but the
waitress returns to take our order. David gestures for
me to go first.

"Um, I'll have two tacos and rice, please."

"Mexican salad," David says, handing his menu to the
waitress, who heads back to the kitchen.

"What's in the Mexican salad?"

He shrugs. "Lettuce, cucumber, black beans, corn."
He strokes his chin. "Red pepper?" When he grins, I
almost lose it.

"I'm so sorry," I blurt out. "I wasn't very nice to you,
David." I manage to make and hold eye contact. "I

mean, I wasn't very nice to a lot of people, but especially you."

He holds his straw between slim fingers and twirls it before sticking it into his glass of water. "I don't want you to beat yourself up over anything. I liked you more than you liked me. It happens a lot in life, you know." He smiles at me, but there's a hint of sadness in that smile, not like the grin he had before I apologized. He sips water, and continues.

"When I was fat, Robin, I didn't like myself much. I could never get a date, not unless I walked into a bar near closing time and found a girl who was really drunk. Then I could score, but the funny thing was, she wouldn't go out with me again. And I was probably one of the few guys who picked up a girl in a bar and actually meant it when I said I'd call her." He shakes his head ruefully. "When I met you, I never thought I'd have a chance, not with someone like you. Then you broke up with your boyfriend, and I saw an opportunity. At least for us to be friends. I was always hoping for more." He looks past me. I turn around to see if someone has walked in, but the place is quiet.

"And then, there *was* more. Like I told you back then, I wasn't looking for a one-night stand. And I thought you felt the same way. But…" He trails off and drinks more water.

Our food arrives, and I'm really hungry, but I wait for him to finish talking. I'll eat the food cold if I have to.

"Look, I was used to the rejection, okay? But I wasn't dangerous, Robin. I never would have done anything to hurt you." His eyes narrow and that imaginary cloud passes over his face, and I know I'd crossed the line with the whole bit about Jenny telling him she'd call the police. He blames me for it, and I deserve it.

He picks up his fork and starts eating. I'm quiet, and my appetite has disappeared like smoke into the air.

"I know," I say quietly. "I do know that. David, I thought Frank and I...well, we've known each other for a long time, and when I came back home last spring, he was here for me. My girlfriends from high school were all away at college, scattered across the country. My father wouldn't speak to me, and Frank was here, and he helped me feel like less of an outcast. We kind of picked up together, even though I can say with absolute certainty that we definitely weren't meant for each other." David sets down his fork and leans back in his chair. I keep talking, ignoring the food on my plate.

"You were nice to me. And yeah, I knew you liked me. It felt good, and I..." I pause, trying to find the right words. *Just tell him the damn truth.* "I enjoyed it. I liked the attention. My father was still mad at me.

And then Frank and I...well, we weren't right for each other."

"And now he's married. How do you feel about that?"

Truth, Robin. "I think he made a mistake." I pick at my food, take a forkful of rice and eat it. "Not that I don't like Melanie. She's wonderful, and I hope they can make it work. Frank does what's expected of him. And his parents are very traditional, they wanted him to meet and marry a nice Portuguese girl."

"And that wasn't you," he points out, unnecessarily. But I bite back a snarky comment.

"No. Definitely not me. His parents liked me fine as long as I was his buddy, but I don't think they approved of me as his girlfriend."

David chews on this for a minute. "So, who broke off your relationship?"

"I did. Come on, you were there that night when I yelled at him. We didn't have a relationship. He came over to eat. And, to have sex."

"So, he used you."

My jaw drops. No, it wasn't like that. Was it?

I say, "Anyway, it doesn't matter. He's married now and everyone's happy."

"Including you. Except that you say the marriage was a mistake." He holds his fork with the tines pointing at me. Four little bayonets aimed at my eyes.

"It's just my opinion. But I hope they prove me wrong." I level my gaze at him to prove I mean it. Because I do. Then I pick up my taco and take a bite. It's barely warm, but I'm starving, and eat half of it before another thought hits me.

"Oh," I mutter, setting down the taco.

"What is it, Robin?"

I try to get control of my emotions. When I finally speak, my throat closes around my voice, strangling it into something unrecognizable.

"I used you, too." He opened the door for me on that one. My truth was staring me in the face.

Fumbling in my bag, hiding my face, I dig at the bottom and pull out the watch he gave me for Christmas. I set it on the table between us. He stops eating to stare at it. A shiny symbol of misunderstanding.

I see his mouth working, as if he's trying desperately to find the words.

"David, this cost a lot of money. I know it's an expensive watch." At the same time, I'm not an idiot. He had it engraved, and he wouldn't be able to return it. But it doesn't have my name on it, so maybe he'd want to give it to a future girlfriend, whoever she might be. So how do I say that without insulting him?

He smiles at his salad, not at me. When he looks up, his eyes are a little shinier, or maybe it's just the light coming through the window of the restaurant as the sun drops in the sky.

I pick it up and turn it over while he watches me.

"I meant that, Robin," he says with a catch in his voice. "I will love you always."

He takes the watch from my hand and fastens it around my left wrist. The metal is cold against my skin, but it feels good. Now who has the shiny eyes?

38

David and I spend two hours in that little Mexican restaurant. I tell him everything, about going back to college, but closer to home, not in Boston. And I tell him all about the book. He feels terrible about the water damage, blaming himself for the destruction of my notebooks, but it wasn't his fault. And I tell him about Andrew, and his wife Barbara, and Maryana Capture. Thank God I tell him all of that, because David thinks of something neither my dad nor I had even considered.

"Just because he's a lawyer, Robin, doesn't mean he works at a law firm," he points out. "He might work for a company, you know. Big corporations have legal departments."

He drives me home that night, and I invite him for dinner the next evening. I want my parents to meet him. Well, my dad already met him, but maybe he won't remember. I want them to see what a good guy he is. I want to be proven wrong, over and over again.

My parents are gracious people with excellent manners. No matter what my father might think of David, based on my previous statements, he is kind and welcoming. My mom doesn't say much, but she smiles at him a lot and tells him he's very handsome. Skip and David seem to get along well, and he's wonderful with the kids. I step back and watch him play outside with Hap and Sammy (apparently Happy has decided that the name 'Happy' is babyish), and he's a natural.

After dinner, David and my dad talk about finding Andrew, and with Skip's help, they make a list of the larger companies based in the area. I call Jenny at home and ask her to keep an eye out for Andrew, in case he ever comes back in, and she agrees to let the others know. She said they'll give him my phone number if they see him.

We have a list of companies, and tomorrow I'll start calling, since I'm the only one who'll be home during the day.

It takes nine misses, but the tenth call is a hit. There's an Andrew Lombardy who is assistant general counsel at IBM. When I describe him to the secretary, and mention that he's a new father, she confirms it. I can hardly believe it. I found him.

"But he's in a meeting. Can I take a message for him?" the secretary asks.

"Yes," I say, breathing out the word as if I've just jogged for an hour. "Please ask him to call me as soon as possible. It's very important." I give her my name and telephone number, and then add that I worked in the diner, in case he doesn't recognize the name. We were first names only, after all.

After I hang up, I stay close to the telephone for the next hour, waiting. My mother is out with Melba, so I make a sandwich. As soon as I take a bite, the phone rings. I chew fast and swallow before picking up.

"Hello?" I half-mumble.

"Robin? Is that you?" It's him. My heart soars to the ceiling.

"Andrew!" I swallow the remainder of that bite and take a sip of water before continuing. "I've been looking for you everywhere!"

"Well, that's comforting," he says with a laugh. "My secretary said it was important. Are you all right?"

"Yeah, I'm fine. Well, no. But yes." I'm making no sense at all. "There's so much to tell you. But you're at work. Now that I found you, I can wait until you have time to speak with me."

"It's my lunch hour. I have plenty of time, Robin. Tell me what's going on."

"Okay, but then I want to hear all about the baby," I say. I tell him everything, the words spilling out of me like a pent-up flood. The book and Maryana, the water damage to my original notebooks, everything. I leave out the part about David. That can wait.

He's quiet for a minute. "Are you still there?" I ask.

"I'm right here. Wow. Well, you're going to need a lawyer, but this isn't my area," he says. I'm disappointed, but if it isn't his area, then I guess I wouldn't want him to handle it. "I can recommend someone," he adds.

"That's probably a conversation you should have with my father," I say. "He wants to do whatever it takes to fix this." And fix *her*, I think. Maryana Capture stole a story from Hap Fortune's little girl, and that was a big mistake.

"Robin, let me call you right back," he says abruptly and I hear the line go dead. Dammit. I scarf down the rest of my sandwich.

He does call back, a half hour later. I'm restless, pacing the rooms downstairs, and grab the phone on the first ring.

"Andrew?"

"Yeah, sorry, Robin, I had to deal with something. Listen, would it be okay if I stopped by your house after work? Are you still living with your parents?"

"Yes, I'm here." I give him the address. "It'll be good for you to meet my dad." I wonder if I should ask him to stay for dinner, but he'll be going home to Barbara and...what's the baby's name again? Helen.

"I'll leave the office early. Five o'clock okay?"

"Sure." After we hang up, I call my dad and speak to his secretary.

"Robin, he's out at the new development, but he should be back in the office by three. Any message?"

I tell her I need to speak with him, that it's not an emergency, not anything to do with my mom, but still pretty important. "Tell him I found the guy we were looking for. He'll know what that means."

"Sure, Robin," she says. "I'll get word to him." She'll probably send a messenger to the construction site. Someday, it would be great to have telephones that you could carry around with you. Ha, I think, like that will ever happen.

Andrew comes to the house right on time, and I introduce him to my dad. We were able to get Mom to visit with Kay and the kids. No need to confuse her with all of this.

"Let's talk in here," my father says, gesturing toward the den. "Come on, Robin."

I join the men and my father closes the door.

Andrew pulls at his necktie. "Robin, after we spoke this afternoon, I called Barbara." He turns to my dad. "My wife edited and typed up Robin's manuscript."

"I didn't know that," my father says.

"She's a librarian, and she was home last summer, looking for something to do. She enjoyed doing the proofing and typing, and she loved the story," he adds, looking at me and grinning. "Anyway, when she'd finished typing, she made a Xerox copy of the entire book, and she sent it to the copyright office in Washington."

What? I spring to my feet. My father jumps up as well. And Andrew, beautiful, darling, princely Andrew, spreads his hands like a saint bestowing blessings.

My dad sticks out his big hand. Andrew stands up and shakes his hand, and my father pulls him into a bear hug. I'm afraid he might crack a bone. Andrew is about a third the size of my dad.

"I want to meet your wife," my father booms heartily.

"Sure, but you can't hug her like that," Andrew says. They both laugh, then together they face me.

"Robin, we'll get your book back. And this so-called author will go down in flames," my dad says.

Maryana Capture. My favorite author of all time, going "down in flames." It doesn't give me a good feeling, even though it should.

39

It's my twenty-first birthday tomorrow. What a year, I think. David said he'd take me to the beach for lobster, but I could share a hot dog with him and be happy. I didn't think I was worthy of his forgiveness, but he offered it anyway. He is kind. He accepts me, the flawed me. I think he always has. I was the problem, because I couldn't see past the outer David to the good and decent man he is.

Maryana Capture's best-selling novel, *The Road to Remembrance*, was withdrawn from publication as soon as our lawyer sent notification to her publisher that the original manuscript (by unknown author Robin Fortune) had been filed with the United States Copyright Office months before her novel was released. There was a write-up about her plagiarism in *The New York Times*, but no one ever contacted me about it. I thought maybe her publisher would offer to publish the book for me, but I guess they were embarrassed about the whole thing. It's okay, though, because they have to turn over all the profits to me, and Madison Peregrine Publishing sent a certified letter to me, telling me they have an interest in publishing my book after all the legal issues are cleared up.

I'm getting ready to return to college in September. I still want to finish and earn my degree. David is moving closer to the campus, and asked me to move in with him. I told him no. Last year, it would have made me feel like a real adult to live with my boyfriend, but I don't want the distraction while I'm in school. He understands (see, he really is a good boyfriend).

My mom and dad continue to find their way back to each other. It hasn't been easy for them, but both deserve credit. My father is a more patient man, and I see a softness in him that I never saw before. The way he steadies my mom when they walk, how he keeps his hand on the small of her back, and sometimes around her thin shoulders. Those little gestures move me.

My brother takes on more and more of the business now, but he thrives on it, and he finds a balance between work and leisure that my father never could. He and Kay bought a boat, and they spend summer afternoons sailing on the bay.

David and I stopped by the Liberty Diner last weekend for breakfast. George's wife hung new curtains at the windows, and there's a new waitress there, a girl who speaks with an accent. George came out from the kitchen to say hello, and after eyeing David carefully, then seeing the tiny nod of my head, he shook his hand and kissed my cheeks, both of them. And, miracle of all miracles, he wouldn't let us pay for breakfast. We left a big tip for the waitress.

Down at Little Beach, we lay on a blanket, fingers entwined, saying nothing and not needing to. I watch an airplane cross the expanse of blue sky above and I'm not envious at all, because I'm exactly where I should be.

About the Author

Martha Reynolds ended an accomplished career as a fraud investigator in 2011 and began pursuing a lifelong dream of writing. She is the author and publisher of four novels, including the award-winning *Chocolate for Breakfast* (book one in The Chocolate Series), *Chocolate Fondue*, *Bittersweet Chocolate*, and the Amazon bestseller *Bits of Broken Glass*.

Her very short poem was featured in Tell Me More's Twitter Poetry Challenge, and she has contributed essays and reflections to *Magnificat* magazine.

She and her husband live in Rhode Island, never far from the ocean.

Connect with Martha:

Facebook: http://www.facebook.com/MarthaReynoldsWriter

Twitter: @TheOtherMartha1

Blog: http://MarthaReynoldsWrites.com